CLOSE TO
THE BONE

BOOKS BY SUSAN WILKINS

Buried Deep

SUSAN WILKINS
CLOSE TO THE BONE

bookouture

Published by Bookouture in 2020

An imprint of Storyfire Ltd.
Carmelite House
50 Victoria Embankment
London EC4Y 0DZ

www.bookouture.com

ISBN: 978-1-83888-520-5
eBook ISBN: 978-1-83888-519-9

This book is a work of fiction. Names, characters, businesses,
organizations, places and events other than those clearly in the
public domain, are either the product of the author's imagination
or are used fictitiously. Any resemblance to actual persons, living or
dead, events or locales is entirely coincidental.

For Sue Kenyon, who makes it all possible.

PROLOGUE

He laughs. Of course he does. Stupid bitch. Is she actually threatening him? He's bigger and stronger than her; it's not a fight she can win. She must know that.

'I get it,' he says. 'You're upset.'

Her body is rigid with rage, her breathing shallow. That may be an understatement.

He lets his gaze stray to the vast plate glass window. The evening sun is sinking over the harbour. A view that certainly justifies the £200k price tag. The door to the balcony stands open and he can feel the light spring breeze. It's warm for early May. The sharp tang of seaweed, the strains of off-key karaoke float up from a quayside bar. When this place is launched on the market in a few days he's going to make a mint. Six luxury apartments. His vision, his graft made this happen. No way will he let the silly cow spoil it with her jealous nonsense.

Perhaps he should just give her a slap. Remind her who's boss. That'll bring her to her senses.

But instead he decides to smile. He's a man of property. He can afford to be benevolent.

'I've got a bottle of bubbly in the fridge. Not the cheap stuff. Got it from my wine club. I was saving it to celebrate the first sale. But let's crack it open now, take it outside, watch the sunset. What do you say? There's no need for this.'

He gives her his aww-shucks boyish grin. *I know I've been naughty again, but you know I'm really a lovable lad.* For most of his forty-three years this has worked with the women in his life, from his mother onwards.

He opens the fridge. High-end Bosch fridge-freezer, included in the asking price. The show flat has been dressed with a selection of cool contemporary furniture to help the punters imagine what it would be like to live there. According to the agent this adds £30k to the value, so worth the effort.

He takes out a bottle of Prosecco. Beaded moisture on the glass. He brandishes it with a smile. *Women need a firm hand but charm goes a long way and costs nothing.* This was his father's advice to him as a teenager and over the years it's proved useful.

The target market for the development is London-based, affluent second home owners looking for a luxury bolthole in Devon. Local yobs need not apply. He had a bit of hassle from the town council with their usual guff about affordable housing for locals. There was a public meeting at which some of the rougher elements got to vent their spleen. But he'd seen them off with a couple of strategically placed backhanders: to the chair of the planning committee, lovely lady who knew the form, and the senior planning officer.

He lifts two elegant champagne flutes off the shelf. And as he turns back to face her he sees it coming straight at him. Dark, blurry, fast. Cold steel. Thwack! Right in the middle of his forehead. Instant pain.

He staggers backwards, head spinning. The glasses fall and shatter. He grabs the granite-topped kitchen counter for support. The second blow is to the temple. He lashes out, makes a grab for her throat. But she skips away out of his reach. He lurches sideways. What is it? A hammer? Where the hell did it come from? She's hitting him with a hammer!

The pain is excruciating. His stomach heaves and he vomits on the floor.

'For Chrissake!' he wails. He raises his forearm to ward off further blows.

She steps back. He sinks to his knees. Is it over?

'You listening now?' she says.

What's she taking about? His head is throbbing. He can hardly think.

'I didn't mean to…'

He tastes bile in his gullet. His vision swims. He's going to puke again. Her face looms over him, tight and red and furious.

Her arm goes up and he sees it. A lump hammer. The square-ended carbon steel head. The builders must have left it, stupid bastards, he'll have to have a word. This is the last lucid thought he has.

The third blow cracks open his skull.

CHAPTER ONE

Wednesday, 7.25 a.m.

Megan Thomas watches the dark, steamy liquid trickle into the cup. First coffee of the day, always the best. Scout, her sister's dog, a Border collie-Labrador cross, comes trotting into the kitchen. He heads straight for her and plonks down at her feet, tail wagging. He gazes up at her, she gazes down at him.

'You can't fool me, buddy. You've had breakfast. And looking at me with those big brown eyes—' She laughs. 'Okay, you're right, I'm a soft touch. But don't tell!'

She reaches for the dog treats jar as Debbie comes in.

'Megan! He's getting fat. You want to haul his dumpy arse up to Berry Head and throw tennis balls for half an hour, be my guest.'

'Sorry.' She gives her sister a sheepish look and pats the dog. 'Coffee?'

'No time. I'm going to be late for my cleaning job. Are the kids up?'

Megan lives with her sister's family in Berrycombe. This was only ever a temporary arrangement when she came down from London to take up a new job. She's a detective sergeant with Devon and Cornwall Police in one of their Major Investigation Teams. But weeks have drifted into months, her family insist they love having her and she loves being there, mostly. Finding a flat of her own remains the long-term plan but not one she's actively pursuing.

She left London, her ex-husband and a gruelling stint working undercover, in a fragile mental state. She was diagnosed with post-traumatic stress disorder but the panic attacks have abated. She hasn't succumbed for months. She focuses on the job and with the help of Dr Moretti, her shrink, she holds her life together.

It's midway through spring and she's up before dawn every day for an early morning swim. The water is still freezing so she wears a wetsuit. It's worth the effort for the exhilaration it brings. The bouts of anxiety and doubt she suffered back in the winter have faded and she's feeling at ease and settled in a way which would have never seemed possible a few short months ago.

Debbie sighs. 'I hate it when Mark's away. Everything falls apart.' Her husband has taken a job as a skipper on a wind farm support vessel in the North Sea; the money's good but he's only home every other weekend.

She goes to the foot of the stairs and yells, 'Amber! Kyle! Ruby!'

'Listen,' says Megan. 'I'll take the kids to school.'

'Don't spoil them, Meg. They'll get used to it. Healthier for them to walk. Amber can take Ruby, Kyle can take himself. Their dad's away, they've got to learn some responsibility.'

Megan scans her baby sister. Her eyes are hollowed out and she looks completely knackered. The holiday season is beginning. It's the time of the year she can make some proper money so she's juggling three jobs: bar work in the evening, cleaning and driving a delivery van.

'What time did you get in last night?'

Debbie sighs. 'I dunno. About one. Late licence and then we had to clear up.'

'Okay,' says Megan. 'What's the point me being here if you won't let me help? Go take a shower. I'll make you some toast and coffee. And I'll make sure the kids get to school. No arguments.'

'I thought you saw the shrink before work on a Wednesday?'

'She's on holiday. So I've got time. Jump to it.'

Debbie grins and gives her a mock salute. 'Yes, Sarge.'
'That's better.'

Megan pulls up as close as she can to the school gate. She slots her small, blue hybrid car in behind a growling monster of a four-by-four. The petrolhead in her still misses her old roaring gas-guzzler. But the mantra of her new life is *responsible not reckless*. Mostly she manages to stick to it.

'Cheers,' says Kyle as he leaps out of the back door.

Amber leans across from the front seat and is about to give her aunt a peck on the cheek when the four-by-four revs its engine and starts to back straight into them. Megan hits the horn. The beast in front shudders to a halt. The driver's door flies open and a large, shaven-headed man in shorts and a vest climbs out.

He walks up to Megan's window and raps on it none too gently. Megan winds it down and stares at him.

He scowls. 'You gotta be fucking kidding me, you stupid bitch!'

'You were about to back into us, you left me with no alternative.'

He leans forward and wags a chunky index finger. 'You're lucky I don't drag you out of that stupid little tin can and then run right over it.'

Megan sighs. Amber and little Ruby, seated in the back, are watching the encounter wide-eyed.

She pulls out her warrant card and holds it up. 'Not a good idea, sir. Because then I would have to nick you. We're a bit short-handed at the moment. It's starting to be a busy time. So you'd probably spend most of the day in the cells before you got processed. But if that's what you want.'

He takes an involuntary step back, the colour visibly draining from his stubbled cheeks. Then he turns, mumbling to himself, and scurries back to his car.

'Have a nice day,' says Megan.

CHAPTER TWO

Wednesday, 8.05 a.m.

Debbie Hayden can't remember the last time she had a day off. Probably back in February when Mark took her out for a Valentine's Day brunch. Snatched moments in a busy life. She loves her three children in a deep, visceral way but they're hard work. Amber, growing up so fast, a sassy teenager but prone to unpredictable mood changes. She'll argue about anything and everything, wearing her mother down. Kyle, on the cusp of puberty. Are boys easier? He's always playing computer games on the internet and completely obsessed with a world she doesn't understand. She assumes Mark does but that's probably wishful thinking. Five-year-old Ruby is her baby and her delight. A mistake – they only ever planned to have one of each – but Ruby is smart and lovable. It's impossible not to adore her. Debbie wonders how long that will last.

She trudges up the hill towards her first job of the day. The luxury apartment block sits in a prominent position above the town. A Victorian terrace was demolished to provide the site. The six flats are practically completed and Debbie has been hired to do the builders' clean and prepare them for marketing. She has three days to finish the job in time for the launch weekend.

The show flat has been cleaned and is now furnished. It was a back-breaking task: hoovering, washing down every surface, hauling all the rubbish to the skip. Debbie did it on her own. The

Amber hoots with glee. 'Yes!' She punches the air. Ruby giggles. 'That was so cool,' says Ruby.

Impressing the kids is childish, thinks Megan. But it still gives her a kick.

'It could've gone either way,' she says. 'There's a lot of angry people out there. Don't mess with them. Best to just walk away.' *Responsible not reckless.*

'Have you ever been really scared?' says Amber.

'Wow! That's a question.' And one she doesn't intend to answer. She isn't about to spoil a lovely spring morning by telling her fourteen-year-old niece about how she was kept prisoner by a psychopathic gangster, trussed up in a cellar and expecting to die. Debbie doesn't know the half of it. No one does.

'I bet you haven't,' says Ruby. 'I bet you're really brave. Like Jessica Jones or Mystique. But braver.'

'She doesn't have superpowers, silly,' says Amber.

'A few superpowers would come in handy,' says Megan.

'I'd like to fly,' says Ruby. 'Like a bird.'

Amber giggles. 'Then when you met a bloke like that idiot in the car you could just shit on his head.'

They all laugh.

other five flats are still filmed in dust and full of decorators' debris. There's a lift but Greg Porter, the developer and her employer, has made it clear he doesn't want 'staff' to use it. He thinks it will spoil the carpet. As a result, when she arrives, she has to cart the clunky old vacuum cleaner up several flights of stairs. Then she has to go back down for the mop, bucket and remaining cleaning materials.

She moves up and down the stairs on autopilot and thinks about her husband. She misses him and, when she's tired and stressed, that longing becomes a physical ache. In the course of their marriage this is the first time he's worked away for any length of time. But jobs locally have become harder to come by. The fishing industry is struggling, fewer boats competing for a limited catch. Mark is an experienced trawler skipper but the only work he can get in Berrycombe is as a deckhand. The decision for him to go and work miles from home is one they took together. The construction of wind farms around the coast is a source of lucrative jobs for someone with his skills. He's skippering his own boat again and Debbie can see how happy that's made him. It will also give them a chance to pay off some of their debts. But the price is separation.

She has to use her pass key to unlock the front door to flat number five. But across the corridor, the door to the show flat stands ajar. She stares at it. She wonders if the electricians are in the building. They could be. Earlier in the week Porter had them in to make sure the built-in sound systems in all the flats worked. While they tested the levels, they'd propped open the doors and blasted a couple of old disco numbers throughout the building. She'd danced round for ten minutes and remembered how much she used to enjoy going clubbing.

Back in London, when she was still a teenager, she and Megan would sometimes go out together. Those were wild times. She'd get completely wasted but knew she could always rely on her big sister to get her home. Now she seems to be galloping towards forty, her life is nearly half over, but where did it all go? Meeting

Mark and falling in love, the births of her children, their first baby steps, all these things have merged into one. She finds it hard to believe how fast the years have flown by. But in herself she doesn't feel fundamentally different. A few grey hairs, a persistent backache that she can't shift. Nothing seems all that different.

She puts on her vinyl gloves and starts to shove handfuls of plaster dust, half-dried filler and paint-spattered rags into a black bin bag. She's never minded hard physical work. Once her body has settled into a rhythm, her mind can drift. She was never much good at school. *Debbie is a daydreamer, she needs to concentrate.* That was the gist of most of her school reports, not that anyone ever read them. She liked sports of any kind. But the school she and her sister attended was a rundown London academy with few facilities. She preferred to bunk off and hang out with her friends in the park. She learnt to skateboard and for a while she was quite good. Megan gave her the board for her birthday, but then it got nicked.

It doesn't take her long to fill two plastic sacks and she drags them out into the corridor. The door to the show flat is still open, the hinge is creaking in the breeze.

Porter has never been an easy man to work for. Truth is she hates the bastard. Tight-fisted when it comes to wages, he's always finding extra things for her to do. Could she pop down to the kitchen shop and get a couple of champagne flutes for the show flat? She's hired to be a contract cleaner but he treats her more like a skivvy who's at his beck and call. He made her do that yesterday morning. It took her half an hour. Put her behind. But he just expected her to work faster to catch up. He'd given her twenty quid to pay for the glasses and examined the change she gave him suspiciously. Luckily she got a receipt.

She stares at the door to the show flat and sighs. The rest of the building is silent. If the electricians are around, they must've nicked off to get some breakfast. She's the only one there, which means she has to sort this out. But she decides to leave it for now. They may come back.

She wedges open the front door to number five and starts to hoover. Then it occurs to her that when she came into the building there was no electricians' van parked outside. In fact the newly tarmacked parking area was empty. *Sod it!*

Switching the vacuum cleaner off, she boots it out of the way with her foot. Anger seeps through her and that helps. Why do people like *Mister* Greg Porter always assume they're a cut above? Because they've got loads of money? Why should that make them so special? Did that give him the right to treat her like shit?

With another sigh she heads for the show flat.

As she pushes open the door the smell hits her. Rank and putrid, it reeks of sick but there's another, sharper smell, almost metallic. It reminds her of some butcher's shops, where the meat is laid out on the counter.

She feels a stab of adrenaline.

The hallway is short, with only a cupboard and two other doors off it before it opens into the main room. She creeps along it. Why the need for stealth? She knows what she's going to see.

CHAPTER THREE

The offices of the Major Investigation Team for South Devon are on the first floor of a repurposed office block on a small industrial estate outside Plymouth. Intended as a temporary solution in a time of cuts it has become a semi-permanent location. The lift is temperamental, the heating system unpredictable and the toilets prone to blockages.

Megan walks into the main office. Open-plan in theory, it's crammed with extra desks. Like everyone else criminals like to go on holiday and many choose the West Country. In spring and summer the crime rate goes up with the huge influx of visitors, and resources have to be juggled to cope with it. In the last week new faces have arrived, mostly eager rookies from uniform anxious to get their teeth into some serious detective work.

Zigzagging across the room, Megan heads for her desk. The regular team is divided into two camps. The youngsters occupy one corner. Vish Prasad and Brittney Saric, once the most junior DCs, are now the most senior. Kitty, the civilian analyst, has the biggest desk, two computers and a bank of screens. Megan sits in no man's land, next to the other DS, Ted Jennings, definitely of the older camp, and next to him is the detective inspector who is theoretically in charge of them all.

Jim Collins has recently returned from long-term sick leave. He's always suited and booted, a punctilious old-school cop, and his presence has had a dampening impact on the office culture. His natural respect for hierarchy has been undermined by the fact he now works for a woman boss, DCI Laura Slater. But he's sly in the ways he lets his antipathy show. The DCs skulk in their corner and keep their jokes and their energy to themselves. A couple of stern reprimands from Collins have put them in their place.

Megan gives him a smile. 'Morning, Jim.'

He doesn't look up from his notebook but acknowledges her with a nod. 'Megan.'

His lack of computer skills and preference for *good old pen and paper* is also an issue. He treats Kitty as his PA and this has led to her stomping into Slater's office and asking to transfer out. The DCI talked her down. She's too valuable. But the resulting rift between the old guard and the new is an ongoing problem. Slater has arranged an IT course for Collins to bring him up to speed.

Megan knows a fragile ego when she sees one, but she can also sympathise with the new DI. He's spent nearly two years battling prostate cancer and has opted to return to work instead of taking medical retirement. His reasons for this difficult decision are kept to himself. It could be about money but he's in his early fifties and perhaps, like Megan, he simply didn't know what else he'd do. The team he worked with previously has gone, only Ted remains. And the quick-thinking kids, with their lightening fingers on a keyboard, can zip round the databases at a dizzying speed. Megan finds their level of skill intimidating at times. A rapidly changing landscape with talk of facial recognition software and the avalanche of available data is challenging for everyone. For a man recovering from treatment it must feel like a mountain to climb.

Megan plonks her bag down, catches Brittney's eye and smiles. Brittney and Kitty are having a whispered conflab about something.

They've learnt to lie low and stay out of Collins's sightline. Megan has discussed the situation with Slater and the boss takes the view that he has to be integrated back into the team. The role of bridge-builder is novel but Megan is trying to embrace it.

She walks over to his desk, points at his outsized Plymouth Argyle football mug and says, 'I'm getting one. You want a refill?'

Collins looks up. His face is pale and still gaunt from the ravages of chemo. He smiles. 'Cheers. Better make it green tea. The wife insists. Some article she read.'

Megan picks up the mug and is about to walk off when he says, 'Isn't Berrycombe your neck of the woods?'

'Yeah.'

'Just had a shout from comms. Uniforms called to a dead body at a new block of luxury flats overlooking the harbour. Head bashed in, so it looks like murder. Property developer, name of Greg Porter. You ever come across him?'

Megan shakes her head. 'I haven't lived there long. I don't really know it.'

'CSI are heading down there.'

'The Crime Scene Manager, Hilary Kumar, is really on it. You can rely on her to be thorough.'

'Good to know.' He nods. There's something creepy about the way he smiles.

But Megan smiles back. It's like pulling teeth. A murder and Collins is up? It's likely the boss will want Megan to hold his hand on it. The prospect doesn't excite her.

Laura Slater comes out of the cubbyhole otherwise known as her office. The morning briefing is about to begin, curtailing any further discussion.

Megan and the boss don't get on exactly but they understand one another. Slater comes over like a woman on a mission and most people assume that mission is to get to the top. She deploys her legal training well, knows how to deal with the lawyers from the Crown Prosecution Service and give them what they need to prosecute. As a result she has one of the best batting averages in the force. Her conviction rate speaks for itself.

She stands at the front and waits for the room to settle. It doesn't take long.

'Okay,' she says with her trademark chilly smile. 'Quite a long list to get through this morning. First up, we have a potential murder in Berrycombe. Jim, you were duty DI, have you been down there?'

Collins shifts in his chair. 'Not yet, ma'am,' he says. He insists on calling her ma'am. 'CSM's gone down, thought I'd wait for their call.'

Slater consults her notes. 'Severe trauma to the head, a lot of blood. You didn't think to send one of the DCs straight away?'

Collins shrugs. 'Didn't think there was any rush. He's not going anywhere, is he?'

Ted Jennings chuckles. A ripple of laughter runs round the room.

Collins gives Slater a smug smile. 'Sorry, ma'am. Bit of black humour.'

But she isn't laughing. She just stares at him. Then she says, 'Vish, get down there now. Talk to the CSM. I'd like to know exactly what we're dealing with. ASAP.'

Vish Prasad jumps up. 'Yes, boss.' He heads for the door.

Like two naughty boys at the back of the class, Collins and Jennings exchange sniggers.

Megan watches them and her heart sinks.

'Megan,' says Slater.

Here we go, thinks Megan. Slater will split the boys up, giving Ted Jennings something routine to do, and she'll be lumbered as Collins's DS on the murder.

'We have been asked to assist on a major NCA investigation into people smuggling. They'll be on our patch intelligence-gathering and carrying out surveillance. You will be the local liaison officer. Depending on how the investigation develops and what they need, you can call on other members of the team at your discretion. But bear in mind we've got a lot on our plate.'

'Yes, boss,' says Megan. *National Crime Agency!* Not what she was expecting.

'Obviously there's an organised crime element here,' says Slater, 'and you'll need to keep me up to speed so we can respond promptly with any additional resources they require.'

Slater is looking straight at her. This is a big deal and Slater is trusting her not to mess it up. Everyone in the room is staring at Megan. Some with respect, others with envy. It's a plum job and Slater would be stupid not to give it to her best officer.

Megan feels a shiver of excitement but also trepidation. Crime falls broadly into two categories: human stupidity and nastiness in its various forms, and crime as a serious and lucrative business with international players who are rarely caught. But the last time Megan played in this league it didn't turn out well for her.

'And, on the subject of organised crime,' Slater says. 'Dennis Bridger has been released from prison.'

'Oh you are kidding me!' exclaims Ted.

'Sadly not. He was sentenced to five years, he's served half his tariff and is being released on licence.'

Jim Collins shakes his head wearily. 'Before your time, ma'am. But you do know that the drug-dealing charge was the only one we could make stick.'

'I've read the file,' says Slater. 'But, since you worked on the case, Jim, it may be useful if you fill the rest of the team in.'

Megan watches Collins. He sits up straight and pulls back his shoulders. Megan wonders if he realises that the boss is managing him by deliberately giving him the floor. She reflects, not for the first time, on what a smart operator Laura Slater is, slackening the leash a little in order to rein him in.

Collins stands up, puts his hands on his hips. 'Okay,' he says. 'Dennis Bridger is a little runt of a bloke but a stone-cold psychopath and dangerous as a nest of vipers. Came down here from Manchester on holiday, liked it and stayed. Drug dealer, rapist, pimp, murderer; he was suspected of several homicides although we never managed to prove it. He ran a gang that terrorised some of the smaller coastal towns. By the time we nailed him he was lording it over quite a little empire. Rob Barker was the DCI in charge of the investigation. Shouldn't think he's best pleased.'

'No, he isn't,' says Slater. 'The surveillance unit from Exeter will be on Bridger 24/7. But they'll be standing off and using GPS tracking to follow him. Plus phone taps and listening devices have been authorised, everything we can legally do.'

'Tosser like him'll get off on that. It'll make him feel important,' says Ted.

'If he even realises,' says Collins.

'In case we're being too subtle for him,' says Slater, 'here's a job you might like, Ted. Pick the three biggest officers you can find, go and knock on Mr Bridger's door and make sure he knows we're on his case. The least infringement, his licence is revoked and he's straight back inside.'

'Pleasure, boss,' says Ted.

Slater sighs. 'According to intelligence from the prison, Dennis made a new best friend while he was inside. A very dangerous London villain with direct connections to the Colombian drug cartels. Our speculation is this is Dennis's new boss and supplier. I'd prefer to stop him committing any further crimes but pragmatically if we can get him banged up again for thumping someone or any other small infringement, before he can set up a new network, that may be a better result.'

Megan feels a shiver up her spine. It's as if someone's just walked over her grave. She knows the answer to her question but she has to ask.

'Who is this London villain, boss?'

Slater peers at the file. 'Zac, not quite sure how you say the last name…'

Yilmaz. Of course it is.

'Yilmaz,' says Slater. 'Possibly Turkish. You know him?'

'No,' says Megan.

CHAPTER FOUR

Wednesday, 9.45 a.m.

Yvonne Porter clutches the cordless phone to her ear as she paces. She's outside on the patio because her son, Aidan, is having breakfast in the kitchen. He's on study leave, revising for his exams. This seems to entail getting up late and lounging by the pool all day, listening to music and chatting on social media. Or whatever else seventeen-year-olds do nowadays. She's not sure she knows. Her three younger children are at school, *thank God*!

The patio is made of York stone and stretches along the entire back of the house. On the wall dividing it from the large terraced garden and swimming pool below, there are terracotta tubs of trailing fuchsias. They're coming into bud but soon they'll produce an explosion of gaudy pinks and reds. Greg hates them, says they're vulgar. This is the main reason she keeps them there.

'I know he's with her. I know it,' she says. 'He didn't come home at all last night. He doesn't even bother to lie any more.'

She's wearing a gaping silk robe over a lace chemise. He can't say she doesn't try. She'd bought some lovely striped cotton pyjamas, really soft and ideal for lounging about in the mornings. And a top brand, nothing tacky. But they'd disappeared. When she asked him if he'd seen them, he said no. Then he added cryptically: 'a wife should always look feminine, not like some old bag lady.' As if she needed reminding.

'Listen to me, Yvonne,' says her sister, on the other end of the phone. 'You've got to stop taking all this crap from him.'

'It's all very well for you to say. I've got four children. How am I supposed to cope?'

'You get a good lawyer and you sue that bastard for half of everything.'

'I feel sick.'

'How much did you drink last night?'

'Honestly, Penny, I don't remember.'

She woke up in the early hours with an empty vodka bottle on the floor beside the sofa. It was probably as well that he didn't come home. He'd have given her hell for that. He prefers her not to drink.

'I'll try and come down at the weekend,' says Penny. She sounds distracted. She's obviously busy. She's always busy.

'Will you? That would be brilliant.'

Penny is two years younger. She was the smart one. She didn't disappoint their parents in the way Yvonne did. University, a career in finance, a life in London. She made sure she had choices. And her own money.

'I have to go, darling,' says her sister. 'I've got a meeting at ten.'

'Okay,' says Yvonne. She imagines Penny in her corner office in a Canary Wharf skyscraper. The only things on her desk will be her phone and laptop. She'll be wearing a tight pencil skirt; she's still thin enough to get away with it. 'I'm sorry I keep phoning up and whinging like this. I'll go and put some coffee on and pull myself together.'

'You're entitled to whinge,' says Penny. 'I hate the way he treats you.'

'Don't worry about me. I'll be all right.'

'Give my love to the kids. We'll take them to the beach at the weekend. That'll be fun.'

'Yeah. They'll love that.'

Hanging up the phone, Yvonne gazes out across the fields. The prospect is calming. Neat acres of English farmland with sheep grazing and rippling fields of oilseed rape down to the river. The house is superb too, everyone says so. She's frequently told how lucky she is to have a developer for a husband. He had the vision to take an old tumbledown barn, really no more than a shed, and turn it into a magnificent detached home, stone-clad and classic on the outside but modern and high-tech within. It's been photographed for *Country Life* and the exterior used in a TV drama. She does love her house. She knows she should be grateful.

Her head is thumping; what she needs is coffee and paracetamol. Can a man really be blamed for straying when his wife is a drunk? This is her fault. She's driven him to it. She needs to clean up her act. The remorse is kicking in; after a wipe-out like last night it always does.

As she turns to go back into the house, her son appears in the doorway. Aidan is her firstborn and she wishes she could cling to him forever. He was such a sweet child and even as a teenager he's retained a softness that she treasures. He's arty and sensitive, not at all the sporty, macho male his father would prefer.

His blond hair is tied in a topknot and shaved up the sides. He has the first hints of a wispy beard. 'Mum,' he says. And he looks perturbed.

'What, sweetheart?' says Yvonne. She doesn't want him to see that she's upset so she rattles on. 'I've just been chatting to your aunt. She was bending my ear about some new man of hers. I despair of her. Nearly forty and still not married.'

The boy nods obediently. She can see the anxiety in his eyes.

Then he says, 'There are two police officers here. They want to talk to you.'

CHAPTER FIVE

Megan parks in the town and walks down to the harbour. She doesn't know Torquay well. And she needs to think. *Zac Yilmaz.* It was only a matter of time before his name cropped up again. Still, it's a shock. She needs to process it and calm her fears.

Think about this rationally.

Villains hook up in jail all the time. The fact a criminal like Yilmaz can continue to run his business from a prison cell is one of the major flaws in the system. Dennis Bridger sounds like the sort of individual he might consider useful. But this is all a coincidence. The connection to Devon is purely random. There's no reason to suppose that Zac knows she's here.

Zac Yilmaz was the target of a major undercover operation carried out by the Met. For reasons she's never fathomed, Megan caught his eye. They became embroiled in an affair. As an undercover officer she knew this was totally against the rules. She also knew the risks she was taking but she did it anyway. And she did it with the complicity of her bosses, who wanted results. It shattered her marriage and nearly cost her life. Her real identity was carefully protected throughout his trial. When he learnt she was an undercover officer, he tried to kill her. He almost succeeded. The broken physical and emotional state he left her in, he would've assumed she'd taken medical retirement. He won't expect her to still be a police officer.

As Megan walks, her anxiety abates and her thoughts become steadier. In the last few months her mental health has improved immeasurably. No more panic attacks. She's proved she's more than capable of doing the job. She can't let something like this throw her off course. It's unlikely she'll even be called upon to deal with Bridger and anyway he will have no idea who she is. She's just another cop.

The day is warm, an early taste of the summer to come, and Slater has tasked her with liaising with the NCA. This is what she needs to focus on and even enjoy.

She walks round the harbour. The marina is large with a striking pedestrian footbridge dividing the inner and outer sections and a tidal cill gate to keep water in the inner harbour and stop it drying out. She's become used to the working port of Berrycombe, where she lives. In Berrycombe they don't mind of a bit of mud exposed at low tide and the stink of seaweed and fish. But this is a posher place; here the boats are bigger and flashier. The pontoons are lined with multi-million-pound gin palaces plus an array of smaller yachts and pleasure vessels of every shape and size.

After the briefing she texted the NCA contact number that Slater gave her and received a curt reply to meet them at a harbourside cafe. There are possibly a dozen to choose from. She walks along the harbour wall scanning the various establishments. Some are fancier than others but they all have tables and chairs set outside on the pavement. Breakfast and coffees are being served to holidaymakers in shorts and beach attire as they enjoy the sunshine. The pubs are popular with plenty of people already on the beer. Alcohol and sun. *Trouble for later*, thinks Megan.

She clocks them at twenty paces. They're wearing black baseball caps and aviator shades. If this is their attempt to blend in with the natives, it isn't working. She stops in front of their table, smiles and says, 'Morning.'

He stares up at her stony-faced, then smiles. 'So, you are a detective.' His accent is northern, maybe Lancashire.

She holds out her hand to shake. 'Megan Thomas.'

He grasps it. 'Danny Ingram. This is my colleague Sasha Garcia.'

Megan gives her a nod. The young woman tilts her head but doesn't smile. Flawless skin, svelte: she looks to Megan like she graduated from university about two weeks ago.

He shrugs. 'We only asked for a couple of uniforms. Just for local info. Don't know that there'll be much for you to do.'

Megan smiles. 'You're running an operation here in Devon and DCI Slater wants to give you all the back-up you might need. I can get some response officers as and when you need them.'

He chuckles and doffs his cap. 'Thank you. We appreciate it. Your boss is a gentleman.'

'No, she's a woman.'

Ingram chuckles again, glances at his sidekick, who smiles for the first time. Some kind of private joke? He doesn't apologise for his assumption. Megan feels her annoyance rising.

'Okay,' he says. 'Well, we're waiting for some kit and a couple of other colleagues.'

It's clear that he isn't about to invite Megan to join them so she pulls out a chair and sits down. She's not about to be patronised.

The two NCA officers exchange looks. He takes off his shades. About forty, weasel-faced and wiry, but fancies himself. Megan stares back. He's absolutely not her type.

He purses his lips, as if she's being deliberately difficult. 'We're staying at some bloody great Victorian pile up the road there,' he says. 'Food's grim. And Sasha's vegan. So can you sort out a couple of restaurants for us? You do have stuff like that round here?'

'Vegan restaurants? No idea,' says Megan. 'But I'll call our civilian analyst and see if she can take some time off from this morning's murder to find out for you.'

CHAPTER SIX

Megan gets home to find her sister sitting in the kitchen and staring into space. On the table in front of her is a pile of utility bills. She looks as if she's been in the same position for a while. Scout is lying on the floor with his head resting on his paws, a few inches from her foot.

'You all right?' says Megan.

Debbie seems to rouse herself. 'Yeah,' she says. 'How was your day?'

Megan bends down and fusses the dog. 'Spent the afternoon looking at incredibly posh boats with a couple of morons from the National Crime Agency down here on a jolly.'

'Oh. Sounds like fun.'

'Not really. They're on our patch so my boss wants to show that we can all play nicely together. But they're being a bit snotty and don't really want us involved in the operation. All I know is it's about people smuggling and they're interested in posh boats in Torquay Marina.'

Debbie gives her a ghostly smile. 'There are a few of those. Mark did some skippering for a bloke who had this enormous yacht. But all he wanted to do was cruise down to the Lizard and back on a nice day, while him and all his mates got pissed.'

'That's why they're called gin palaces.'

Megan scrutinises her sister. She appears to be making a huge effort to chat and be normal. But a sixth sense is telling her that Debbie is in trouble. She knows about the financial problems. She's offered a loan but her sister refused. She's married to a man who would not take kindly to the notion he can't support his family. Megan contents herself with providing treats for the kids: new trainers, outings, takeaways.

'How's your back?' she says. 'Still giving you trouble?'

Debbie sighs. 'A bit.'

Megan takes up a position behind her sister's chair and starts to knead her shoulders.

Debbie leans back and exhales. Then she says, 'I've just lost two of my three jobs.'

'Shit. What happened?'

'This afternoon I was supposed to be doing deliveries. But I was late. Third time it's happened, so I got canned.'

'That's a bit harsh. Couldn't you talk to your boss?'

'He's got no leeway. Company policy. Decided in Milton Keynes. And the reason I was late was because of your lot.'

'My lot?'

'Your DC, the really fit one.'

'You mean Vish?'

'Yeah, Vish. He was nice and very apologetic. I gave him my witness statement. But then I had to hang around because the DI wanted to talk to me and he just asked all the same questions. And they wanted fingerprints and DNA.'

'Good grief,' says Megan. 'This murder at the luxury block of flats, is that where you've been working?'

'Yep. I discovered the body.'

'Oh Deb, that's awful.' Megan puts her arm round her sister and gives her a hug.

'Gets worse. Now that Porter has snuffed it, I probably won't get paid for any of the work I've done there. It was a contract job. Payment at the end.'

Megan shakes her head. 'I don't know what to say.' She goes to the fridge and pulls out a bottle of white wine. 'I think you need a drink. I think we both do.'

'I'm afraid if I start drinking I won't stop.' Debbie's chin trembles. 'What am I going to tell Mark? He's slogging his guts out so we can pay off the bloody credit cards and get ourselves out of debt, and now this.'

Megan unscrews the wine and pours it into two glasses. 'Start at the beginning and tell me what happened.'

Debbie accepts a glass of wine. 'I found the stupid tosser in the show flat. At first I thought maybe he was passed out drunk. Then I saw his head.' She grimaces. 'He's pissed someone off, that's for sure.' She takes a hefty slug of wine.

'Presumably you just called the emergency services?'

'Yeah.'

'And the paramedics confirmed he was dead?'

'Yeah! I suppose they did. I can't remember. Don't go all cop on me, Meg, I've had enough bloody questions for one day.'

'Hey, I'm sorry.'

Debbie puts her hand over her mouth, her body shudders and the tears start to flow.

Putting down her own glass, Megan kneels in front of her and cradles her sister. They remain like this for several minutes.

Finally Debbie says, 'I know I should feel sorry for him, but I don't.'

'You feel how you feel.'

'He was a nasty bastard. Treated me like I was a lower form of life. He was one of those blokes who can't have a conversation with you without staring at your tits.'

'That's always annoying.'

'And he expected me to be ever so grateful that he was paying me minimum wage to clean his bloody flats. I know I'm going to be out of pocket, but the truth is I'm glad he's dead. Does that make me a bad person?'

'No. I think you've been under huge stress. And finding a dead body, whoever it is, is a shock.'

Debbie gazes directly at her and there's a steeliness in her look. 'Between us we've encountered a few monsters over the years, haven't we? You more than me. But trust me, Meg, whoever whacked Greg Porter has done the world a favour.'

CHAPTER SEVEN

Thursday, 5.45 a.m.

Megan swims slowly across the bay. Ahead of her a family of cormorants bobs on the gentle swell, diving for fish then popping up again through the shimmering surface. She doesn't want to disturb them. The rising sun glitters on the water. This is the perfect moment in her day and she likes to savour it.

She's never really thanked her therapist, Dr Moretti, for bullying her into it. But she figures that, as secret addictions go, her obsessive early morning swimming is acceptable. She has acquired all the kit: wetsuit, cap, goggles, float. She charts her progress on an app. And she's made a few acquaintances among the small posse who share this mad pastime. The etiquette is to recognise that, for most of them, this is a solitary pursuit. On the rare occasions they meet, all that's required is a friendly nod. Of those she sees on a regular basis, there's only one couple. She's exchanged a few words with them, about the amount of seaweed or the size of the waves. He's tall and rangy, looks to be about seventy; she's possibly younger. They have voluminous dry robes they use for changing afterwards. Megan has eyed these garments enviously.

But today she has the bay to herself. Just her and the flocks of seabirds. It's barely dawn, and chilly, but she's got used to that. Her body has adapted remarkably well to the shock of icy water. Her first few strokes are vigorous then she slows down, lets her mind empty and drifts on her back for a few moments before heading out across the bay.

As she glides along, she thinks about her sister and feels guilty. She should have been more aware of just how close Debbie is to the edge. Debbie and Mark are an inseparable item and have been such a solid fixture for years, that she's forgotten what her sister was like before she met Mark. Debbie has always been emotionally volatile. She often reacts without thinking and that has led to trouble in the past. And last night there was something about her sister's mood and manner, when she talked about the discovery of the body, that Megan finds disturbing.

The issue of money is a delicate one. Megan's divorce has provided her with a sizeable lump sum from her share of a London flat. Paul bought her out and installed his new partner immediately without changing a single thing. Megan walked away with a couple of suitcases of clothes, a few personal keepsakes and some books. She's invested the money with the plan that she'll use it eventually to buy her own place. But she's not ready for that yet.

She reminds herself that worrying about Debbie is her default setting; she's been doing it since their childhood. Sorting out her little sister's problems was always an easier option than tackling her own. And, as she swims, she knows this is what she's doing. Using Debbie to block out her darker thoughts, thoughts about Zac, the danger he will always pose and the fear that one day he might catch up with her.

Thursday, 8.30 a.m.

Megan arrives at the office early with a view to getting a jump on the day. She left Debbie at the breakfast table in full mother mode, fussing over the kids, stopping her son from sneaking a can of Coke and making sure Ruby – always a live-wire in the mornings – sat down for long enough to eat. In Megan's opinion all three children were subdued, Amber scanning her mother anxiously. They knew the sketchiest of details about her discovery of a dead body. But they also sensed her tension and fragility. No questions were asked.

As she expected, Megan finds Slater in her office. The boss is usually the first to arrive. She looks up as Megan pauses in the doorway.

'Morning,' Slater says. 'How are our esteemed colleagues in the NCA?'

'Chippy. They don't appear to have got the memo saying we work as partners.'

Slater sighs. 'That's a pain. Particularly for you.'

'I can cope. Also, I wanted to flag up the fact that it was my sister who found the body in the flats. She was hired to do the builders' clean.'

'Okay. Duly noted. I've yet to hear Jim's initial thoughts. Post mortem is this afternoon.'

'I'm presuming you want me to stick with the NCA?'

Slater leans back in her chair. 'I'm afraid so. I did have a chat on the phone with an old colleague who works there now. According to him, Danny Ingram has a bit of a reputation. His police career was in Manchester and he did some excellent undercover work against the gangs. But he's known to be temperamental, bit of a one-man band.'

Megan smiles to herself. This explains why Slater gave her the job. She thinks they've got something in common, so they'll get on.

'Right,' says Megan. 'I'll try and be charming.'

Megan is on her way out when Brittney appears.

'Just got a shout from comms,' she says to Slater. 'Response has been called to Blackpool Sands. There's a very distraught woman on the beach with a little girl. She's wearing a hijab. Officers attending think she may have been brought ashore by smugglers in the night. Appearance and language possibly Middle Eastern. She was kneeling on the beach and rocking back and forth as if someone's died. Border Force has been called. But they thought we should know too.'

'Interesting,' says Slater. 'Go down there and take a look. And you go too, Megan. This may well relate to the NCA's inquiry. When we know what's going on, you can let Mr Ingram know. Perhaps it'll be a useful lesson for him in how agencies should co-operate.'

Megan chuckles. 'You want me to tell him that?'

Slater smiles. 'I think he'll get the point.'

CHAPTER EIGHT

Blackpool Sands, contrary to what the name suggests, is a crescent-shaped stony bay overlooked by steep wooded hills. The road to it is a narrow switchback. Brittney drives and her habit of looking away from the road as she talks to her passenger unnerves Megan. The dips and loops of the road are demanding, with a sheer drop in places. Megan glances out of her side window apprehensively. She's not normally a nervous passenger.

Brittney is oblivious. '… and he said, do you fancy going for sushi. So I thought why not. It's no big deal, we're just mates.' She pushes her owl glasses up her nose. She's describing her latest romantic encounter, which has been the talk of the office.

'But do you like him?' says Megan, trying to get into the spirit of the discussion.

'He's all right.'

'Do you fancy him?'

Brittney screws up her nose. 'I don't really know what that means.'

'Yes you do.'

'He's quite big.'

'As in overweight?'

'No, sort of solid. But I suppose what I'm thinking is he's big enough not to be overwhelmed by someone like me.'

Megan glances at the young DC. She's plump and curvy and hugely self-conscious about her weight and appearance. She jokes about being called Miss Piggy at school. The pain of those jibes never leaves you.

'You're not a bloody elephant, Brit,' says Megan. 'Most blokes prefer curves.' She finds herself suddenly with a vision of Sasha Garcia, Ingram's perfect, model-thin sidekick. It's obvious what he prefers.

'I've lost half a kilogram in the last month,' says Brittney.

'Any bloke who went out with you would be a lucky man. I hope whatever his name is—'

'Matt.'

'Yeah, I'm sure Matt knows that. Or else why did he ask you to go for sushi?'

Brittney turns into the car park adjacent to the beach. Two squad cars and an ambulance are parked up. A few curious holidaymakers are milling around.

'We swapped numbers. But I don't expect I'll hear from him.'

They pull up next to the ambulance.

'Be optimistic,' says Megan, as she gets out of the car.

Megan shows her ID to the uniformed officer and he leads her to the back of the ambulance, where a young woman, not much different in age to Brittney, is wrapped in a space blanket. She's clutching a child to her, a girl of about four, and rocking gently. Her dark eyes fix on Megan; they're full of fear. She whispers something in a foreign tongue. *Leaving your homeland, putting yourself in the hands of criminals and crossing the sea to an unknown destination, that puts optimism into a whole new dimension*, thinks Megan. Or is it desperation? The line between the two can be thin.

She gets into the back of the ambulance and sits down so she and the woman are on the same eye level. Pointing to herself, she says, 'I'm Megan.' She takes out her warrant card and holds it up. 'I'm a police officer.'

The woman starts to cry. Tears course silently down her cheeks. Brittney has been talking to the paramedics. She joins them.

'They found her kneeling on the beach and staring out to sea. Took them ages to even get her to move.'

'Look at her hijab,' says Megan. 'That's pure silk. She's not poor. And if she was brought here by smugglers, she wouldn't have been on her own. But if there were others, they've gone. Why did she stay?'

Megan reaches out slowly and touches the woman's knee. She flinches. Megan pats her gently. 'It's okay,' she says softly. 'I think you've lost someone, haven't you?' She turns to Brittney. 'Ask one of the PCs to get some coffee from the cafe.'

Brittney heads off. Megan calls after her. 'And put sugar in it. She's in shock.'

Megan holds out her hand, palm upwards. 'Come with me, let's go back onto the beach and see if we can figure out what's happened.' She nods and smiles. 'It's okay. Come on.'

The woman hesitates then nervously takes Megan's hand. They get up and Megan helps her down the step and out of the ambulance. Still holding hands, Megan leads her and the child back to the beach.

The nature of the terrain makes it slow going. Shingle soon gives way to pebbles and larger flat stones. The woman's shoes are black ballerina pumps. They're muddy and wet but the silver embroidered toe caps suggest they were once fancy. She clutches her little girl's hand. The child is numb and bewildered.

The beach is largely empty. A few tourists are eating breakfast on the cafe terrace. They watch the little cavalcade pass them. Someone films it on a mobile phone. Further down the beach a couple in swimwear are lying on towels. They've erected a windbreak. Megan can feel the hostility of their gaze.

Close to the shoreline, Megan stops. She points to the woman and then out to sea and back. 'You came in a boat? Yes?'

The woman nods, her lip trembles and she starts to cry. 'Hassan,' she whispers.

'Hassan?' says Megan. 'Your husband? Your son?' She points to the little girl, holds out her hand to measure a child's height.

The woman nods. 'Hassan.' She brushes away her tears and suddenly a torrent of explanation pours from her. The words are fast and furious. She waves her arms about, points to the sea, pleads with Megan, points to the sea again.

Megan looks out to sea too and points. 'Hassan fell in the sea?' She mimes swimming.

The woman shakes her head and holds out her hand to indicate the height of a small child.

'Hassan is your son. He can't swim, he's too young?'

The woman gets down on her knees and grabs Megan's arm. She's begging. 'Hassan.' She keeps repeating her child's name.

Megan pulls the woman to her feet. 'It's okay. We'll look for him.' She nods vigorously. 'I understand. It's okay.'

Brittney comes across the beach towards them. She's carrying a takeaway coffee and a carton of juice. Megan takes the coffee and hands it to the woman. Brittney gives the juice to the little girl. They stare at it in a bemused fashion.

Brittney grins. 'Drink,' she says, miming the action.

'It's her little boy,' says Megan. 'Fell in the sea, maybe as they were landing. I'm not sure. We going to need the coastguard to start looking, although my guess is we're looking for a body.'

'Okay,' says Brittney. 'The natives are getting restless. The bloke sitting on the beach back there asked when we're going. Apparently we're spoiling his holiday.'

'Really,' says Megan. 'Can't he see how upset she is, stupid plonker?'

Brittney shrugs. 'You know what some people are like. I'll get onto the coastguard.' She hurries off.

Megan starts to escort her charges back up the beach. She gives the sunbathing couple a wide berth.

But the bloke calls out. 'You wanna put them on a plane and send them straight back where they come from!'

Megan knows she should just keep walking and ignore him. But something in his spiteful tone stops her in her tracks.

She walks over towards the couple and says, 'I'm afraid you need to leave, sir. The beach is now a crime scene and will need to be cordoned off.'

'Oh, sod off!' he replies. 'I just paid six quid for the car park. Means we get to stay all day. I'm not shifting because of her. You just need to shove her in a van and get her out of here.'

'We're looking for the dead body of a child. If you see it floating in the water, what are you going to do? Just swim round it?'

She turns and walks away. *She shouldn't have said that. It was unprofessional.* She should've just left it to the uniforms to clear the beach.

CHAPTER NINE

Thursday, 10.20 a.m.

Megan sits in the car waiting for Ingram and Garcia to turn up. She's brooding. Annoyed with herself for her outburst. It demonstrates that her temper is more volatile than she thought. A salutary reminder that she lacks self-control. Officers on response get to deal with this kind of crap from members of the public every day. And she used to be able to do it too. But she's out of practice. And the last thing she needs is a complaint that could lead to disciplinary action. She suspects that Slater is a stickler for *proper procedure* when it comes to complaints which could lead to bad publicity. Or is she just being neurotic? Maybe she is. The spectre of Zac Yilmaz has thrown her off kilter.

As she returned to the car park from the beach with the woman and her little girl, the cafe manager appeared and invited the refugees inside for some food. This helped Megan tell herself that not everyone is a self-obsessed idiot. Brittney went with them to the cafe. The response officers have been clearing and cordoning the beach. It's given Megan some time to calm down.

Ingram arrives driving a brand new Range Rover Evoque. He's abandoned the baseball cap but is still wearing the shades. Garcia is wearing a skintight top and black jeans. Her hair is cropped short with bleached tips. She looks Megan up and down and smiles as she gets out of the car. It's hard to tell if the look is judgemental or friendly. But it leaves Megan feeling self-conscious and old. A middle-aged cop in a boring trouser suit.

'Morning,' says Ingram. 'Thanks for the heads-up. We appreciate you bringing us in on this.'

Yes, thinks Megan. *Now it's your turn to do some grovelling.*

But she says, 'Well, I think this woman could be a valuable source of intelligence. But we're going to need a translator.'

'We brought one,' says Garcia, patting her stylish faux leather bag.

'Okay, let's do this,' says Megan.

They find Brittney and her two charges at a corner table in the cafe. The mother stares blankly into space but the little girl is slowly eating some soup.

Garcia walks straight over to them, smiles at the woman and says, '*Marhabaan.*'

The woman's eyes flick with surprise, she inclines her head and mumbles a reply.

Ingram turns to Megan. 'I believe that's Arabic for hello. We thought it might be a good place to start.'

'You mean Sasha speaks Arabic?' says Megan.

'Just a smattering. It's not one of her main languages.'

'How many languages does she speak?' *This woman gets more annoying by the minute.*

'Five, I think. Her mum's Russian, so she speaks that fluently. One of the reasons the NCA hired her. We've got too many Russian gangsters treating London as a laundromat for their ill-gotten gains.'

Garcia opens her bag and takes out her laptop. Ingram stands back, arms folded and lets her perform. Megan and Brittney watch.

'What's she doing?' Brittney whispers.

'I dunno,' says Megan. 'She speaks some Arabic and I guess she's got some kind of translation app on her computer. Have you found any witnesses?'

'Just the manager who called it in.'

They head for the kitchen where the manager is talking to the chef. The place is small and steamy and busy serving breakfasts. Megan wonders if, when CSI arrive, they're going to want them to shut for the day. It seems unfair at this juncture; they don't even know if it is a crime scene.

The manager comes straight over to them. He's young with a goatee beard, and wears a white apron over his jeans, as he doubles as the waiter.

'This is Evan,' says Brittney.

He smiles sadly and says, 'It's a cruel world. Makes your heart break if you think about it too much.'

Megan nods. 'When did you first see her, Evan?'

'Well, I get in about seven, for the deliveries. Usually there's not many people about. I noticed her right down on the beach, just sitting there facing the sea. I thought maybe she was meditating or just chilling out, y'know.'

'What time was that?'

'Seven fifteen, maybe. Bit later this dog walker comes in. We weren't open but he says he thinks she's some kind of illegal immigrant person, I dunno.'

'So what did you do?'

'I wasn't sure what to do. I didn't want to jump to any conclusions.'

'You thought he might be being racist because she was wearing a hijab?'

'Exactly. So I left it for a bit. Then I thought, well she's been there a long time, perhaps she is in trouble. And I went to take a look.'

'What did you find?'

'Her and the little girl looked quite bedraggled. There were lifejackets on the beach next to them. I asked her if she was all right. But she didn't understand me. She looked in a bad way. Really upset. I tried to get her to come back to the cafe. She just sat there rocking back and forwards. So I came back and called the emergency services.'

'Call was logged at 8.06,' says Brittney.

'Now I feel really bad,' he says. 'I should've done something much sooner. When the dog walker told me.'

'Don't feel bad,' says Megan. 'The dog walker could've called us. Do you know who he is?'

'No. Bloke about fifty with a big German shepherd. Dogs aren't allowed on this beach after the first of May. But a few people still come down early. Maybe he didn't call because he didn't want anyone to know he was breaking the rules.'

Megan nods. 'That's possible. Thanks for your help.'

She and Brittney turn to go.

Then Evan calls after them, 'Y'know, I've been wondering about something else. I don't know if it's connected.'

'Okay,' says Megan.

'I live with my mum and dad, just up the road there, overlooking the bay. I sleep like a log, but the last couple of nights my mum says she woke up because she could hear jet skis.'

'Jet skis?'

'Yeah, jet skis. In the middle of the night. Down here in the bay. She says there were several of them, making a hell of a racket.'

'Did your mum say what time?'

'Oh, like two or three in the morning.'

Like the pin tumbler in a lock, when the last one slots into place, it opens. You never know when it's going to happen, thinks Megan. But it's one of the pleasures of being a detective.

'Right,' she says briskly. 'We may need to talk to your mum about that. Can you give DC Saric your address?'

Brittney gets out her notebook.

Megan hurries back into the main part of the cafe, goes over to Ingram and says, 'Can Sasha ask her if her little boy fell off the back of a jet ski while they were being brought ashore?'

He raises his eyebrows. 'A jet ski?'

'Yes. I think your people smugglers are coming into the bay in a boat, then ferrying people ashore on the back of jet skis. Does that make sense?'

Ingram stares at her for a moment, then grins. 'Yeah, that makes sense.'

CHAPTER TEN

Thursday, 11.46 a.m.

Yvonne Porter stares out of the kitchen window. She reflects on her excellent decision to erect a pergola in direct line of sight of the window. It's absolutely covered in *Arabella*, her favourite purple clematis. The flowers are beginning to open. She focuses on the vibrant colour, lets it sink into her. She's always loved flowers, ever since she was a child. She's supposed to be going to the Chelsea Flower Show with her sister next month. It's the sort of outing Greg approves of.

'Can I make you a cup of tea, Mrs Porter?' The voice jars; she hates the accent.

That bloody woman! Why can't she just go away?

She turned up yesterday afternoon, said she was the Family Liaison Officer and her name was Christine. Yvonne hates having people she doesn't know in the house. Christine is one of these middle-aged, mumsy types. Her hair's a mess, she smells of cigarettes and she never looks quite clean. She's supposedly there to provide support. But when she unpacked the dishwasher, she just dumped the cutlery in the drawer. The forks were all out of alignment. Some of the teaspoons the wrong way round. How is that supportive?

The children are all home from school, which is stupid. What the hell is she supposed to do now? She has no idea.

Aidan is skulking round the house. Several times she's caught him watching her. She hates being watched. And he's always got his phone in his hand.

She caught him videoing her earlier. She was in her bathroom, nose inches from the mirror, struggling to get her contacts in. It caused a small explosion.

'Oh for fuck's sake, Aidan,' she said. 'What the hell are you doing?'

'Just checking you're all right,' he replied.

All right? What does that even mean?

The doorbell rings.

'I'll get it,' says Christine brightly. She disappears into the hall.

Yvonne sighs. The most annoying thing about Christine is that whilst she's around it's impossible for Yvonne to have a drink. There are two bottles of Chablis in the fridge. When it gets to lunchtime she'll have a glass. It's a perfectly civilised thing to do. No one can criticise her for that. The police may have sent this awful woman to spy on her but they can't arrest her for drinking a glass of wine.

She can hear whispered voices in the hall and then suddenly her sister Penny appears.

Penny throws open her arms and rushes towards her. 'Oh my God, darling! I got the first train I could this morning. I wanted to come last night but—'

Yvonne collapses into her arms.

'I'll give you two some privacy,' says Christine.

Yvonne clings to her sister, the dam breaks and she sobs. Penny strokes her hair. They remain like this for some time.

'Sssh,' says Penny. 'It's all right, darling. I'm here now.'

'I don't understand any of it. What am I going to do?'

'It'll be okay. We'll get through this together.'

Finally they let go of each other. Yvonne wipes her face with her hand. 'Oh God, I must look a fright.'

'That doesn't matter. You look fine.'

'Let me make you a cup of coffee. I've managed to keep that stupid woman away from the coffee machine. I don't want her grubby finger marks all over it.'

Penny puts a gentle hand on her shoulder. 'Now let's not start with that nonsense, Yvonne. She looks perfectly clean to me.'

'It's not nonsense,' wails Yvonne. 'You should see the cutlery drawer. It's a complete mess.'

'Remember what Dr Davenport said. It's a compulsion. It happens when you get very stressed. Now obviously you're stressed. Who wouldn't be? But you mustn't fixate on these things.'

'Do you think the police have got this right? A suspicious death? How do they know it's suspicious?'

'Darling, once they've done the post mortem, they'll know how he died.'

Yvonne stares at her sister. She's always so sensible. The relief of having her there is enormous.

'Do you think we can have a glass of wine instead of coffee?' says Yvonne.

'Of course we can. Have you got some in the fridge?'

Yvonne nods.

Penny goes to the fridge and takes out a bottle. 'Petit Chablis, how lovely.'

'It's just the ordinary stuff from M&S. Greg reduced my housekeeping budget because he says I spend too much on booze.'

Penny chuckles cynically. 'Well, you're not going to have that problem any more, are you?'

Yvonne smiles. 'No, I suppose not.'

Penny places the wine on the marble counter and takes two glasses from the cupboard. Then she opens her palms and grins. 'Darling, this all belongs to you now. None of your fifty-fifty split and a long drawn out argument with his bloody accountants trying to hide his assets. You get the lot.' She unscrews the top of the wine and pours it into the two glasses. 'All I'm saying is,

I know how wretched you feel. But there is light at the end of the tunnel.'

Yvonne isn't listening. Her attention is focused on the lovely pale liquid. She seizes her glass with a shaky hand and takes a large mouthful. Then another.

The relief!

CHAPTER ELEVEN

Thursday, 2.35 p.m.

The nearest thing the Major Investigation Team has to a conference room is at the end of the corridor. Random pieces of unwanted furniture and junked computer monitors tend to end up there. There's a large wooden table in the middle and a mismatched selection of chairs. Megan watches Ingram and Garcia looking around. There's a whiteboard which could do with a proper clean. They're probably used to something much more posh and high-tech.

Slater takes the chair at the head of the table. Chief Superintendent Rob Barker sits down next to her. But it's Slater's meeting.

'Okay,' says the DCI. 'I hope you understand, Danny, that May into June is a difficult time for us down here in the South West. There's a real pressure on resources. We have one murder investigation ongoing and my DI is dealing with that. CID can't spare anyone. So I shall be asking Megan to step up.'

Ingram shrugs. He doesn't look at Megan. 'No problem with that. I'll let Sasha fill you in on what we found out from the woman on the beach.'

'Fine. Go ahead,' says Slater.

Sasha smiles. She seems totally comfortable. No hint of nerves. It's the kind of self-possession that Megan envies.

'Her name is Ranim, she's Syrian and comes from Idlib, where her husband was a businessman. He was killed in an air strike.

But he'd put money aside, in dollars, for her and her two children to escape. They got over the border into Turkey and were able to pay people smugglers.'

Ingram chips in. 'This is where it connects to the intelligence we've gathered from some of our European partners. The people-smuggling market is huge and diverse. It's like a lot of things, it caters for all budgets. We've been following the online marketing put out by an organised crime network, who specialise in a premium, bespoke service. Summer is high season for them too.'

'Jesus,' says Barker. 'Sounds like they're bloody travel agents.'

'They're a criminal enterprise that makes millions every year,' says Ingram. 'We think they're operating between Spain and the West Country. They deliberately avoid the usual routes.'

'Ranim isn't willing to tell us what she paid,' says Sasha. 'But we think it could be up to twenty thousand dollars each.'

'That's ridiculous,' says Slater. 'Sixty grand for three of them. Do illegal immigrants have that kind of money?'

'Some do,' says Ingram. 'Some were quite well off before the war and they've managed to liquidate assets. The smugglers have identified a gap in the market.'

Megan watches the interplay between Ingram and Garcia. They make a slick team, riffing off each other.

'These are people,' says Garcia, 'who are not rich enough to buy a fake passport and visa. That would set you back much more. But they don't want to risk dying at sea in a leaky dinghy or freezing to death in a refrigerated lorry. This lot offer them a door-to-door service. They collect them in northern Spain, drive them up the coast of France to Brittany. The crossing is at night in some kind of luxury yacht. They're picked up on the beach and driven to their nominated address in the UK. Probably a family connection. The smugglers' USP is safety. That's what people are paying top dollar for.'

'All right until it all goes wrong,' says Megan.

'Yeah. And we've been waiting for an opportunity like this,' says Garcia gleefully. Ingram tries to subdue her with a look. This amuses Megan. *As if they hadn't already realised his brilliant sidekick is a heartless bitch.*

Ingram steers the discussion in another direction. 'We think that the boats they're using are based at marinas here on the south coast of Devon and Cornwall. They may be owned by a shell company. Or leased from someone else.'

'Makes sense,' says Slater. 'They come into one of our bays at night, offload their passengers using jet skis or dinghies, then return to their moorings. Nothing shows up on CCTV.'

'Problem is,' says Barker, 'this is a hell of a lot of coastline to put under surveillance. We simply don't have the manpower. I can give you Megan, maybe a DC, plus one surveillance unit from Exeter – they've got a couple of drones they can deploy – and a few uniforms.'

'I appreciate that, sir,' says Ingram. 'We know this has to be intelligence-led. But our breakthrough today came from a good old-fashioned bit of legwork by your sergeant.'

He smiles at Megan. She wonders what Slater's thinking. Probably the same as her. Danny Ingram is a politician.

There's a tap on the door. Brittney comes in.

'Sorry, boss,' she says to Slater. 'I thought you'd want to know that the coastguard have spotted a body. Below some cliffs down the coast from Blackpool Sands. It could be a child.'

'Thanks, Brittney,' says Slater. 'That tells us pretty clearly who these people are, I think.'

'It does,' says Ingram.

The mood in the room is sombre. No one says anything for a moment or two.

'Right,' says Barker, standing up. 'Let's get on with it.'

CHAPTER TWELVE

Thursday, 3.50 p.m.

The path to the hidden cove is steep and rocky. It's quite a scramble. As local liaison, Megan leads the way, even though she has no idea where she's going. Luckily the track is obvious. A small ravine dips down; clumps of pink and purple sea thrift cling to the stony hillside and patches of bluebells are still in evidence. Garcia follows her and Ingram brings up the rear.

Since there's no vehicular access, CSI have lugged their gear down to the beach by hand. An impressive feat in Megan's view. But speed is of the essence if they're to recover the body ahead of the rising tide.

'Wow! This is so beautiful,' says Garcia. 'You could be in Italy or even Greece. It's so unspoilt.'

Megan bristles. She feels defensive of her adopted home. *Why would that be better?* It is beautiful. Devon is beautiful. Why can't the stupid woman settle for that instead of making some snobby comparison?

They pause on a ledge above the cove. The last part of the descent is the steepest. Loose scree makes the path treacherous.

Garcia sits down on a rock to check her phone.

Ingram takes his cap off and wipes his face. 'Phew!' he says. 'You need to be a bloody goat round here.'

Megan ignores him. She's thinking about Ranim. Her own longing for a child was the ghost in her marriage. Paul always insisted it didn't matter to him. But now he's the one with a baby; obviously it did. The only consolation for Megan is she will never feel the kind of pain Ranim is feeling.

Garcia gets up and moves up the hill in an attempt to get a better signal.

Ingram turns to Megan and smiles. 'I think you and I got off on the wrong foot,' he says.

Megan shrugs. 'I assume from what you said in the meeting that Ranim confirmed they were transferred from the boat by jet ski.'

He nods. 'Twenty passengers. They wanted to get them off as quickly as possible. She sat behind the jet ski driver, holding her daughter in front of her. The boy was on the back with his arms round her waist. There were some big waves, he fell off. They tried to find him but couldn't. He did have a life jacket. She thought he could've survived. That's why she refused to leave the beach.'

Megan finds it hard to imagine that kind of despair, sitting on an alien shore, waiting for the sun to come up and hoping against hope that somehow your child is alive.

'What's next?' she says.

'We need to press her for more information. But not right away. If this is him, I don't know how she'll react.'

Megan nods. She can feel Ingram scanning her. She finds it unnerving.

'Look,' he says. 'I know I come over as a dick at times.'

Megan says nothing.

He grins. 'Yeah, well you probably agree.'

She folds her arms. *What the hell does he want?*

He ploughs on. 'I treated you like a gofer, which was rude. It's clear you know what you're doing. Very much so.'

'Fine,' she says. 'Apology accepted. Can we move on?'

'Let me buy you dinner. Peace offering.'

Megan stares at him. *More politics.*

'I appreciate the gesture,' she says. 'But I'm not much of a vegan. I'm more burger and chips.'

'And a cold beer, yeah, me too. You pick a venue, text me, I'll meet you there. Deal?'

'I'll think about it,' says Megan.

She starts on the trail down to the beach.

They scrabble and slide for a couple of hundred meters until they reach the cove. The sand is coarse and red, matching the soil.

A stiff easterly breeze is driving the crashing waves onshore and the tide is rapidly rising. Megan recognises Hilary Kumar, the Crime Scene Manager, up to her knees in the waves. She and two colleagues, all in protective gear, are lifting a small body from the sea. They've spread a plastic sheet on the sand. They lay the child down on it. Dark hair, bare feet; he's still wearing a yellow life jacket, which is too big for him.

Hassan.

As Megan watches the small corpse being carefully arranged in its plastic shroud, she thinks of Ranim. How will she survive this?

She becomes aware of Ingram standing beside her.

'For Chrissake!' he says. 'Doesn't matter how many times you see it…'

He's right about that.

Megan glances at him. The baseball cap is pulled low over his face concealing, she suspects, the tears in his eyes.

CHAPTER THIRTEEN

Thursday, 8.10 p.m.

Megan doesn't intend to arrive late; that's not her style. But when she got home she found Debbie in a strange mood. The kids were hungry and no one had walked the dog. Megan, Amber and Scout took a circuitous route to the fish and chip shop.

Once she'd settled the family in front of the television with the takeaway, Megan went to get ready. The problem was she didn't know what she was getting ready for. Dinner with a colleague? Or colleagues? She'd selected an upmarket burger joint in Torquay. She had no idea what Sasha was going to eat. But they probably did some kind of soya-based veggie burger.

Megan's wardrobe is not extensive. Before leaving London, her old home and her marriage, she'd thrown most of her clothes away. She'd lost weight. Many things didn't fit. And the colours jarred. She used to like bright, sassy outfits. But she'd realised that standing out in a crowd was not something she wanted any more. She'd chucked all her party dresses out. But dinner with a couple from the NCA was hardly a party dress occasion. In the end, she opted for low key rather than low neckline. Skinny black jeans. *Garcia wasn't going to have the monopoly on cool.* And a white shirt with a black and grey geometric pattern.

As she was about to leave the house, she asked her family's opinion.

'Is it a date?' said Debbie.

'No, absolutely not!'

'You look really fit,' said Amber. 'I'd fancy you.'

It's a hassle to park. Torquay is busier than Megan expected. The season is beginning and the promenade is busy. It's nearly dusk, the lights are twinkling on the water and a mild evening is encouraging many people to take a stroll.

Megan arrives at the restaurant, flustered, to find a queue. She knew she should've booked. But then she sees that Danny Ingram has already secured a booth at the back. He gives her a wave. He appears to be on his own.

As she approaches the table, he gets up.

'No Sasha?' says Megan.

'Past her bedtime, don't you think?' he says with a grin. 'This is an outing for the grown-ups.'

Megan sits down opposite him. He has a half-drunk Pilsner glass of lager in front of him. A smart shirt. He looks freshly showered and shaved.

'What can I get you to drink?' he says.

She indicates his glass. 'A beer's fine.'

The waiting staff are buzzing between the crowded tables but Ingram obviously has the knack. He catches the eye of a passing waitress and orders two more beers.

They face each other across the table. He smiles but it feels awkward. Megan wonders what the hell she's doing there. She smiles back and picks up her menu.

'I hear you're from the Met,' he says.

'Yeah,' she replies. 'What about you?'

'Manchester. Laura Slater mentioned you worked undercover.'

Laura Slater is a blabbermouth.

'I just did a bit,' says Megan. 'No big deal.'

Ingram chuckles. 'Okay. I see. I'm not trying to ask any awkward questions.'

They both stare at their menus in silence for several minutes. The waitress comes and they order. Megan is trying to calculate how quickly she can eat and leave without being rude.

'I'm surprised that someone with your kind of experience and ability isn't a DI,' he says.

What the hell would he know about her experience?

He continues, 'Strikes me your bosses think that too. Have you taken the exam?'

'Nope,' she says. 'I'm crap at exams.'

'Me too.'

'So what rank were you before you joined the NCA?'

'I was a DCI. And I know what you're going to say. But I'm still crap at exams. I left school with three GCSEs and one of those was woodwork.'

He grins. Megan scans him. His hair is short and mousy and receding at the temples. He was probably blond as a kid. But the most arresting thing about him are the eyes. Cornflower blue. He has a habit of tilting his head when he smiles. It gives the impression of a detached but wry take on life.

'Sasha has a double first from Oxford,' he says. 'I'm supposed to be teaching her the ropes. She'll probably end up with my job before too long.'

'She seems extremely capable.'

'She's certainly clever. But she's never been in a back alley in Moss Side facing a fifteen-year-old crackhead with a shiv. As a result she tends to fixate on facts and results. She's a bit short on empathy.'

'I thought you and her were, I dunno, good friends?'

He laughs out loud. 'My God!' he says. 'You think I'm shagging her.'

'It's none of my business, I'm sure.'

Megan feels self-conscious. Is he laughing at her? And the way he's looking at her is way too direct. She doesn't usually have a problem with eye contact. But Danny Ingram is not turning out to be what she expected.

'Megan,' he says, chuckling. 'Sasha's got her eye on you. You're right up her street. Bit older than her; tough, cool and contained. Intriguing history.'

Intriguing history?

'Sasha's a lesbian?' says Megan.

Ingram throws up his palms. 'I'm not going to label her. I wouldn't dare. She doesn't "do" labels. Queer, pansexual, bisexual or something, I dunno. She thinks I'm beyond the pale. Didn't you see the look she gave me when I assumed your boss was a man?'

'I thought it was a private joke.'

'Yeah. I'm the joke,' he says with a shrug. 'But, hey. She's educating me as much as I am her. And that's not a bad thing.'

Megan smiles. 'You can tell her I'm straight.'

'That'll just encourage her. She's been round half the straight women in our office, and probably a few of the men. I mean, seriously, you know what she looks like. Drop-dead gorgeous. There's not many that say no to her.'

'I'll bear that in mind,' Megan says with a smile. This is turning into a very peculiar evening.

He laughs, tilts his head. Then he says, 'That was a smart piece of police work this morning. The jet ski thing.'

She's relieved to get on to a safer topic.

'Just luck really. A witness remembered something.'

The waitress arrives with their food. They've both ordered burgers. But Megan has ordered salad instead of fries.

'Wow!' says Ingram. 'This looks good. I'm starving. But, hey, share my chips.'

He places the small metal tub on the table between them.

'I'm fine.'

The blue eyes are staring right at her. 'C'mon,' he says. 'You know you want to. They're triple cooked.'

She looks straight back at him. It hits her. *That fluttery feeling. No!*

He's an NCA officer, down here on a job. She's not going to be stupid about this. Keep it professional. That's what she tells herself.

CHAPTER FOURTEEN

Friday, 9.05 a.m.

As she drives, Megan wonders if she has a special talent: knowing you're about to do a really stupid thing and doing it anyway. She and Danny had breakfast in bed, which is why she's late now. His hotel room is enormous, with a bay-fronted window overlooking the sea. As she snuck out past the concierge, she prayed she wouldn't bump into Sasha. As far as she's aware, she made her escape unseen. She also narrowly avoided getting a parking ticket.

She feels an odd combination of confusion, embarrassment and elation. She wasn't drunk – she only had two beers – so she can't use that as an excuse. And it's no exaggeration to say that Danny Ingram is nothing like her usual type.

How did it even happen? This is the conundrum she's struggling to solve. He turned out to be amusing and self-deprecating. He asked her opinions about things and listened to the replies. He was easy to talk to. They laughed a lot. And he insisted she ate half his chips. By the time they shared a dessert – sticky toffee pudding and ice cream – she felt every nerve ending was primed. Her whole body was zinging. The last time she'd had sex was in another life. But she knew she wanted this. She was ready.

There was no assumption on his part. He didn't push it. He waited for her to come to him. And she did.

They were standing outside the restaurant, inches apart, joking about the couple who'd left just in front of them, and she reached out and touched his arm. She was curious. He didn't appear to be a tough bloke. He wasn't big and muscular like her ex-husband Paul and so many of the other men who had featured in her life. But his body was reassuringly solid. In response he put his hand on her shoulder and she stepped into his arms.

Now she has to face the fallout. Sexual entanglements with a work colleague are a bad idea for so many reasons. The stupidity of what she's done is beginning to dawn on her. It's not that she thinks Ingram will boast about sleeping with her. In any event he's not likely to have much contact with the rest of the team. She's been given the job of liaison officer – and that's the problem. It's totally unprofessional and Megan does not want to be that kind of cop. Nor does she want to be that kind of woman. Not any more. She can't afford to be.

The moral wilderness she inhabited in her undercover years has left her with a need for way-markers that she can rely on. This is a subject she's discussed with her therapist, Dr Moretti. Every boundary in her life was destroyed when she was imprisoned in that rat-infested cellar. She expected death. She welcomed it. The euphoria of her escape was immediately followed by a spiralling descent into darkness and despair. Everything failed her. Her marriage, the job, people who'd been her friends. Her sister was the only one who was there for her. Debbie refused to walk away. She and her family provided Megan with a lifeline. And it was only by grabbing that thin rope that she managed to haul herself up and out. It brought her to Devon, a new job and her new home by the sea.

By the time she's on the A38 heading for Plymouth, she's formulated a plan. When she gets a chance to speak to Ingram privately, she'll tell him that it was great. But it's something she can't repeat. She likes him but...

She sighs. On the outskirts of the city, the traffic is bunching at some roadworks. Megan checks her watch. She's going to be late for the morning briefing. This demonstrates to her – as if she needed it – that bad decisions have a knock-on effect. They ripple out. But…

But what? It definitely feels like there's a but.

The car crawls in the slow-moving column of traffic. And her mind drifts back to the sex. She never expected to end up having sex in a ridiculous four-poster bed in a Gothic hotel room in Torquay. And she never expected to enjoy it quite so much. It's been a long time since she experienced this sort of intimacy, a long time since she would even let a man touch her. She's experienced attraction from afar. But the last time that happened it was a disaster.

She runs up the stairs to the office and slips into the back of the room. Her work outfits are variations of the same thing; she doubts anyone will notice she's wearing the same shirt as yesterday.

Slater is at the front, addressing the team, and it sounds as if she's winding up.

Noticing her arrival the DCI pauses, sighs and glances at Megan.

'Sorry, boss,' says Megan. 'Traffic was awful.' It's not entirely a lie. Several people crane their heads round to look at her. Brittney gives her a ghostly smile. But there's a tension in the room. Something isn't right. Jim Collins is seated at the front. Megan can only glimpse the back of his head. He doesn't turn.

'Okay,' says Slater. 'We'll leave it there.'

Megan decides to go and apologise to Slater properly. But she finds Vish standing in front of her. He's frowning and looks nervous.

'What's going on?' says Megan. 'There's a horrible vibe in here. Has Slater just given someone a bollocking?'

'I'm sorry,' says Vish. 'There's no easy way to say this. We've brought Debbie in for questioning.'

'You mean my sister Debbie?'

'Yes. She's been cautioned and—'

'Cautioned? What the hell do you mean? What are you talking about? You've arrested my sister?'

'Megan, she's our prime suspect for the murder of Greg Porter.'

CHAPTER FIFTEEN

Friday, 10.25 a.m.

Megan storms into Slater's office. The calm professionalism she's spent months cultivating is gone. This is her sister, her baby sister, and the anger is raw and unfettered.

Laura Slater is standing behind her desk. She's checking her phone. But Megan gets the impression she's waiting. And bracing herself.

She looks up at Megan and says, 'Come in and close the door.'

'Are you fucking serious?' says Megan.

'I know you're angry—'

'That broken-down excuse for a police officer, that we're all carrying, has come up with some lazy, half-baked notion and you've bought it.'

Laura moves round the desk and edges past Megan to close the door herself. The outer office is like a frozen tableau; everyone has stopped what they're doing. They're all listening. They can't help it. The partition walls are plywood-thin.

'What's his bloody theory then?' says Megan. 'That my sister killed this douchebag and I'm in some way complicit?'

'No, of course not—'

'Of course nothing. We're probably people smuggling in our spare time too. Part of this mob that the NCA's chasing. After all, my brother-in-law can skipper a boat. So that's it. Both crimes solved. We can all pack up and go down the pub for a pint like in the old days.'

'Megan,' says Slater, 'you need to sit down and listen to me.'

'When was she arrested?'

'Earlier this morning. I don't have a note of the precise time.'

'And you've searched the house?'

'Yes. Obviously.'

'Were the kids there?'

'They were at school.'

Megan imagines a posse of her so-called colleagues going through the house, her house. Opening doors and cupboards, rifling through all their personal possessions. And Scout? What about Scout?

She should've been there. *Sod's law! The one night…* But she can't think about that now.

'Please, Megan. Sit down and let me explain,' says Slater.

Megan has run out of steam but she's too wound up to sit. She stands in the corner and folds her arms. It's all she can do not to hit something. *Take a deep breath.*

'Okay, boss. I'm listening.'

'Your sister has been arrested and is being interviewed under caution because some disturbing facts have come to light.'

'What sort of disturbing facts? My sister is not a killer. Wasn't his head bashed in? Debbie would not do something like that. I know her. She just wouldn't. Where the hell is she? I need to see her.'

Slater returns to the desk and opens her laptop.

'You need to listen to me first. You know how this goes, Megan. We follow the evidence.'

Megan starts to pace. Her brain has gone from anger to overdrive. 'You must have the results of the post mortem by now. What's the estimated time of death?'

'Tuesday evening between eight and midnight.'

'There you are then. She's got an alibi. She works behind the bar at the Duke of York from six thirty usually until the early hours. They've got CCTV all over the bloody building so you can see when she arrived and when she left. Plus, this time of the year, it's pretty busy. So there'll be a slew of witnesses who can confirm she was there all evening.'

'We have looked at the CCTV,' says Slater. 'Brittney and Kitty went through it all yesterday. And you know they're thorough. Debbie left the pub by the back door at eight fifteen and she didn't return until nearly nine o'clock.'

'Well,' says Megan. 'There'll be some logical explanation. Some problem with the kids, I don't know.' She realises she's grasping at straws.

'Where were you on Tuesday evening?' says Slater. 'Weren't you at home with the kids?'

Megan's floundering. She thinks back and realises that she was. She watched television with the girls and coerced Kyle into doing his homework, which he was trying to avoid. There was no crisis, no emergency her sister was forced to rush home for. But already, in a secret part of her brain, Megan knows she could invent one. *Lie to protect Debbie? No question.*

Megan's head is in a spin. 'Maybe she needed a break for some reason. It can get manic. Have you ever worked behind a bar?' *Course she hasn't.*

'Vish has already spoken to the manager,' says Slater. 'He says she just disappeared without any explanation. He also said they were very busy, she's a hard worker and this is out of character.'

'And is this the "disturbing facts that have come to light"?' Megan can't keep the disdain out of her voice. 'Debbie went out for some fresh air? Collins has excelled himself with that stunning piece of evidence.'

'No,' says Slater calmly. 'The victim's phone was recovered. On it we found a recording. I can play it for you if you like. But it may be better if I summarise.'

Megan stares at the boss. She's wearing her professional poker face. *This is going to be bad.*

'Yeah, summarise if you prefer,' Megan says. She's trying to sound casual and get a grip on her fury but she realises it's her turn to brace herself.

'Greg Porter made a recording on his phone of a conversation between himself and your sister. It seems likely that he did this covertly. The date on it is Tuesday, the day he was killed. The phone's being forensically examined to see if we can get more specific with the time.'

Get on with it!

Slater continues. 'The discussion was about money. Specifically the contract payment they'd agreed for the builders' clean. Debbie said she was having to do much more work and it was taking much more time than they'd initially agreed. His response was...' Slater sighs. She's searching for the right word.

'I already know that he was a difficult, tight-fisted employer. Debbie's told me as much.'

'His response was salacious in tone. He offered to increase the fee in return for a blowjob.'

'What!' Megan stares in disbelief.

'It seems from the tenor of the conversation that he'd made such a request before.' Slater hesitates. 'But that, in this instance, she probably complied.'

Whoever whacked Greg Porter has done the world a favour. Megan can hear her sister's words. And she agrees.

'I want to hear this recording. Please,' she says.

'No, Megan. Trust me. You don't. Not right now.'

'What are you saying? She did it? She... she gave him... and it's on...' Megan feels sick and angry.

'That's our conclusion. He does provide some commentary on what's happening.'

Motive. Opportunity. He forced her to do this so she killed him.

Megan puts her hand over her mouth to stop the tears. Finally she manages to say, 'You've got her in an interview room? What's she saying to you?'

'She won't talk to us. When we confronted her with the recording she just said "no comment".'

'Can I speak to her?'

'I wish you would. Because if she makes a full confession—'

Could she have done this?

'Yeah, I get it, boss. Mitigating circumstances. Reduced sentence. You don't have to spell it out.'

CHAPTER SIXTEEN

Friday, 10.35 a.m.

Megan follows Slater out of her room. As they walk through the open-plan office no one looks at her directly but she can feel the covert glances of her colleagues, their curiosity and their pity. Her stomach is churning and she reflects ruefully that if Debbie hadn't bashed Greg Porter's brains in, she might well have done it herself.

The interview rooms are along the corridor. Small, pokey and airless. Debbie is seated at the table; in front of her, the remains of a cardboard cup, which she's shredded. She looks up as Megan enters. Their eyes meet.

'I'll leave you to it,' says Slater. 'We'll regard this as an informal chat.'

'Thanks,' says Megan.

Slater leaves. Megan crosses the room and throws her arms around her sister. For several moments nothing is said. Megan can feel the warmth of her sister's skin, the familiar smell of her hair.

Then Debbie pulls away and says, 'I just feel like shit.'

'Sssh,' says Megan. 'They told me about the recording and what he made you do. If the bastard wasn't already dead, I'd've done it myself.'

Debbie's chin quivers. 'What's going to happen when Mark finds out? He'll know I did it for the money. He's just gonna think I'm a whore, isn't he? 'Cause that's how it is, isn't it? But the bastard just kept badgering me, Meg. Blokes like him, they think sex for money is normal. First time I told him to fuck off. Then he'd find a whole load of other shit for me to do. Rubbish to shift. More cleaning. I know I should've just walked away and told him to stick his fucking job. But we've got a stack of utility bills. The bank's just put up the interest rate on our overdraft. I was just… I dunno. It sounds pathetic.'

The tears are rolling down Debbie's face.

Megan clutches her by the shoulders. 'I wish you'd told me you needed money.'

'I didn't want to put it on you. How could I? You've had a tough enough time. I'm so sorry.'

'No, I'm sorry that I wasn't there for you. But we'll get you a bloody good lawyer, don't worry.'

Debbie wipes her face with the back of her hand. She seems surprised. 'I didn't kill him.'

Megan hesitates. 'Okay. So what did happen?'

'Nothing. I just went there to clean on Wednesday morning. And I found him. I told you.'

'Have you said that? Why have you been saying "no comment"?'

'Of course I said that. Several times. But they just kept repeating the same bloody questions. *What happened? When did you go back there? Were you angry?* Yeah, I was fucking angry. But I didn't kill him. I told them. They obviously didn't believe me. So I gave up and said no comment. I just want to get out of here, Meg. Please.'

'Just explain one thing to me. Tuesday night, when you were at work. You left the pub for three quarters of an hour. Where did you go?'

'How do you know about that?'

'The CCTV's been checked. You went out of the back door at eight fifteen, came back at nine.'

Debbie stares at her in horror. 'You think I did it too.'

'No—'

'Don't fucking lie, Meg. Slut I may be, but I'm not a murderer.' Debbie folds her arms tightly and turns her face away.

Megan stares at her. She's at a loss. He sister is a complicated character. Sunny and breezy on the surface but there's a dark undertow to Debbie. Marriage to Mark and having three children has grounded her. But before that her life was full of ups and downs. She's always been useless with money. Her teenage years involved a lot of drugs. And there's one thing Megan knows about her sister: Debbie is a virago when her blood's up. She fights back. There have been some nasty incidents in the past: the boyfriend she attacked with a frying pan. He ended up in A&E but decided not to press charges. On another occasion Debbie got into an argument in a pub. She was queuing at the bar when a bloke groped her. She went ballistic and would've shoved a glass in his face if Megan hadn't stopped her.

Megan sits down opposite her at the table. 'Listen to me, Deb, your word is good enough for me. Always has been, always will be. Because what else is there but trust? You've seen me at my worst. You were the one who stuck with me. And I'll stick with you now. That's the bottom line. If you say you didn't kill him, then you didn't kill him. That's where we start. Okay?'

Debbie meets her gaze. 'Okay.' She reaches out her hand, Megan grasps it and squeezes it.

'Okay,' Megan says. 'But I need ammunition to get you out of here. "No comment" is not going to work. It's like an admission of guilt. So why did you leave the pub?'

Debbie sighs. 'I've been getting headaches again.'

'Migraines? Like you used to get?'

'Yeah. So I went to the doctor. She said it was probably stress and sleeping badly, as if I didn't know that. But she gave me these pills. Not painkillers but you take one if you feel it coming on. Suma… tripta… something or other. They sort of relax your blood vessels. Stop the migraine developing. On Tuesday night, I went to work. But I could feel my head getting bad. I didn't want to just go home, because I'd lose a night's pay. So I thought, if I slip out, take one of my pills, I could walk it off in about half an hour.'

'And that's what you did? Did you tell anyone?'

'No, I just walked round the town. Up and down some of the back streets. And the pill worked. I started to feel better and I went back to work.'

'Can you remember any of the route, the streets you went up?'

'I dunno. I was on autopilot. You know a place, you can just wander round. I sat on the steps overlooking the harbour for a bit, because there was a cool breeze.'

'It all makes sense. And you've got a prescription from your doctor giving you these pills.'

'Yeah.' Debbie seems distracted. She fidgets.

'Look at me, Deb. You sure? Because these details will be checked.'

Debbie meets her gaze. This is the technique she's always used. A surly look, challenging Megan to call her a liar. 'I'm sure, okay.'

'Okay.' She can sense Debbie's desperation, which is not a good sign.

'I've got to get out of here, Meg. Mark's coming home tonight for the weekend. I don't know what the hell I'm going to say to him.'

Megan gets up and paints on a smile. 'Just sit tight. I'm going to go and talk to my boss.'

She walks calmly out of the door but her heart is pounding. Could Debbie have done this? She has to force that thought out of her mind.

CHAPTER SEVENTEEN

Friday, 10.50 a.m.

As Megan walks towards Slater's office she sees that Jim Collins is already in there having a conversation with the DCI. He's wearing a crisp white shirt, silk tie neatly knotted. They both see her approaching. She decides to go in guns blazing. There's no point messing around.

She pauses on the threshold. 'She says she didn't do it and I believe her.'

Collins huffs, puts his hands on his hips and faces Slater. 'Megan should not be involved in this, ma'am. It's completely inappropriate.'

Slater sighs.

'Your evidence is circumstantial,' says Megan. 'You've homed in on a single suspect. She has a perfectly reasonable explanation for why she left the pub.'

'Then why didn't she give it to us?' says Collins. He turns back to Slater. 'I reiterate, ma'am. This is not appropriate.'

'Oh for heaven's sake, Jim,' says Slater. 'This is her sister. What do you expect?'

'I expect not to be vilified for doing my job. And I expect you, as the SIO, to support me. Ma'am.'

'Then do your bloody job,' says Megan. 'What have you actually found out about Greg Porter? Does he have a wife? What's her story? What about business associates? Who else could he have pissed off?'

'You have no idea what we've been doing,' says Collins evenly. 'I've been looking into your sister's finances. Do you know how deeply in debt she is?'

'That doesn't make her a murderer.'

'It makes her desperate. And having agreed to perform a sexual act she later regretted, and of which she's ashamed, it gives her a very good motive for murder. I think you have to consider, Megan, that in the circumstances, she's probably lying to you as well.'

He could be right. Megan bats this thought away.

'What sort of man was Porter?' she says. 'If he was capable of bullying and blackmailing a female employee into giving him a blowjob, then it strikes me his lifestyle and connections warrant some investigation.'

'And that is in hand,' says Collins, checking his watch. 'I have an appointment to speak to his father at eleven. His wife and children are being looked after by the family liaison officer. Questionable morals or not, he is the victim here.'

'He's not the only victim,' says Megan.

'She could've just said no to him,' says Collins with a shrug. 'This is not a rape or a sexual assault. There's no evidence of coercion. She did it for the money. So you could argue that both parties have questionable morals.'

Megan is within a hair's breadth of losing it. *Calm down. Play it smart.* She catches Slater's eye. The boss is tight-lipped. But Megan's guess is she'll hedge her bets.

'All right,' says Slater. 'This is not getting us anywhere. Jim is right about one thing, Megan, we need some very clear boundaries. You cannot be involved in this inquiry. You have every right to speak on behalf of your sister but you do so in a personal capacity.'

She inhales. 'I accept that, boss. But the evidence against my sister is circumstantial. At present I don't see that there are grounds to charge her.'

'I agree with that,' says Slater. 'We're not ready yet to take this to the CPS so I propose to release her under investigation, while we pursue other lines of inquiry.'

'I think that's a mistake, ma'am,' says Collins. 'I think we should continue to question her. I think that when the seriousness of her situation is brought home to her, she will tell us the truth. You let her go home, regroup, get her story straight' – he glares at Megan – 'and you lose the initiative.'

'You're talking about it as if it's a psychological game,' says Megan bitterly.

'And you would too,' says Collins. 'If you had no personal involvement.' He looks at his watch again. 'I should go, ma'am. If you'll excuse me. Barry Porter will be waiting for me.'

Slater gives him a nod and he leaves.

Megan and Slater are left facing each other.

The boss sighs and says, 'He is just doing his job.'

'And loving every fucking minute!' says Megan.

'I know you're upset and I would be too. But if you want to help your sister, you've got to take a step back and look at the overall situation and the evidence. Attacking Jim Collins is spiteful and will get you nowhere.'

'Oh come on, boss. Ma'am this, ma'am that. He's a supercilious bastard and he pisses you off as much as he does me.'

'I'm not going to comment on that. Take your sister home, let her calm down and then talk to her. If she did this, then her best defence is to make the court understand why. Now this is just between you and me, and I'm only speculating, but a defence of coercive control might be applicable in this case. It's uncharted territory but you get a really good lawyer to argue it and you might get it down to manslaughter.'

Megan nods. She knows Laura Slater is going out on a limb here. 'Okay. Thank you.'

'Also, on a different note, I spoke to Danny Ingram on the phone. He's been talking to his boss and the NCA are keen to ramp up their people-smuggling investigation down here. They're bringing in more resources. Ingram seems very impressed with you so I'm reluctant to take you off the case. But I will if you want me to.'

Megan exhales. What the hell does she want? She has a maelstrom of thoughts and fears spinning in her brain. *What if Debbie's lying? What if she is guilty?*

'It's your call,' says Slater. 'But, if you take my advice, you'll carry on with the NCA case. Why? Because it'll keep you occupied and out of trouble. And I know you, Megan. I don't want you interfering with some covert investigation of your own. And I don't want another set to with Collins. You have to let the murder inquiry take its course. And we will be looking at all potential suspects. Be assured that as SIO, I will be keeping a close eye on it. Do we understand one another?'

Megan nods. *Cold-hearted bitch!*

'Yes we do,' she says. 'And thank you.'

She looks at Laura Slater and wonders what she's thinking behind that icy façade. Does she have a sister? Megan has no idea. But she knows one thing: at the end of the day, Slater's priority will be a result that leads to a conviction.

CHAPTER EIGHTEEN

Friday, 11.15 a.m.

Megan walks back to her desk. The office is half empty; no sign of Collins, Ted or Vish. Brittney is making coffee. She gives Megan a sidelong glance, picks up her mug and wanders over.

'Are you okay?' she says.

Megan isn't. She can feel her lip trembling. She has to swallow to suppress a tear. Rage has morphed into despair. She needs time to collect her thoughts and make a plan. What Debbie has told her sounds plausible. The migraine, the pills. And she wants to believe her. She wants it desperately. But she also knows her sister. Debbie knows how to spin a line. She's good at it. Always has been.

Megan forces a smile. 'Have you got a sister?'

'Two brothers, both younger. They can be a bit of a pain.'

Not as much of a pain as this.

Brittney holds out her mug. 'Fancy a coffee? You look like you could do with it. And I've drunk about four already this morning, so I'm buzzing.'

'I'm fine,' says Megan. 'Slater is releasing Debbie under investigation. I need to take her home.'

'Well,' says Brittney. 'Good luck.'

Megan knows she shouldn't ask, but she can't help it. 'Has he actually got a case? I know I shouldn't ask you—'

'Megan, I don't really know what they're up to. And I'm not just saying that. I'm not that involved in the inquiry. He's got me and Kitty doing back office. Putting all the post mortem stuff in the system. Typing up his stupid handwritten notes. To tell you the truth, I'm a bit bored.'

Typical bloody Collins. Megan feels incensed on her behalf.

'You're a DC, Brit,' she says. 'Not a civilian analyst. And certainly not his bloody secretary. If Collins is running a boys' club and cutting you out of the loop, you should tell Slater.'

Brittney shrugs. 'She'll just think I'm whinging though, won't she? And that'll piss her off.'

Megan knows she's right. The boss takes a tough line with whingers.

'Are you still on the NCA thing?' Brittney says with a tentative smile.

'Theoretically,' says Megan.

'How's the woman we found on the beach?'

'I don't know.'

Brittany's angling. Megan can feel it. She knows what's coming next and so she says, 'Look, I'd like to rescue you but I've got a lot on my plate at the moment.'

The young DC bristles. 'I wasn't going to ask you to.'

'Yeah, you were. But you've got to learn to stick up for yourself. Front up to Collins. Tell him straight. He needs to do his own typing and treat you and Vish exactly the same.'

Brittney stiffens. 'Right. I will. No problem.' She walks away.

That went well.

Megan slumps down at her desk; she feels mean. Brittney didn't deserve that. *Spiteful?* That's the word Slater used. Is that what Megan does when she gets wound up? Lashes out. It's stupid and short-sighted.

She checks her phone. There's a text from Ingram. *Briefing at the hotel at 3. Hope you can make it.*

Debbie is being processed by the custody officer. Megan wonders what she's going to do with her sister. She can't just take her home and dump her. But, on the other hand, leaving her some space to reflect might be a good idea. If fear and panic have driven her into a corner and made her lie, she might think better of it once she's in her own place and can calm down. *And she could well be lying.* That's the reality Megan has to face.

Megan glances across the room. Brittney is standing next to Kitty's desk. The two young women are chatting. Megan looks across at the boss's office. The door is ajar. Slater is on the phone.

Sod it! Megan comes to a decision. If she knew the truth, at least she could work out what to do next. She gets up and, with one eye on Slater's office, she strolls over to Brittney and Kitty's corner.

'Listen, Brit, I'm sorry,' she says.

Brittney shrugs. 'You're right, I'm a wuss. Kitty agrees.'

The analyst nods and smiles. 'I've told him to get his own bloody coffee. And now he doesn't ask me.' She gives Brittney a pointed look. 'And I would rat him out to Slater. In fact I'd make a formal complaint.'

Brittney gives her friend a sheepish grin. Kitty is small and fierce and takes no prisoners.

'Anyway,' says Megan. 'There's still no excuse for me being a bitch.'

'Hey,' says Brittney, reaching out and touching Megan's arm. 'It's okay. This must be horrible for you. I get it.'

Brittney is soft and warm-hearted, which makes Megan feel worse.

'It's just all such a mess,' she says.

'Yeah, we know,' says Brittney. 'Do you think she did it?'

Megan avoids the question. She can't even answer it in her own mind. 'How much CCTV have you actually got from Berrycombe?'

'First lot is round the immediate area of the flats,' says Kitty. 'But it's patchy. Builders' security for the site. The block has got its own system, but that's not up and running yet. Collins also asked us to concentrate on the area round the pub.'

'The Duke of York, where Debbie works? So you've got her leaving and returning?'

Brittney nods. 'By the back door.'

'But you don't have her entering the flats?' says Megan.

'We have her on Wednesday morning, using the front door, where there is a camera. But there's also a service entrance through the basement car park where the camera isn't connected up yet.'

Megan sighs. 'Thing is—' She hesitates. She knows she shouldn't do this. *But it's for Debbie.* 'My sister has problems with migraines. She took a pill and left the pub to try and clear her head. She says she wandered through the back streets around town and ended up sitting on some steps near the harbour.'

Megan has a tight knot in her stomach. If Slater gets wind, she's stuffed. But she doesn't care.

Kitty and Brittney exchange glances.

'Well,' says Kitty. 'If we could track her phone…' She turns to Brittney. 'Who's got it? Has it gone to the lab?'

'Dunno,' says Brittney. 'Ted was in charge of the search.'

'That's only one layer of data,' says Kitty. 'And it's not going to be that accurate in the centre of town. CCTV is much better. We can certainly widen the trawl and get more granular. It may take a couple of days to access some of the cameras.'

'And they don't all work,' says Brittney.

Kitty's fingers skip across her keyboard. 'Some belong to private businesses, but the council has a map. Plots where they all are. So we can go round and ask them to show us.'

The map of Berrycombe pops up on Kitty's screen. It's covered in red dots.

'We'll start around the harbour and work outwards,' says Brittney. 'Do you know which side of the harbour?'

Megan shakes her head. She's skating on thin ice. But they don't need any encouragement.

Kitty points at the screen. 'Harbour steps there and there. And at the end. There's a restaurant on the corner with three outside cameras.'

Brittney is leaning in and frowning through her glasses. 'That would probably cover those steps. Depending on the angle of the camera. I could go and look.'

Megan watches. Then she says, 'You realise I shouldn't be—'

'Megan,' says Brittney with a smile. 'We're sitting here twiddling our thumbs. It's logical to extend the search area. I'm acting on my own initiative. As you rightly point out, I am supposed to be a DC.'

The dimpled cheeks, the owl glasses; Megan could hug her.

'Thank you,' she says softly. Then she adds, 'The NCA are expanding their inquiry. They'll probably need more help. I'll get you back on it.'

Brittney turns to look at her. 'You don't have to do that.'

'Yeah I do,' says Megan. 'Because it's a complex investigation and Slater's going to want us to keep our end up. So I'm going to need you.'

CHAPTER NINETEEN

Friday, 12.45 p.m.

Yvonne has taken refuge in the conservatory. She's wearing an old wash-faded pair of pyjamas and a towelling robe. As Penny has pointed out, there's no one to answer to any more. She can do as she likes. The doors stand open to the garden and the smell of cut grass is drifting through on the breeze. She's settled herself on a lounger and she has a bottle of white wine in a cooler on the table next to her. It's a Chevalier Montrachet, from Greg's wine club stash, and ridiculously expensive.

Penny has put the awful Christine in charge of the children. She makes a passable nanny. She gave them breakfast and then for the rest of the morning they've been settled in front of the television. They probably think it's Christmas. Yvonne knows she should speak to them. But she's been putting it off. The truth is she's not used to having serious conversations with her own children; that was Greg's department. He didn't like her to interfere.

Aidan understands what's happened to his father. In many ways Aidan understands far too much. But the younger three have only been told that Daddy's gone away on business. This seems to have satisfied their curiosity for the time being. But they're being good. They know not to make a mess.

The huge fronds on the indoor palm are whispering. Yvonne prefers the company of plants to people. They're cleansing. The conservatory is full of old friends that she knows individually. Turning her head she realises that Penny is standing in the doorway watching her. Her hands are neatly folded. She always looks so perfect. How does she do it? Yvonne is envious. Men like Penny, they always have.

Penny smiles. 'A car's just pulled up,' she says. 'It's Barry.'

Oh shit. Yvonne reaches for her wine and takes a hefty slug.

Her relationship with her father-in-law is detached and cordial. To him she's simply Greg's wife. If he's ever given her any thought in the last eighteen years it's only that.

'Want me to deal with him?' says Penny.

Yvonne sighs. *Yes.* But it's too late. The ever-efficient Christine has already opened the front door to him and is ushering him through the kitchen towards the conservatory.

Barry Porter is large and bluff. He's over seventy but still has a full head of wavy silver hair with untidy sideburns. He favours open-neck shirts and cavalry twill trousers in khaki or pink.

He sails through the door from the kitchen with his meaty paws outstretched. She hates his hands. They never look clean and the backs are matted with hair like a gorilla. He ignores Penny and homes in on Yvonne.

'My *poor poor* darling, you must be absolutely devastated! I would've come yesterday but Marion's in pieces. Well, you can imagine. Her only child. It's just so… I don't know where to begin.' His eyes are bloodshot; booze or tears, probably both.

Yvonne is lugged into an awkward embrace. He smells of cologne and whiskey.

As he releases her, tears well in his eyes. 'My God, you're wearing his bathrobe.' He shakes his head sorrowfully.

Yvonne pulled it out of the charity bag because it was clean and soft and snuggly. It probably once belonged to her husband. But she can't remember him wearing it.

Barry greets Penny with a nod and, uninvited, plonks down on a basket chair.

'Well,' he says. 'I've spoken to the police. A detective inspector. He seems a very competent fellow. Such a terrible business. Awful for you. And you must've spent the night worrying when he didn't come home.'

'Not really. I assumed he was with her.'

Barry sighs and wipes his nose with the back of his hand. 'Yvonne, Greg was my son and I know he wasn't perfect. But he adored you and the children. You were the absolute cornerstone of his life.' His chin quivers. 'I have no doubt of that and I know in his heart he was always faithful. The rest was meaningless.' He glances at Penny, she turns away.

Yvonne's head feels woozy and relaxed. Most of a bottle of wine has loosened her tongue too.

'Does she know?' she asks.

'I'm not sure I know who you're—'

'Oh come on, Barry. His current bit on the side. The Spanish woman.'

'If you mean Elena, I can assure you that she was a business associate, pure and simple. There was absolutely nothing untoward in her relationship with Greg.'

Yvonne considers this as she takes another mouthful of wine.

'Oh, I see,' she says. 'You thought she was just shagging you?'

Barry glances at the wine. Then he gives Penny a reproachful look.

'I think you're a bit tiddly, my dear,' he says. 'Understandable. The stress of it all. I've had a few glasses myself.'

'Could Elena have bashed him on the head?' Yvonne pours the remains of the bottle into her glass. 'I've been wondering about that. Lover's tiff?'

He sighs. 'You're upset, Yvonne. But you really need to be careful what you say and who you say it to.'

'Do I? Why?'

'Okay. Well, I didn't want to go into this. Because I didn't want to upset you more than necessary. But the police know who did it.'

'This detective inspector told you?' says Penny.

'No. But I managed to have a word with his sergeant. Chap called Ted. I don't know him that well but he plays golf at the club. We have friends in common. He's a good, reliable sort. He spoke to me in confidence and has promised to keep me updated. They expect to charge this person very soon.'

'Who is it then?' says Penny.

'A woman who worked for Greg as a cleaner. Some sort of dispute about money. She lives in Berrycombe, has something of a reputation as a tart. Trust me, you ladies do not want to hear the sordid details.'

Yvonne takes a large swallow of wine. 'Well, that's that, then.'

He reaches over and puts his paw on her knee. 'We're all devastated. I'm not sure his mother will ever recover.'

Yvonne pictures her mother-in-law. Marion is a strange woman. Hard to fathom. But, like Yvonne, she loves gardening. It annoyed Greg that the two women always had something to talk about. He said it made him feel like he'd married his mother. It wasn't a compliment.

'Do give Marion my love,' says Yvonne.

'Of course I will. I don't know when the body will be released but, don't worry, I'll make all the arrangements. You don't need to be bothered with any of that.'

The old man likes to be in charge. That was Greg's view of his father and it turned their relationship into a battleground. They bickered continually about everything from politics to golf.

'Thank you,' she says meekly. Now she just wants him to go. Leave her in peace. His sheer physical presence nauseates her.

But he goes on, 'And I'll speak to Greg's lawyer. Wills, money, it's all going to be rather complicated with his various business interests. But I'll deal with all that for you.'

Yvonne glances at her sister. 'No,' she says. 'Penny's got a lawyer in London who'll help me sort out my husband's estate.'

Penny looks at her with some surprise.

But Barry stares in disbelief. 'Really? I don't see why. That's totally unnecessary.'

He glares at Penny. She smiles and follows Yvonne's lead. 'You've got your own grief to cope with,' she says. 'And Marion to look after.'

'I'm not sure it's what my son would've wanted. But we don't have to come to any firm decisions now. I'm sure we're all in shock.' He gets up. He seems annoyed. 'Would you like me to speak to Aidan?'

Aidan was in the kitchen earlier but made himself scarce as soon as his grandfather arrived.

'He might be in his room,' says Yvonne. *He's probably hiding out in the pool house until you leave.*

'Okay, I'll go up. We'll discuss the estate another time, when you're in a better frame of mind. I think you must accept, my dear, that I have a better grasp of your husband's business affairs than you do.'

Yvonne stares at him. What he's saying is true but she's in no mood to give in.

She says nothing.

Barry gives them a curt nod, stomps back through the kitchen and disappears.

Yvonne heaves a sigh. 'I think I'll open another bottle.'

Penny folds her arms and says, 'Well, that's certainly rattled his cage. You haven't said anything to me before about a lawyer. Is that what you want?'

Yvonne gets to her feet. 'Yes,' she says. 'You may think I've been sitting here getting pissed but I've also been thinking. Can you help me find someone?'

'Of course. Though I suspect, if you don't want to get screwed over by your father-in-law, we'll need a firm of forensic accountants too.'

'Fine. Then that's what I want.'

CHAPTER TWENTY

Friday, 2.30 p.m.

On the drive home, Megan and Debbie spoke little. Debbie seemed unreachable in her misery.

'What time is Mark due back?' Megan asked.

'His train doesn't get in until seven,' her sister replied.

'It will be all right, you know.'

'Don't talk rubbish, Meg. This time I've fucked it for good. There's no way out.' She turned and gave Megan a pointed look. 'C'mon, you know that better than anyone.'

They continued for another half mile in silence. Then Debbie added, 'Probably better if I had killed him and I went to jail. Easier for everyone.'

Was that self pity or something more? Megan wasn't sure she was ready for the answer so she didn't ask.

She dropped Debbie outside the house and drove to Torquay for her meeting with the NCA. For the whole journey her brain pecked away at her sister's last statement. Was it the precursor to an admission of guilt? Was Debbie searching for a way to confess that she'd lied? As a teenager, she was always silent and sullen before finally coming to her big sister full of contrition and fessing up. Was that about to happen here? It sounded like it. Megan wondered if she should start to look for a lawyer.

*

Danny Ingram greets her in the foyer of the hotel. Megan has the impression he's been lying in wait. He has his hands in his pockets and a boyish grin on his face.

'Well, here we are again,' he says with a big smile. Then he scans her face and frowns. 'Are you all right?'

'Not really.' She has an overwhelming desire to collapse in his arms and sob on his shoulder. But Garcia is approaching.

'We're all set up in one of the meeting rooms—' says Garcia.

He raises an index finger. 'Hang on, Sash.'

'You may as well both know,' says Megan. 'My sister has just become the prime suspect in a murder investigation.'

It's out there. Megan scans their faces for a reaction, a judgement. But all she sees is concern.

'Shit!' says Garcia. 'Who's she supposed to have murdered?'

'A sleazebag she worked for. She was doing a contract cleaning job. She asked him for more money. He said only if she gave him a blowjob. She and her husband are in serious debt.' Tears well in Megan's eyes. 'So she agreed.'

'Jesus wept!' says Ingram.

'You can see where they're coming from in terms of motive,' says Megan. 'That same evening, when the murder took place, she went AWOL from her other job in a pub and can't really prove where she was. Next morning he's discovered with his head bashed in.'

'What do you think?' Ingram asks.

'She says she didn't do it. She's my sister and I believe her.' *Hollow words.*

'I believe her too,' says Garcia.

Megan and Ingram both stare at her.

'You sound very convinced and you don't even know her,' he says. 'Why?'

'Anger leads to violence against others, shame leads to violence against oneself.'

It sounds to Megan like something she read in a book. But it's a straw worth grasping.

Garcia goes on. 'How do you know about the blowjob? From her?'

'No, he recorded the whole encounter on his phone. I suppose he got off on it.'

'And she only admitted it when confronted with the recording.'

'Yes,' says Megan. 'I haven't heard it. My boss just summarised.'

'Well,' says Garcia. 'Killing him draws attention to her shame. It's the opposite of covering it up. If he says "give me a blowjob" and she says "fuck off, how dare you" and attacks him that's a much more logical prelude to violence. If she gave him what he wanted, she's much more likely to keep it secret.'

Megan ponders this. Then she says, 'But what if she didn't know he made a recording? She kills him to conceal what she's done.'

Garcia sighs. 'Yeah, you got me there. Who found the body?'

'She did. When she went to clean the next morning.'

Garcia opens her palms. 'There you go then,' she says. 'Unless she's totally stupid, which I'm assuming she isn't, that's the last thing she'd do. If she is guilty that draws the immediate attention of the police to her, which she'd want to avoid. It's a common psychological fault among police officers to over-connect a witness with a crime. Our brains like to join up the dots of what we know. But most perpetrators, unless they're psychopaths and want to be at the centre of the drama, go out of their way to distance themselves from what they've done. Common sense, if you think about it.'

Megan smiles. Garcia is right. Annoyingly arrogant, but logical. Megan has been so wound up in the emotion of what's happened to her sister, that she hasn't been looking at the whole situation clearly. Now Debbie's attitude and behaviour makes more sense. She's just deeply ashamed about the blowjob. Of course she is.

Megan feels a surge of panic. *Shame leads to violence against oneself.* She left Debbie alone deliberately. But maybe that's the last thing she should've done. *There's no way out.* That's what her sister said.

'Can you give me five minutes?' she says to Ingram. 'I need to make a phone call.'

'No problem, we'll be in the conference room. We've got a couple more colleagues who've arrived.'

As he and Garcia turn to go, Megan grabs her arm and says, 'Hey, thanks, Sasha.'

Garcia beams. 'My pleasure.'

Megan goes out onto the hotel terrace and dials her sister's number. It rings and goes to voicemail. She presses it again, her anxiety rising. Voicemail again. She presses it a third time. How could she be so stupid? Debbie's desperation was clear to see and she ignored it. All she was focused on was whether or not her sister was lying to her. She presses the phone again. Voicemail. And again. Her hands are sweating. What if she's too late? It doesn't bear thinking about.

Finally Debbie answers. 'Meg?'

'Where the hell are you? I've called about five, maybe six times.'

'I'm up on Berry Head. The signal's crap.'

'What are you doing up there?'

'I thought I'd take the dog for a walk. Fresh air, a chance to clear my head.'

Calm down. She's not about to throw herself off Berry Head if she's got Scout with her.

'Listen, Deb. I've been thinking all this through. It's just bullshit, them arresting you. They have not got a case. And we'll sort it out, I promise.'

'I know it's bullshit.'

'But I'm worried about you.'

Debbie sighs. 'If he divorces me, he divorces me.'

'Mark is not going to divorce you. He's going to be upset. But he's mainly going to be upset with himself because you were so desperate for money that you agreed to this.'

There's a silence on the line.

Then Debbie says, 'You're probably right. The whole thing's a fucking mess.'

'But we'll get through it. All of us. Together.'

'Yeah.' It sounds as if Debbie's crying.

'I promise,' says Megan.

'I've been thinking about Amber. What sort of example am I setting to my daughter? She's just going to think—'

'She's fourteen. She doesn't need to know the details.'

'But what if there's a trial?' says Debbie. 'Then it'll all come out in court.'

'Trust me,' says Megan. 'There'll be no trial. It won't get that far. I'll make sure of that. We're going to prove your innocence. Do you want me to come home now? Are you going to be all right?'

There's a sardonic chuckle on the end of the line. 'Don't worry, Meg. I'm not going to top myself. I wouldn't do that to my children.'

'I hope you wouldn't do it to me either,' says Megan.

CHAPTER TWENTY-ONE

Friday, 3 p.m.

Megan sits at the oval table. There are five of them; Ingram and Garcia are joined by two colleagues from the National Crime Agency. The room has a high, ornate ceiling. It was once the hotel ballroom and has been partitioned down the middle and repurposed as a conference suite. Danny Ingram is opposite her. He probably thinks he's being discreet but she can feel his eyes tracking her. She's not sure if she finds his concern reassuring or intrusive.

In her lap, under the table, she's holding her phone. She's texted Brittney for an update but has received no reply. She's resisting the temptation to hassle. Brittney and Kitty are on it. They'll be checking all the CCTV they can get their hands on. But what if Collins has found out and stopped them? Except Brittney is canny. *But what if…?* Her anxiety is in overdrive. *Get a grip.*

'Right,' says Ingram. 'Let's start with an update from Bibi.'

Megan has been introduced to the new arrivals: a young man with a shaved head and a goatee beard, the techie, and a small, stout woman in her fifties.

Bibi, the woman, smiles. She's wearing pearlescent pink lipstick. 'We've interviewed Ranim with the aid of a translator,' she says. 'The loss of her son is obviously a huge source of distress. However, that seems to have motivated her to help us. She thinks the smugglers could have rescued him and is angry that they didn't. She regards that as a breach of faith. So we have a co-operative witness, which is unusual. Illegal migrants picked up in these circumstances tend to be unwilling to give information.'

'Has she been offered any incentives?' says Garcia.

'We assume that she'll be asking for asylum,' says Bibi. 'But as yet she hasn't mentioned it.'

'So you think her information is untainted?' says Garcia.

'Yes. I read her as an angry mother who wants to punish those she holds responsible for the death of her son.'

'That should make her very useful to us,' says Ingram. 'She may be able to ID members of the gang.'

Megan is trying hard to stay focused on the discussion. But her mind is wandering. She keeps surreptitiously checking her phone. She thinks about Debbie and the desperation that drove her into Greg Porter's net. If only her sister had confided in her. *Why didn't she?* This is the question torturing Megan. Why didn't Debbie trust her? What's happened to the tight bond that's sustained them since childhood? Is it Megan's fault they're no longer as close as they were? Her brain keeps nattering away. *If they can just find some CCTV...*

'... and so factoring in the timings and the fuel needed that does suggest that the boats being used could be moored, at least overnight, in a local marina,' says Bibi.

'Megan?' says Ingram.

She starts. Her gaze meets his. He's smiling.

'Sorry,' she says. 'Yeah, the boats. We can start with the harbour office. They'll have a pretty good idea about the comings and goings.'

'The boat that Ranim was on was piloted by a man in his early fifties, bushy beard,' says Bibi. 'There were two crew, both much younger men. She thought they might be brothers. All dark-haired, Mediterranean appearance and spoke the same language. The older man gave the orders, the younger ones drove the jet skis that brought them ashore.'

'Family business maybe?' says Garcia.

'Could be,' says Ingram. 'Does she know what language they were speaking?'

Bibi shakes her head.

'The crossing was from France, so they could be French,' says Megan. She feels the need to throw something into the mix to prove she's paying attention.

'We know they weren't speaking Arabic,' says Bibi, 'but Ranim has a smattering of French. She spent time in Lebanon and it's still widely spoken there because of the former colonial connection with France.'

'Not French then,' says Megan. 'What about Spanish?'

'I think that's a good bet,' says Garcia. 'And it would tie up with our intel. If a Spanish crew moor their vessel in a local harbour, how noticeable is that going to be?'

'I've really no idea,' says Megan. 'But we can certainly find out.'

As the meeting breaks up, Ingram approaches Megan. They face each other with a degree of awkwardness.

'If you need to slip off—' he says.

'No,' she replies. 'I need to do my job and keep Slater onside. If I go off-piste, I'll lose her sympathy.'

'You're quite a strategist,' he says. 'I wish I had you on the team permanently.'

She folds her arms and sighs. 'Listen, Danny,' she says, 'what happened last night was…'

He holds up his hand. 'Hey, don't say any more. You don't have to.'

'I don't want you to think… I mean, it was nice—'

He shoves his hands in his pockets and hunches his shoulders. 'Yeah, it was fun, but I get it, you've got a lot to contend with. And I'm a grown-up. It's fine. There's no need for explanations.'

He's grinning inanely and looks more like a teenage boy getting the brush-off than a grown-up.

Megan shifts from foot to foot. Upsetting him is the last thing she wants. *More guilt.*

He tilts his head, gives her a wry smile. 'Well, we're still colleagues. Maybe a bit more than… anyway, this situation with your sister, if you need a sounding board, someone to talk things over with, I'm quite a strategist myself. I may be able to help.'

'Thank you,' she says. 'I appreciate that.'

He dips his head. 'That's okay.'

Megan feels a surge of relief. One less problem to deal with. But as she watches him walk away she feels a pang of disappointment.

CHAPTER TWENTY-TWO

Friday, 4.15 p.m.

Megan calls ahead for an appointment with the harbour master. As the four of them walk down the hill from the car park towards the harbour, Megan falls into step beside Garcia. Ingram is several paces behind, deep in conversation with the techie, Rodney. Bibi has remained at the hotel.

'So,' says Garcia. 'Did you and Dano have a nice dinner?'

Dano? She remains annoying but Megan reminds herself that Garcia has been helpful.

'Yeah,' says Megan. 'We went to a burger joint. Don't think you would've liked it.'

Garcia chuckles and gives Megan a sidelong glance. 'He's a sneaky operator. He cut me out of the loop.'

Megan responds with an innocent shrug. 'Don't see why. We talked mainly cop war stories. You'd've probably been bored.'

Garcia smiles sadly. 'I irritate you, don't I? I irritate most people.'

'No—'

'Yeah, I do. It's okay, you don't have to lie. He's probably told you I'm some predatory dyke, which is a bit unfair. I'm just interested in interesting people. And you, Megan, are an interesting woman.'

'Trust me,' says Megan. 'You'd be disappointed.'

'Queen's Police Medal? That's not a gong they give out every day. You must've done some serious shit to earn that.'

'It was an undercover job and I got lucky. It could've easily gone the other way.' That's an understatement.

'So is this your bolthole? A quiet life in Devon. An escape from all that?'

She's right, she is irritating.

'Has anyone ever told you that you ask too many questions?'

Garcia nods. 'Yep, I get told to go fuck myself on a fairly regular basis. But curiosity is the essential component of intellect. In my humble opinion.'

Megan laughs. Here's a very beautiful young woman looking her over appreciatively. It's hard not be flattered. Garcia is clever, no question. She exudes confidence and privilege. Megan wonders what it would've been like to grow up with just a bit of that. Life is such a lottery. Garcia was born with a winning ticket. You'd have to be a saint not to be envious and Megan knows she's far from that.

The harbour master's office is located on the first floor of a modern two-storey block overlooking Haldon Pier, which forms the southern arm of the outer harbour.

'Call me Alan,' says the harbour master, as he offers Megan his hand to shake. He's young and casual and not very nautical in appearance. 'We see the local police down here quite often. Drunks falling in the harbour. And we help the coastguard too,' he adds. 'But you're my first serious detectives.'

'That's probably a good thing,' says Megan, 'but we're just making some general enquiries. Nothing to be excited about.'

'Whatever I can do to help,' says Alan. He obviously is excited. Garcia has run a check and discovered he's only been in post a few months.

Out of the corner of her eye, Megan watches Ingram. He's reverted to the baseball cap and the aviator shades. This is her first chance to observe how he operates. And he's taking his time, wandering round the office, hands in pockets, gazing out of the window. Alan's gaze keeps flicking in his direction. Ingram knows how to subtly attract attention.

Megan can guess what he's up to. They have a problem. The marina itself is run by a private company. Going through official channels to access private data can be complicated and time consuming. The company may be wary and will probably want to protect the privacy of the millionaire owners of the posh yachts in their care. What Ingram needs is a shortcut.

He takes off his sunglasses, focuses on Alan and smiles.

'We're interested in the comings and goings, possibly later in the day, or maybe even after dark,' he says. 'Do visitors have to contact you before they're allowed to dock their boats?'

'This time of year we get a lot of visitors,' says Alan. 'For average size vessels – cabin cruisers, yachts – we don't require people to contact us in advance. We have a visitors' pontoon which is down there.' He points out of the large panoramic window at the jetty below. 'And we offer two hours' free mooring before they have to pay.'

'Better than the parking round here,' says Megan.

'It's to encourage people to visit the town, go in the shops and restaurants.'

'What about CCTV?' says Garcia.

'There are cameras mounted at the ends of the piers and at all the access points to the pontoons. We have over six hundred berths in the outer harbour and marina and two hundred in the inner harbour. You may have noticed there are some pretty expensive vessels out there. So security is a big issue.'

'Mind if we take a look at your set-up?' says Ingram casually.

'Of course. So who are you after? Drug dealers?'

Ingram chuckles. Then he gives Alan an avuncular pat on the shoulder. 'You'll appreciate I can't go into specific details. But you're obviously an astute bloke.'

Megan watches the young harbour master beam with pride at the flattery.

'We have to keep our eyes open,' he says. 'This is a commercial port as well as a leisure facility. Lots of things going on. But if we see anything untoward, we're on it.'

'I'm sure you are. And, actually, what would be a real help is if my colleague, Rodney, could take a closer look at your digital recordings.'

'I don't see any problem with that,' says Alan.

'Good man. Thank you,' says Ingram, giving him another gentle pat on the arm.

Rodney stands waiting near the door. He has a black backpack looped over one shoulder. Before they left the hotel Megan saw him assembling his box of tricks. A laptop, cables, several mysterious devices. She wonders what he's going to do.

Alan grins. 'Through here, mate.'

Rodney follows him into the control room. The bank of monitors can be glimpsed through the open door.

Ingram meets Megan's gaze. 'That was slickly done,' she says. 'Are we breaking the law?'

'Good Lord, no,' says Ingram. 'Just cutting a few corners. There's such a lot of stuff to trawl through. This'll make things easier.' He doesn't go into details and she decides not to ask.

'Let's go and get a coffee while Rod does his thing,' says Garcia.

'I'll stay here,' says Ingram. Megan has a feeling she's being managed. But she follows Garcia out of the door.

They walk along the harbourside in search of a cafe. Megan is expecting another raft of questions, so she's relieved when she sees Vish Prasad sitting on a wall in the sunshine, scrolling on his phone.

'Hey, Vish,' she says, walking over.

He looks up and beams. 'Megan, hi.'

Garcia is at her elbow, so she's forced to make introductions.

'DC Vish Prasad. Sasha Garcia from the NCA.'

'Cool,' says Vish with his best smile.

Megan watches them checking one another out. *Both so young and unscathed.* It doesn't improve her mood. She wishes she didn't feel so stressed and grumpy.

Vish sighs. 'Y'know, Megan, I'm really sorry about all this. I know she's your sister. And I spoke to Brittney. It's all a bit... well, y'know.' He seems embarrassed.

'It is what it is. The investigation will have to take its course. But what are you doing down here?'

'Oh,' he says with a huff. 'Just waiting for Ted.'

'Stopped off for a snack, has he?' The DS's appetite and need for frequent refuelling is well known in the office.

Now Vish seems even more embarrassed. 'No. He's talking to Barry Porter, the victim's father.'

'What? Interviewing him?'

'No. Collins did that earlier. But Ted knows Porter. I dunno, they're some sort of golf buddies. Ted said he's worried about him. Obviously the guy's upset. So Ted's gone to have a word with him. He's on his boat.'

'On his boat?'

'Yeah, it's that one down there.' Vish points down at the nearby pontoon. 'Third one along.'

Megan and Garcia look in the direction he's indicating. It's a sleek forty-footer, white with chrome trim, and it looks brand new.

'That's quite a toy,' says Garcia.

'Why didn't you go with him?' says Megan.

'He didn't want me to, told me to wait here.' Vish shrugs. 'I didn't want to argue with him.'

Megan nods thoughtfully. 'Okay.'

'You think I should've gone?' says Vish. 'But he's the sergeant, I'm just a DC.'

'I know,' says Megan. 'I'm just wondering why he didn't want you to?'

''Cause he's an arsehole,' says Vish.

'Yeah,' says Megan. 'You're probably right.'

'Still,' says Vish. 'I got to go and play a heavy with Dennis Bridger.'

Megan has spaced all that out in the emotional turmoil of her sister's arrest.

'How was that?' she says. *Has Bridger made a deal with Zac Yilmaz?* That could cast her problems in a whole new light.

'Pretty routine,' says Vish. 'He's a smarmy little creep. But you know what Ted told me? A murder charge against Bridger got dropped because some of the forensic evidence disappeared. Faulty procedures got blamed.'

'I've heard that one before,' says Garcia cynically.

'You think Bridger paid someone off?' says Vish gleefully.

Megan frowns at Garcia. 'Cock-ups happen far more often than conspiracies, Vish.'

Garcia shrugs. 'Statistically speaking, Megan's right.'

CHAPTER TWENTY-THREE

Friday, 5.45 p.m.

Megan is bone weary. She heads home, having declined Garcia's invitation to go for a meal. It's hard work batting away the smart questions and the scrutiny. All she wants to do is escape.

The events of the day have worn her to a frazzle. The awkwardness of her discussion with Danny, the machinations of her NCA colleagues, the accusations against her sister, all continue to spin round in her mind. And what the hell is Ted Jennings up to? Not to mention the shadow of Zac Yilmaz. She hasn't the headspace to think about that. She's also anxious to see Debbie and check how she is. The children will be home from school too and Megan is wondering what Debbie will have said to them. They're bound to be confused and worried.

She has the added irritation of having to drive round the block several times before she can find one of the few residents' parking slots. By the time she puts her key into the front door, her brain is ticking with annoyance. Scout comes trotting to greet her and she rubs his head.

'Good boy!'

That's when she hears her sister's raised voice.

'This is bloody ridiculous,' shouts Debbie. 'How am I supposed to manage?'

Megan walks through the door into the kitchen and is surprised to see Brittney standing there, looking uneasy and sheepish.

Debbie immediately turns to her. 'Did you know about this? Did you know they want my fucking phone?'

Brittany glances at Megan and readjusts the owl glasses on her nose. She seems embarrassed.

'I've been trying to explain,' says Brittney, 'that if we can—' She doesn't get a chance to finish.

'Can they do this, Meg?' says Debbie. 'Just walk in here and take my phone, my private property? They've already been through the whole bloody house.'

'I discovered that the phone wasn't found during this morning's search. And we do have a further warrant,' says Brittney. 'And I've been trying to explain that this could help her.'

'Help me, how?' says Debbie. 'It's bullshit.' She turns on her sister. 'You said you could sort this. How is it sorted? How can I manage without my phone? What if the kids need something? I can't afford to just get another one.'

Through the double doors into the sitting room, Megan can see the children sitting in a tight defensive line on the sofa. Amber has her arm around little Ruby. Kyle is just watching, wide-eyed and frozen. They all seem terribly young and vulnerable to Megan. The dog wanders back and takes up his post at their feet, head on his paws, but watchful.

'Listen to me, Deb—'

'No, you listen to me.' Debbie slams her hand on the kitchen table. 'Either I'm nicked or I'm not nicked. Which is it? You lot can't have it both ways.' She stares defiantly at Megan.

Megan sighs. 'Deb, it's more complicated than that.'

'Complicated, how?'

Brittney shifts from foot to foot in the background. She has her hands neatly clasped in front of her. She gives Megan a beseeching look. *She wants rescuing. They all want bloody rescuing!*

Megan turns to her sister. 'You've been released under investigation. They explained to you what that meant, Deb. The investigation is continuing and, as part of it, that means that they can take your phone.'

'You mean you want me to give it to her?' says Debbie. Her rage seems to be ebbing or perhaps she's simply run out of energy.

Brittney steps forward. 'What I was trying to explain,' she says, 'is that by examining Debbie's phone, we may be able to establish her location more precisely at the relevant time. And this in turn may confirm her account of events and exonerate her.'

'She's telling you the truth,' says Megan.

Debbie stares at them. She has a mulish expression which reminds Megan very much of how she was as a teenager. She glances at her children then slumps down on a kitchen chair and puts her face in her hands.

'What I wanted to ask you,' says Brittney gingerly, 'was about when you sat on the harbour steps. Could you have used your phone? Sent a text? Checked for messages?'

'What business is that of yours?' says Debbie. But the fight has gone out of her.

'Think, Deb,' says Megan. 'This could be important. After you left the pub. Did you use your phone at all?'

Brittney pushes her glasses up her nose again. 'The harbour steps that you sat on, were they the ones next to the restaurant? I think it's called the Fisherman's Kitchen.'

'Yeah,' says Debbie. She's entered the sullen phase; Megan remembers it well.

'Okay,' says Brittney. 'It's possible that your phone could've done what we call a "handshake" with the Wi-Fi in the restaurant.'

Debbie stares at her. 'What does that even mean?'

'It means,' says Megan, 'that we may be able to prove that you were where you say you were.'

Debbie sighs. She extracts her phone from her pocket and offers it to Brittney.

'Thank you,' says Brittney as she takes the phone.

'I did sit there and scroll through a few things,' says Debbie. 'To distract myself from the headache. I can't actually remember but I think I was looking for a new pair of trainers for my son. Something not too expensive. His feet are growing so fast at the moment...'

She glances through to the sitting room and meets Kyle's gaze. She smiles at him, he smiles back.

'Okay,' says Brittney, 'well, you'll get a receipt for the phone.'

Debbie dismisses this with a wave of her hand.

Brittney heads for the door. 'I'll be off.'

'Thanks, Brit,' says Megan. 'I'll see you out.'

As the two police officers move into the hall, Brittney mouths *I'm really sorry.*

Megan shakes her head and whispers, 'What about CCTV?'

'We've got a couple of bits but they're just fragments. Kitty's trying to track down some dash cam footage from a council rubbish truck that we think drove past her.'

'I really appreciate it,' says Megan. She keeps her voice low. 'And I'm sorry.'

Brittney shrugs. 'No problem. She's stressed.'

Megan opens the front door and takes an involuntary step back. Mark is standing on the doorstep, rummaging in his pocket, a holdall and backpack at his feet.

'Ah, brilliant,' he says with a big grin. 'Can't find my bloody key.'

Megan takes a deep breath and says, 'Mark! We didn't expect you until later.'

He picks up his bags and steps inside. 'Managed to get the early train. Had to run for it. And I'm starving. Hope there's something good for tea.'

He gives Brittney a friendly nod as she slips out of the door.

Debbie has got up from the table and stands framed in the kitchen doorway. From the hallway Mark catches the desolate expression on her face.

'What's up?' he says. 'Somebody die?'

CHAPTER TWENTY-FOUR

Friday, 6.10 p.m.

The glass and wood dining table is by an up-and-coming Scandinavian designer. Yvonne bought it from Heal's. At the time Greg moaned about the cost, but it seats ten, twelve at a pinch, which makes it ideal for dinner parties. Not that they've had any dinner parties lately. Greg prefers to eat out. More often than not she isn't invited. Business. That's his usual excuse. When he's feeling nasty, he blames her drinking.

Yvonne has settled herself at the head of the table in her husband's place. She's been drinking steadily for most of the day. She's stashed the empties behind a large plant pot in the conservatory. But does white wine really count as booze? It's not the same as gin or vodka. It's a light beverage that just takes the edge off things.

The awful Christine has gone and Penny has cooked supper, which is obviously good of her, but, truth to tell, she's not the best cook in the world. Yvonne dreads to think what kind of state the kitchen is in. But she can't worry about that now. Her thoughts are drifting around in quite a pleasant way. She hasn't felt this relaxed for a long time.

Penny ordered one of those recipe boxes, where they give you all the ingredients and tell you what to do. As a result she's produced a passable chicken casserole. Yvonne stares down at the plate in front of her. It really doesn't look too bad. The problem is if she tries to eat anything she'll probably throw up. And being sick is awful. Not to mention the mess.

Her gaze skates round the table. The children are sitting in their usual places. Has she told them about Greg? She's been meaning to. Imogen is on her left. She's nine and such a sweet child, she never gives Yvonne any trouble. The twins, Harry and Lucas, are on the other side of the table but Aidan's place remains empty. *Where is Aidan?*

Penny is facing her at the other end of the table. That's usually her place. Near the kitchen door. But today Penny is being mother. The very idea of her sister in a maternal role amuses Yvonne.

'Do you think I should take a plate up to Aidan?' says Penny.

Now she remembers. They had a small spat. He was watching her again and she told him not to. Told him to go away. Possibly she was a bit harsh. Now he won't come out of his room.

'No,' says Yvonne briskly. 'It's teenage nonsense. If he wants to eat he can come down here and do it in a civilised fashion.'

Teenager! It's used as an excuse for everything.

'Darling,' says Penny gently. 'Don't you think that maybe, in the circumstances, we should cut him a little slack?'

Circumstances? Oh yes, the circumstances. Greg is dead. For some reason that's the thing that keeps slipping out of her mind. *He's gone!* But, yes, she did tell them. This morning. Now she remembers. Imogen cried.

Yvonne takes another sip of wine.

Imogen forks the chicken around her plate, she's hardly touched it.

Yvonne meets her daughter's gaze. She's such a neat, pretty child. Or she can be when she doesn't frown like that.

'Don't be troublesome, Imo,' says Yvonne. 'Auntie Penny's made us a lovely dinner. Eat it.'

'But you're not.'

'That's because I'm finishing my wine. Then I'll eat it.'

Penny gets up from her place at the other end of the table and walks out into the hall. Yvonne can hear her calling up the stairs.

'Aidan! Supper's ready. Come and eat it before it gets cold.'

Penny returns to the table and picks up her napkin.

Harry and Lucas haven't had any difficulty clearing their plates. They're only six. Do they know what death means? Probably not. Their father's gone but they'll always have each other and Yvonne is glad about that. Now Harry is jabbing his brother in the arm and both boys are giggling. It occurs to Yvonne that her daughter, her lovely daughter, rarely giggles. *Girls should giggle.*

Penny smiles at the boys. 'And you two can behave yourselves,' she says. She glances up the table towards her sister. She seems really tense. *Why can't she have a drink and relax?*

Yvonne chuckles and raises her glass in a toast. 'You tell them, Pen,' she says. 'You be the mother and fucking tell them!'

Yvonne can feel a stillness around her. A deep silence. Everyone seems to be watching her. *Why?*

Imogen is staring at her. Suddenly she puts Yvonne in mind of her own mother. Pursed lips, that disapproving scowl.

'You have no right to judge me. No right!' she shouts.

Imogen flinches. *Silly girl.* Yvonne would never hit her. She's never hit her children. And she told Greg, if he ever raised his hand to them, she would leave.

Suddenly Penny is right next to her, tugging at her elbow. 'Listen, darling,' she says. 'Why don't you go and sit in the conservatory while I give the children some ice cream? Would you like some ice cream, boys? I think we've got toffee pecan or chocolate.'

'Chocolate!' say Harry and Lucas in unison.

Yvonne nods. She is possibly a little pissed. 'I'm sorry,' she says to no one in particular.

Penny is trying to haul her to her feet when Aidan walks into the room. His face is pale, his hair limp and greasy. He's wearing an awful rag of a T-shirt and baggy shorts.

'Sit down and have something to eat, darling,' says Penny. 'I've kept a plate hot for you.'

Aidan is staring at his mother. 'I'm not hungry,' he says.

'You have to eat something,' says Penny.

'Can I have a glass of wine?' he says.

'Absolutely, darling,' says Yvonne with a shrug. 'Your father's left us a whole fucking wine cellar. I'm never going to get through it on my own.'

Aidan walks over to the sideboard and takes out a long-stemmed glass. He picks up the bottle from the table and fills it. Penny sighs and shakes her head.

'At least have something to eat with it, Aidan,' she says.

'If he's not hungry, he's not hungry,' says Yvonne.

Aidan sits down next to Imogen. She gives her brother a nervous sidelong glance. He smiles at her and pulls her into a hug.

'All right, kiddo?' he says.

'Is Daddy really dead?' says Imogen.

'Yes,' says her brother.

Yvonne is aware of her son's eyes resting on her. Such a soft boy, never critical. Except for the watching. She regrets arguing with him.

She looks at her daughter. Such a smart little thing. And the twins. Those two sweet little boys. But such a handful. She smiles at them all fondly.

Greg kept on at her. He wanted more children, another son. Yvonne didn't. Aidan and Imogen, they were enough for her. One of each, just right. But her husband disagreed. He threw away her birth control pills. He told her not to be stupid. When Yvonne found out she was pregnant again, she was close to despair. Then she discovered she was pregnant with twins, which made the whole thing worse. The delivery was by Caesarean. Greg absented himself, couldn't stand the sight of blood. But Penny was there. Penny held her hand. After that she was ill for a long time. Then came the OCD and Dr Davenport.

Yvonne never imagined she'd end up with four children. But then what did she imagine? She wanted to be married, she always wanted to be married. Surely it's what every girl wants. But you have to pick the right man. That's the trick.

Penny returns from the kitchen – Yvonne didn't even notice she'd disappeared – with a plate of food and puts it down in front of Aidan. She smiles at her nephew.

'Come on,' she says, 'you must be starving. Have something to eat.'

Aidan looks at his aunt. 'What happens now?' he says.

'What do you mean?' says Penny.

'You know what I mean,' says Aidan. 'What the hell are we supposed to do? What am I supposed to do? Look at her. She's absolutely drunk as a bloody skunk. So what do we do now?'

Yvonne tries to focus on them. They're talking as if she's not there.

Penny reaches out and touches his arm. 'We just need to give her some time, darling,' she says softly.

'How's that going to work? The police know what happened to him, or they suspect,' says Aidan. 'I phoned Granddad and asked about it, but he wouldn't tell me the details. Why not?'

'Okay. You want the details?' says Yvonne. 'Someone bashed his bloody head in. That's why Barry didn't tell you. Made a real mess apparently. I suppose they must've really hated him. Can't imagine why.'

Imogen starts to snivel.

Yvonne pats her daughter's hand. 'It's all right, Imo,' she says. 'Everything's going to be fine.' She takes another mouthful of wine and paints on a smile.

Aidan stares at his mother in horror. Then he turns to Penny and says, 'We have to do something.'

CHAPTER TWENTY-FIVE

Friday, 7 p.m.

Berrycombe is basking in a burst of early evening sunshine. Megan leads Ruby by the hand. Amber walks beside them. Kyle is a few paces ahead. He has Scout on a leash and the enthusiastic dog is towing him along. They stop outside the new pizza restaurant, which has recently opened on the harbourside.

'Well,' says Megan. 'What do you reckon? Shall we get some pizzas to take away and go and sit on the breakwater and eat them?'

Amber nods. All three children are uncharacteristically subdued.

'So what does anyone fancy?' says Megan. She's trying to sound upbeat. She knows she's failing.

'Whatever,' says Amber with a shrug. She appears to be speaking for all of them.

'I'll get a couple of the large margaritas,' says Megan. 'Then we can share them. Okay?'

'And a Coke?' says Kyle, hopefully.

'And Coke,' Megan says with a smile.

As Megan queues at the takeaway counter, she glances out of the window at the three children. Except Amber is not a child, she's fourteen and old enough to understand exactly what's going on between her parents.

Things were already getting fraught when Megan hustled them out of the house; she wanted to give her sister and brother-in-law a chance to talk in private. Mark is a reasonable man. He loves his wife and he loves his family. Megan keeps reminding herself of this. But it's going to be a tough conversation. A catalogue of bad decisions made by Debbie, followed by a raft of unlucky coincidences, have created a situation which would test the love and tolerance of any reasonable man. It doesn't help that Debbie has wound herself up into an emotional turmoil. She's angry and guilty in equal parts. But however much Megan loves them, she's an outsider. It's their marriage, they have to sort it out. She can only watch and wait.

She comes out of the restaurant, carrying two large pizza boxes and four cardboard cups of Coke. Scout's nose twitches. *At least the dog is happy*, thinks Megan. But it's clear that no one else is.

Megan hands out the drinks. Ruby clutches her hand as they walk along the harbour wall towards the breakwater. It's a glorious spring evening, the tide is high, a family of swans is bobbing around in the inner harbour. A few people are still lounging on the decks of their boats, catching the last few rays of sun. A couple of lads on jet skis are cruising back from the outer harbour towards their moorings.

When they reach the beginning of the breakwater, Kyle hands the dog's leash to his sister and hoists himself up onto the wall. Megan lifts Ruby up to sit beside him. Amber perches on the end of a nearby bench with the dog at her feet. Megan opens the first pizza box. She separates out a couple of slices and hands one each to Kyle and Ruby. She offers a third slice to Amber. But Amber shakes her head.

'Do you think they'll get a divorce?' says Amber.

'No,' says Megan. She extracts another slice of pizza for herself, folds it over and starts to eat it. It's a messy business. She ends up with tomato sauce running down her chin. She wipes it away with the back of her hand.

'Are you sure?' says Amber. She's glaring. The look is full of confusion but also accusation.

'Yes, I'm sure,' says Megan.

'Mum's in a right state. She says he'll never forgive her. But what has she actually done?' says Amber. 'And why did she have to give the cops her phone?'

Megan takes another bite of pizza. *She gave her boss a blowjob for money.* There's no way she can answer the question so she evades it.

'She may think that he'll never forgive her,' says Megan, 'but I actually have more faith in your father. He loves you all and he loves her.' *For better or worse?* How many marriages manage that? Hers certainly didn't.

Kyle has devoured his pizza. Megan hands him another slice. He tears a piece off the corner and tosses it to Scout. The dog gobbles it up greedily.

'Kyle,' says Amber, 'that's so stupid. He shouldn't be eating pizza.'

'Why not?' says Kyle. 'We're eating it. Why shouldn't he?'

''Cause he's a dog, you dipshit,' says Amber viciously. 'It's bad for him.'

'You're the dipshit,' says Kyle.

Megan raises her palm. 'Okay, you two,' she says. 'That's enough of that. This is the last thing we need at the moment.'

'Well,' says Amber. 'He can't just feed crap to the dog like that. It's stupid and it's not fair on Scout.'

'How can it be crap if we're eating it?' says Kyle.

Megan looks at the two of them. The anger bubbling up inside them is bound to find a way out. Two confused and frightened kids, who are waiting to see if their world is about to fall apart. Where else is all that pent-up emotion supposed to go?

'Listen,' says Megan. 'I know we're all finding this a bit difficult. But the two of you need to calm down and stop squabbling.' Is she sounding more like a cop than a parent? She's trying for something in between.

'She started it,' says Kyle.

'I don't care who started it,' says Megan. 'I'm finishing it, okay.'

They all lapse into silence. Scout licks his lips and looks up at Kyle hopefully. Kyle huffs, jumps down from the wall and strokes the dog's head.

Megan wonders if she should say something more. But what? She's not exactly sure what Debbie may or may not have told them. How do you say to your children: 'I've been arrested and accused of murder?' The reality is you probably don't.

Megan digs in her pocket and brings out some clean tissues. She takes one of them and wipes Ruby's mouth. Ruby pushes her hand away.

'I'm not a baby,' says Ruby indignantly. Even she is tetchy and not her usual sunny self.

'I know you're not,' says Megan. 'But you don't want to get tomato sauce all over your T-shirt, do you?'

Megan turns to Amber. 'You sure you don't want any pizza?'

Amber shakes her head.

Megan takes a deep breath. She knows she has to take the plunge.

'What did Mum say to you when you got home from school?' says Megan.

Amber shrugs. 'She didn't really say anything. I asked her what the matter was and she said she was really sorry. I said sorry for what, but she wouldn't say.'

Amber is looking straight at her. Megan feels the weight of the responsibility. She must find a way to get them all through this. But they have different levels of understanding. Amber: alert, critical and ready to pounce. Kyle: avoiding eye contact and wary. Ruby: trusting but terrified.

'Well,' says Megan. 'This is a rather difficult situation to explain. You know that your mum was doing a cleaning job at that new block of flats that they're building on the top of the hill. The man that she was working for was killed.'

'We know that,' says Amber impatiently. 'And Mum found him. That happened the other day.'

'His kid goes to our school,' says Kyle. 'Her name's Imogen and she's a right snobby little cow.'

'That's not a very nice thing to say about her,' says Megan. 'And I'm sure you don't really mean it.' *Playing for time. Get on with it.*

Kyle just shrugs.

'I'm sure he does,' says Amber sourly.

'The thing is,' says Megan, 'before he died, he and your mum had a bit of an argument about money. And sometimes arguments about money can get quite nasty and complicated.'

'We're broke,' says Kyle. 'That's why Dad has to go away to work. On the wind farm.'

'Yes,' says Megan. 'And it's why your mother has several different jobs.'

'I don't get it,' says Amber. 'Why would Mum having a row about money with this contractor she was working for, lead to a big problem between her and Dad? It doesn't make sense to me.'

Megan sighs. Amber is too old and too smart to be fobbed off with the simple story.

'Because she had a row with him and because he was found dead, there's some suspicion that your mother might have been involved,' says Megan.

Kyle and Ruby look at her blankly.

But Amber says, 'Do you suspect her?'

'No, of course I don't,' says Megan. 'I know my sister and she would never harm anyone.' *Sounds convincing, but is it?*

Amber is scanning her. The kid is way too smart.

'Then who suspects her?' says Amber. 'The police?'

'It's complicated. We have to prove her alibi,' says Megan. 'But I'm trying to help sort that out. And now your dad's home, things are going to be easier.'

'Is he going to stay at home?' asks Kyle.

'Maybe for a bit,' says Megan.

'Whoopee!' says Kyle.

Amber frowns and stands up. She tugs on Scout's leash.

'Mum needs us, and we're sitting here, eating stupid pizza,' she says. 'I'm going home.'

CHAPTER TWENTY-SIX

Saturday, 7.10 a.m.

Megan is in her pyjamas, making herself coffee and toast. Her brother-in-law wanders into the kitchen in a T-shirt and boxers. When she and the children returned to the house the previous evening, Debbie was tight-lipped and Mark had disappeared altogether. All Debbie knew was that he'd gone to the pub. Megan did hear him return in the early hours, clattering around, shushing the dog.

She smiles at him. He looks haggard and hungover and appears to have slept on the sofa.

'Coffee?' she says.

'Cheers,' he replies. 'Been swimming?'

'I was going to. Decided I didn't have the energy.' She refills the coffee maker with water and slots a pod in. It starts to gurgle and deliver a fresh stream of coffee into a cup. She wishes she had gone swimming. But she spent a restless night trying to solve other people's problems and getting nowhere fast. On top of all that she kept seeing a small body washed up on the beach. Hassan. But what if it was Ruby or Kyle? Or even Amber?

Mark gazes out of the window. 'It's a lovely morning. But I don't think it'll last. Rain later.' *He reads the clouds with a seaman's eye*, thinks Megan.

They look at one another; neither knows what to say.

Megan sighs. 'Listen, Mark—'

He raises his hand. 'I know she's your sister. But you don't have to defend her. This is my fault.'

'I don't know about fault. But I do know she never meant to hurt you.'

'That's a bit irrelevant, don't you think?'

'It's crucial. The impact on you and the kids is all that matters to her.'

He smiles sadly. 'Well,' he says. 'Good job that bastard Porter is dead. 'Cause if I'd got hold of him…'

'You'd've had to join the queue,' says Megan.

They smile at each other. She lifts the brimming coffee cup from the machine and hands it to him.

'I think I'm going to need several of these,' he says, cradling it in both hands.

Suddenly there's a loud hammering. They both start. The unremitting rat-tat-tat is repeated. It's coming from the front door.

'What the hell?' says Mark. 'Can't they find the bloody bell?'

Megan's heart sinks. *Oh no, surely not!*

'I'll get it,' she says. 'Just stay here.'

'Why? What's going on?' says Mark.

Unfortunately she knows exactly what's going on.

Megan walks down the hall to the front door. Kyle is coming down the stairs. The hammering continues.

'Kyle, go back to your room,' says Megan.

'Why?' says the boy.

'Tell Amber and Ruby to stay upstairs too. Just do it, okay.'

He reads her tone and scampers back upstairs.

Megan takes a deep breath and opens the front door.

Jim Collins is standing on the doorstep, flanked by Ted Jennings and two uniformed officers. Several cars are parked outside on the double yellow line.

He holds up his warrant card and says briskly, 'Good morning, Megan. We're here to question Mark Hayden.'

'Really?' says Megan. 'And you hope that by coming mob-handed at seven o'clock on a Saturday morning, you'll intimidate both him and my sister?'

'You know very well, Megan, that this is a murder inquiry. I'm merely following normal procedure.'

'Normal procedure? What are the uniforms for? In case they make a run for it? Are you doing this to every suspect? Or, let me guess, you're still targeting my sister. Is that your blinkered version of normal procedure?'

Mark comes up behind her. He's frowning. 'You can let them in,' he says. 'We've got nothing to hide.'

'It's not a question of that,' says Megan. 'This is a tactic. And one that's out of date. Does Slater know what you're up to? My sister was released under investigation, you're not entitled to question her without a lawyer present.'

'You're not involved in this, Megan. And you should step aside,' says Collins.

'I live here. So I am involved.'

'Please, Megan, let's just get this over with,' says Mark.

She sighs. 'The uniforms stay outside,' she says.

'I don't have a problem with that,' says Collins. Megan glances out of the door. Vish is sitting in the driver's seat of one of the cars, looking embarrassed. He's been dragged into this farrago too.

Megan opens the front door wide. Collins steps inside. Jennings follows. He gives Megan a smug grin. Mark leads them down the hall into the sitting room.

'We're just wondering, Mr Hayden,' says Collins, 'if you were aware of your wife's intention to put financial pressure on Greg Porter?'

Megan is about to follow them in, but Jennings stands in her way.

'Come on, Megan,' he says. 'You heard what Jim said. You need to step aside and let us do our job.'

'And were you doing your job, Ted, when you paid a visit to Barry Porter on his boat?'

Jennings seems taken aback but he says, 'Yeah. Obviously.'

Debbie appears at the top of the stairs. She's wearing only a T-shirt and knickers.

'What the hell's going on?' she says sleepily.

'Maybe your sister would like to put some clothes on and come down?' says Ted.

'No she would not,' says Megan.

He grins, disappears into the sitting room and closes the door behind him.

Megan bounds up the stairs two at a time to the landing, where Debbie is standing.

'What's going on?' says Debbie. 'The kids just came and woke me up.'

Megan shepherds her sister back into the bedroom. 'DI Collins has decided to try and bully you into submission. He's come here supposedly to question Mark, which he hopes will put pressure on you and persuade you to *tell the truth.*'

'I have told the truth,' says Debbie sullenly.

'I know. This is a scam. And I think Slater will agree with me. I doubt she knows about this.'

Debbie sits on the bed and sighs. 'I feel like I'm stuck in some nightmare and I can't escape. When I told Mark what happened with Porter, he just looked at me. He didn't say anything. But his face, Meg, the look on his face…' Her lip trembles and she starts to cry.

Megan puts a hand on her shoulder. 'Oh, babe!'

'And the worst thing is, he blames himself!' She wipes her face with her palm. 'Because he couldn't provide for his family and we got into debt.'

Amber puts her head round the door. She has tears in her eyes too. 'Mum?'

Megan beckons her in. 'Come and sit with your mum,' she says. 'I need to phone my boss.'

Amber sits down on the bed beside Debbie. 'I'm all right,' says Debbie. 'I don't want you upset too. I need to put some clothes on and go downstairs and deal with this.' She stands up. 'I'll be fine.'

'No,' says Megan. 'Absolutely not. Stay here.'

'But I don't want them putting this on Mark—'

'Deb, let me deal with this.'

Megan hurries back down to the kitchen to retrieve her phone. Through the double doors into the sitting room she can eavesdrop on what Mark is saying to Collins and Jennings.

'…what happened to me, happened to plenty of people in the fishing industry. The business went broke, I was made redundant. That's when we started putting things on credit cards…' He sounds calm and in control.

Megan scrolls her contacts for Laura Slater's number. She clicks on it. She gets a busy signal.

She walks out into the hall, glances up the stairs. Redials. Still busy.

Debbie appears on the stairs. She's barefoot but now wearing jeans. She rakes back her hair.

'Fuck this!' she says. 'I'm not having them walking in here like this. Treating my husband like he's a criminal.'

She comes thundering down the stairs.

'No, Deb,' says Megan. 'Let me handle this.'

But Debbie goes straight past her and flings open the door to the sitting room.

Megan has no option but to follow.

Mark, Collins and Jennings are standing awkwardly round the coffee table, Jennings using his phone to record. They all turn at Debbie's abrupt entrance.

Debbie fronts up to Collins. 'Why are you here?' she says. 'And why are you questioning my husband? He's got nothing to do with this. He was on a bloody boat in the middle of the North Sea.'

'Deb,' says Mark. 'It's all right—'

'No, it's not bloody all right. Meg says he's doing this to bully us. And that's not all right.'

'Mrs Hayden,' says Collins. 'You seem very agitated. I would suggest you take your husband's advice and calm down.'

Red rag to a bull, thinks Megan. But she suspects that's Collins's intention.

Debbie takes a step forward. She stops inches from Collins face. 'I'll calm down when you and your fat sidekick get out of my house.'

Megan reaches for her sister's arm. 'Deb, you can't do this—'

Debbie shrugs her off. 'I'm not doing anything. I'm just telling your colleagues to leave.'

Collins stares right back at her but he's smiling. 'You really would like to hit me, wouldn't you, Mrs Hayden? Is that what happened with Greg?'

'Oh fuck off!' says Debbie, turning away.

'You're clearly a woman with a violent temper,' says Collins. 'You find it hard to control, don't you?' The tone is teasing.

'She does not,' says Megan, pushing forward between the two of them. Then she fixes her sister with a steely look. 'Let it go, Deb. He's a tosser. This is what he does.'

Debbie meets her gaze and connects. Megan watches her exhale. *She's got the message. Thank God!*

'Your sister will feel much better once she tells us the truth,' says Collins.

Megan rounds on him. 'You're totally out of order. You want to ask her any more questions, it will be with a lawyer present and at a proper time. There's no justification for this.'

Collins retreats, takes a turn about the room and puts his hands on his hips. 'You know very well, Megan, that I'm perfectly entitled to question Mr Hayden on matters that might relate to his wife's motivation.'

'Are you questioning him as a suspect or a witness? And has he been cautioned?'

'That's hardly your concern. I am the senior officer.'

'And I'm supposed to trust you to do the right thing?' She can't keep the sarcasm out of her voice.

The doorbell rings. Collins gives Jennings a nod. He goes to answer the door.

Megan folds her arms and positions herself strategically between Collins and Debbie.

Collins says, 'I'm happy to arrange a time for Mr Hayden to come in and answer further questions—'

Jennings reappears in the doorway. He has Vish in tow.

Vish holds out his phone. 'Sorry, boss,' he says to Collins. 'I've got the DCI on the line. She wants to talk to you urgently.'

Collins grins and shakes his head. As he walks across the room past Megan he says sarcastically, 'You are quick off the mark, aren't you, sergeant?'

'Not really,' she replies. 'I couldn't get through to her.' This is true. Slater's phone was busy. *So what's urgent?*

Collins takes the phone from Vish and goes out into the hall, followed by Jennings.

Megan looks at Vish. She doesn't even have to ask.

As soon as Collins is out of earshot he blurts it out. 'Guess what? Aidan Porter, Greg Porter's seventeen-year-old son, has just presented himself at the police station in Torquay and confessed to his father's murder.'

CHAPTER TWENTY-SEVEN

Saturday, 1.15 p.m.

Danny Ingram suggests they meet at a country pub on Dartmoor. Although Megan is supposed to be the local, she's never discovered the village of Widecombe before. However, after a morning of stress and mayhem, the possibility of escape appeals to her. So she agrees to his suggestion. Debbie and Mark didn't need to hear her ranting about Collins. She realised the more she said about that the less it helped. Leaving them in peace to recover seemed the best idea.

As she drives into the village, she finds Ingram leaning on a wall near the church. He appears to be alone and just soaking up the sunshine. He gives her a wave. She parks in the car park and strolls across the village green towards him.

'It's amazing,' he says. 'Have you noticed how high the church tower is?'

Megan stares up at the imposing granite tower. For a tiny village, it is a big church.

'A hundred and twenty feet,' he says. 'That's why they call this place the Cathedral of the Moors.' He holds up a small booklet. 'I went in the National Trust shop round the corner and got all the gen. In 1638, during a church service, it got struck by ball lightening. Four people were killed, sixty injured. Local people reckoned it was the work of the devil.'

Megan smiles. She wonders what he's up to, because if there's one thing she's learnt about Danny Ingram, it's that he's always got an agenda. Sometimes several.

'I didn't take you for a history buff,' she says.

'I like to learn things,' he says. 'Didn't do enough of it at school, so I'm still playing catch-up. Anyway, I don't see why we shouldn't mix business with a little pleasure. And I hear you've had a difficult morning.'

'Who told you that?' she says.

'I keep my ear to the ground.' He gives her a mischievous grin. 'But the truth is I had a phone call from Barker.'

'What did he want?' says Megan. *Checking up on her?* He probably wanted to know if the trouble with her sister had sent her off the rails.

Chief Superintendent Barker had sponsored her transfer from the Met. She'd been diagnosed with post-traumatic stress disorder and faced retirement on medical grounds. As a favour to an old friend, he'd offered her a job so she could continue as a police officer. But he'd imposed stringent conditions to keep an eye on her mental health.

'He wanted an update on the investigation,' says Ingram. 'I told him that things were going pretty well and that your input had been extremely valuable. He said he was glad to hear it. Said you're a very capable officer.'

She smiles and shakes her head at him. She knows she's being flattered.

Ingram shrugs. 'I'm only telling you what he said. Let's go and get a drink.'

Widecombe-in-the-Moor is picture-perfect. Besides the magnificent church there are several gift shops, two cafes and two pubs dotted round a neat village green. The garden of one of the cafes has been overrun by a gaggle of cyclists; middle-aged men in fluorescent Lycra, on a gruelling mission to hang on to their lost youth. But Ingram makes a beeline for the pub. He selects the less fussy of the two and leaves her sitting at a wooden table outside while he goes in to buy drinks.

Megan looks around her. She's still completely hyped. The day has been manic, and it's not even half over. As she drove across the moor to this ridiculous rendezvous, her brain had continued to seethe with anger and resentment and plans of revenge. How dare Jim Collins pull a stunt like that? He wasn't going to get away with it, that's for sure. As soon as he'd spoken to Slater on the phone, he was out of the door without even an apology and with Ted Jennings, his poodle, hot on his heels. Debbie and Mark were left upset and confused.

Mark was aggrieved that the police had garnered so much detail about his personal financial affairs so quickly. Collins had accessed all his bank accounts, knew the outstanding debt on his credit cards, the state of his mortgage and the interest rate on his personal loans. He dealt with the police calmly enough at the time. But once they were gone he was steaming.

Debbie was worse. Collins had taunted her and it took half an hour and two cups of coffee for her to calm down. But the incident did serve one useful purpose. It united the couple in anger and solidarity. Mark felt that both he and his wife had been mistreated and his instinctive response was to protect her and defend his family. Aidan Porter's confession proved Debbie had told the truth all along.

By the time Megan left the house, the Haydens were all seated around the kitchen table. Mark and Debbie were still awkward with each other but at least they were speaking and the children were back under their parents' wing: Amber and Kyle squabbling, Ruby on her father's knee. It wasn't going to be plain sailing but it was a start, Megan reflected.

Ingram comes out of the pub carrying half a pint of shandy for himself and a ginger beer for Megan. He places them on the wooden table in front of her.

'I'm not trying to get you drunk,' he says, 'but if I was you, I think I'd be wishing this was something stronger.'

Megan scans him. 'Well,' she says, 'if you will insist on meeting in the back of beyond, you don't give me any option.'

He has a ready smile and there's a calmness about him which brings a feather lightness to their banter. She feels as though she doesn't need to be on full alert. Just being with Ingram makes her relax. It's not a feeling that she's had with any man for a very long time.

Ingram sits down and extracts an iPad from his bag. He puts it on the table.

'Right,' he says. 'Let's get down to business. This is what I wanted to show you. Rodney downloaded a week's worth of CCTV from the harbour office. A ton of data. It took a while to break it all down. But we have some whizzy software that speeds up the process. Don't ask me how it works, I leave all that to Rodney. But we extracted a little sequence that's rather interesting.'

He taps the screen of the iPad and a dark, grainy image pops up. It is possible to identify the outline of the pontoon and some boats, rocking gently. Megan screws up her eyes and peers at it.

'This is about 3.30 a.m.,' says Ingram. 'Early hours of Thursday morning, which is when Ranim and her children ended up on our beach. Now, if you wait for a moment, you'll see three figures appear.'

Megan stares at the dark, pixelated image but she can make out very little: a few flickering reflections from a harbourside lamp dance on the water. But suddenly a floodlight comes on, illuminating the whole jetty.

'There's a motion sensor on the pontoon,' says Ingram, 'which is convenient because now we can see our guys more clearly.'

Megan focuses on the screen. A heavy-set male figure comes into view. He's the one who's tripped the light switch. He's carrying a backpack and walking towards the CCTV camera. As he gets closer, it's possible to see more of his face. His hair is receding but long and straggly at the back. He has a full beard and looks to be around fifty. Another figure follows, much slighter and looser in his gait. His hair is short and fashionably shaved, definitely a much younger man. A third figure, he's young too, trots to catch up.

Megan feels a stab of excitement.

'They match Ranim's description of the people smugglers,' she says.

Ingram nods. 'We need to go and see her, show her this. I'm thinking we'll drive up to the detention centre tomorrow morning.'

'Absolutely.'

Megan returns to the screen. The pontoon is separated from the jetty by a metal gate with a keypad lock. The first man taps in the code, the gate clicks open and they pass through. The angle of the shot changes. A camera, set higher up at the entrance to the pier, picks them up as they head towards the roadway. The harbour is quiet. There's no one around. But a car is parked on the road near the entrance to the pier. It's a darkish Range Rover Discovery. The eerie glow of the street lamps washes out the exact colour. The three men hurry towards the car. The older one climbs into the passenger seat. The other two jump into the back. The car drives off.

Megan turns to Ingram. 'Hard to be sure,' she says, 'but I'd say that the driver is a woman.'

'I would agree,' he says. 'We tracked the vehicle on ANPR.'

'Did you get the number plate?' asks Megan.

'Yes. Unfortunately, we discovered this morning that it's a cloned plate. Taken from a Vauxhall Astra scrapped in Southampton a month ago.'

'That tells us one thing,' she says. 'Whoever they are, they're up to no good.'

'They also know how to disappear. We tracked them until they left the main road and drove up onto the moors where we lost them. I've put an information marker on the vehicle, so as soon as it pings off another ANPR camera we'll get an alert. But if they're careful, and it looks like they are, that'll be a long shot.'

'Unless they get careless.'

'They've probably got more than one vehicle. And that's why I wanted to meet here in Widecombe. Seems the devil may have taken up residence in the locality again. Rodney's done a projection. Given the route they took and where they left the main drag, we think they may have been heading for a bolthole round here somewhere.'

'There are lots of farms dotted about,' says Megan. 'I could talk to the local uniforms, find someone who really knows the patch.'

'That would help. But I've already asked Barker if he can lend us a drone. He's agreed. We'll put it up, scan the whole area and see what we can see.'

'You might get the car. But a Range Rover Discovery is going to be a common vehicle round here. Lots of people who live up on the moor have four-by-fours.'

Ingram sighs. 'That is a drawback. And we've got to wait for the drone. So I've got Sasha and Bibi driving round, posing as tourists. It's a bit of a needle-in-a-haystack job.'

'And we need to be careful not to be too obvious.'

Ingram chuckles. 'Bibi drives a decrepit Volvo estate. She's brilliant at passing under the radar. People tend to assume she's some mad old bat beetling about. She opens the bonnet and pretends it's broken down. All kinds of people stop and talk to her and offer help. It's a great way to gather intel. No one would ever imagine she's from the National Crime Agency. She's just a woman out with her daughter.'

Megan laughs. 'I'm glad to hear you lot do a bit of old-fashioned legwork. It's not all whizzy gadgets.'

'I was thinking we could always play at being tourists too, if you fancy it. It's a nice day for it.'

A couple driving around, seeing the sights. What could be more normal? *That's how life could be. Part of a couple again.* Megan wonders why she finds that so seductive. She was certainly right about Ingram and his many agendas.

Her phone buzzes. It's a text from Slater.

She reads it and sighs. 'Slater wants me back in the office. Says it's urgent.'

'Oh well,' he says sadly. 'Another time.'

CHAPTER TWENTY-EIGHT

Saturday, 2.30 p.m.

Megan finds the office busy for a Saturday afternoon. A couple of new DCs have been drafted in for the murder inquiry and Brittney is having a cup of tea and chatting to Kitty and one of the newbies. Megan gives them a nod but heads straight for Slater's office. The DCI is on the phone but she beckons Megan in.

Hanging up, she says, 'That was the Crime Scene Manager. They've found a hammer in a skip down the road from the Greg Porter scene. It's got dried blood on it, so there's a good chance it's the murder weapon.'

Megan nods but wonders why Slater is sharing this information with her. She's not part of the murder inquiry, in fact she's been specifically excluded from the team.

'You said in your text it was urgent, boss?'

Slater gives her a chilly smile. 'We've managed to establish the exact route your sister took during the period of time she was absent from her job at the pub,' she says. 'I thought you should know.'

It sounds ominous. But that could be Slater's manner. She's a cold fish at the best of times. And Aidan Porter has supposedly confessed to killing his father.

'Okay,' says Megan. *Wait and see.*

Has her sister been exonerated? After Collins's attempt to strong-arm Mark and Debbie this morning, Megan is not in a mood to trust her colleagues.

Slater looks at her. She seems about to say something else but hesitates and fiddles with her hair. It's pinned up in a neat French twist. *Is she nervous?* Then she walks to the door of her office and calls across the room, 'Brittney! Have you got a moment, please?'

Megan is well aware that she must be radiating resentment. Slater can obviously feel it. But Megan doesn't care. She's not about to apologise for her attitude. And she's certainly not going to back off. She continues to stare at her boss.

Brittney joins them in the office.

'Could you run through the findings for Megan?' says Slater briskly.

Brittney pushes the owl glasses up her nose and smiles. Slater stands back and folds her arms.

'We've mapped the route Debbie took from the time she left the pub at 8.15 to when she returned at 8.57,' says Brittney. 'The security camera in the yard of the pub covers the back door and confirms her exit and re-entry. As she said in her statement, she walked round the harbour to the other side. A council rubbish truck was emptying bins and picked her up on its dash cam. This time of year they do a run every evening to pick up refuse from the day. There's an ice cream parlour on the far side of the harbour to the pub. She was picked up on their security camera walking past that at 8.26 and back at 8.45.'

'So there's no record of her walking up the hill towards the flats?' says Megan.

'We calculate that it's a brisk ten-minute walk up a steep hill from the pub to the flats where the murder took place,' says Brittney. 'And we can definitely place her down in the harbour area for virtually the whole time she was absent from the pub.'

Megan smiles warmly. 'Thanks, Brit.' She ignores Slater.

Brittney adds, 'In her statement she said she sat on some steps and we think that we can locate her there too.'

'Next to the Fisherman's Kitchen?'

'Yes,' says Brittany. 'Forensics looked at her phone and it did do a handshake with the Wi-Fi in the restaurant. At 8.38.'

Megan turns to face Slater. She knows her expression is probably more defiant than it needs to be. She should be glad. Her sister is exonerated. But she wants to hear Slater say it.

The boss merely turns to the DC and says, 'Thanks, Brittney. You've done some excellent work.'

'And Kitty,' says Brittney.

'You've both gone the extra mile,' says Slater. 'And that's duly noted.'

'Unlike Jim Collins,' says Megan.

Brittney beats a hasty retreat. Megan is left facing her boss.

'I understand why you're upset,' says Slater. 'But as I told you before, this is a process in which we follow the evidence.'

'Oh come on, boss,' says Megan. 'Collins turned up at my sister's house at seven o'clock this morning with uniformed back-up in order to try and pressurise her and prove what was essentially a hunch on his part. Do you really call that proper police work? I'm not sure I do.'

'You've never followed a lead based on a hunch? Be honest, Megan. Instinct and guesswork are sometimes the only starting points we have. I totally understand why you would believe and support your sister, but you also have to look at this as a police officer.'

'Why? It's not my case.'

'I'm not defending Collins's judgement on this. It was way off the mark—'

'But you still backed him. Luckily you've got a DC who can do her job.'

Slater sighs. 'Okay. This is not getting us anywhere. You can let your sister know that she is no longer under investigation or a suspect in this case.'

'Shouldn't Collins go round there and tell her that himself? Possibly apologise?' says Megan.

'Please, Megan. Don't be difficult,' says Slater.

'If I felt like being difficult, you'd know about it. Because I'd be telling them to get a lawyer and sue.'

The two women stare at each other. Megan knows she's probably said enough. She has to dial this down. Pushing Slater's tolerance to the limit is not a smart move.

But the DCI shakes her head wearily. 'What am I supposed to do? I've got an officer who was seriously ill, nearly lost his life to cancer. He's trying to get back to the only job he knows. But he needs help. His judgement is off kilter. He struggles with the technology so he reverts to old habits and attitudes. That's where he feels comfortable. Force him into retirement, is that the only answer? You resisted that for yourself and rightly so. If this hadn't involved your sister, what would your attitude be?'

Megan is well aware she's being guilt-tripped. But she's nothing like Jim Slater. There's no comparison. *Say that!* She doesn't.

'C'mon,' says Slater. 'I'm asking. If you were in charge what would you do?'

Megan hesitates.

'I'd split him and Ted Jennings up for starters,' she says. 'They make each other worse.'

'That's good advice,' says Slater. 'Only that leaves me short of a DS on the murder inquiry.'

Megan realises she's walked straight into the trap.

She glares at Slater. 'You are kidding me! You want me to be Collins's babysitter? Can't you get someone from Exeter?'

The DCI smiles and shrugs. 'Your sister's no longer involved. Why not? Think about it.'

Megan can think of a zillion reasons. She realises that she's been snookered. She was angry and emotional and Laura Slater has played her. The boss probably had the whole thing planned out before she even walked into the office.

'I don't need to think about it,' she says. 'I want to stick with the NCA investigation.'

Hassan. The CSIs lifting his small body from the waves. *Ranim.* Desperately pleading with Megan to find her son. There's no way she's abandoning them to clean up Jim Collins's mess.

'You can still be a point of contact with the NCA to ensure continuity,' says Slater. She's using her reasonable tone. 'But Brittney can replace you on the day-to-day. The experience will be good for her. And I think you'll agree she's earned it.'

This is classic Slater.

'She has earned it. She should be on it too. But it's not just about continuity. Boss, we've got a dead child. Hassan was his name. I know that because I was the first one to deal with his mother, Ranim. We've got some CCTV footage to show her. We'll be doing that tomorrow. I really want to see this through.'

Slater sighs. Then she smiles. 'Okay. Fair enough. But first I'd like your opinion on something.'

Has Slater just given in? Megan doubts it.

CHAPTER TWENTY-NINE

Saturday, 3 p.m.

Megan stands beside Slater in front of the bank of monitors in the murder inquiry incident room. They're watching the interview with Aidan Porter which is being live-streamed. Vish Prasad is asking the questions. Collins sits beside him, arms folded, looking bullish. There's a woman next to Aidan. Middle-aged, expensively dressed. And a bored-looking bloke, scribbling in a notebook.

'Who's the appropriate adult?' says Megan. 'Doesn't look much like a social worker.'

'His aunt,' replies Slater. 'The mother's sister, not the father's. Her name is Penny Reynolds. When Aidan was offered his call, he phoned her. I didn't want to hold things up any more than we had to. Seemed like he was busting to talk. I ran it by the interview advisor in Exeter. He agreed. So I pulled in the duty solicitor and they finally started about half an hour ago. But it's been slow going. I don't know, maybe when it's come to it, the boy's lost his nerve.'

Either that or Jim Collins glaring at him is freaking him out, thinks Megan.

Out of the corner of her eye she's aware of Ted Jennings, at his desk in the corner, pretending to work but with a sulky look on his face. He's probably not thrilled to see that Slater has got Megan in tow.

Aidan Porter is pale, a skinny teenager with hunched shoulders. He must be stronger than he looks, reflects Megan, if he beat his father to death with a hammer.

In the interview room no one is speaking.

Megan turns to Slater. 'What has he said?'

'Basically, "I killed my father". Then he clammed up. I've told Vish to break it down and get specific with the questioning.'

Megan returns her attention to the screen.

'So, tell me,' says Vish. 'How did you know where your father would be on Tuesday evening?'

The boy shrugs and says, 'I knew he'd be down at the flats. He was getting ready for the launch.'

'The launch?' says Vish.

'Yeah,' says Aidan. 'This weekend. They were having an open weekend to market the flats.'

'What made you decide to go down there?'

'Because it was away from my mum and my sister and brothers,' says Aidan.

'And that was important why?'

Aidan shrugs. 'I dunno.' He's avoiding eye contact. He has a multicoloured, plaited band on his left wrist which he twists obsessively.

'Did you want to talk to him?'

'I just felt like going down there.'

'Tell us what happened when you arrived,' says Vish.

'He was in the show flat,' says Aidan.

'What was he doing?'

Aidan hesitates. Megan gets the feeling he's trawling around for an answer. *Does he not know or is he simply filling in the blanks?* Everyone fills in the blanks; it's the unconscious impulse to embellish, make the story sound better.

'I can't remember exactly,' says the boy. 'But I think maybe he was sorting furniture and stuff out. He'd got furniture for the show flat. He was, y'know, making sure it looked all right for the launch.'

'Let's talk about how you were feeling,' says Vish.

'Don't remember,' says Aidan.

'What were you thinking?'

'Nothing much.'

'But you went down there to see him?'

Aidan nods. Then he adds. 'Thought maybe I could help.'

'You wanted to help your father prepare for the launch?'

'Yeah. Move stuff around, y'know.'

Megan transfers her attention to Penny Reynolds. The aunt looks tense. She has her arms folded, and she's frowning as she follows the proceedings. It's natural that she's concerned for her nephew, but Megan has an odd sense of something else.

Megan turns to Slater. 'What do we make of the aunt?' she asks.

'Not sure yet,' says Slater. 'I phoned her about coming in. She was very brisk and businesslike.'

'Surprised?'

'Hard to say. You're wondering if she knows the boy's guilty?'

'I'm not sure,' says Megan. 'There's a vibe. She knows something.'

Slater gives her a sardonic smile. *Hunches!* The boss doesn't need to rub it in.

Megan turns her focus back to the screen. This is the last thing she wants to be doing. She wants to go home and talk to her sister. She sent Debbie a text, short and to the point. Her sister knows that she's no longer a suspect. But for Megan now that's the least of it. Her family is in a mess, they need her and she's stuck here.

She resents the way that Laura Slater has twisted her arm. There's also a missed call and a text on her phone from Danny Ingram. He's set up an interview with Ranim.

Megan forces herself to concentrate.

'Tell us what happened when you got to the flat,' says Vish. His questioning of the boy is even and calm. Collins, by contrast, is sitting back in his chair and staring. Cold and hard and unremitting. It's another old-school technique from his bag of tricks. Make the suspect feel the scrutiny and the pressure. That's the theory. But Megan wonders if this is what they should be doing with a seventeen-year-old boy. He's a kid in a trouble, not a hardened villain.

The prospect of working with Jim Collins fills her with despair. She's determined to resist it.

Aidan sighs. He looks at Vish. 'It was just a stupid fight. He had a go at me. He's always doing that. Pulls my hair, says it's sissy.'

He wears his hair in a topknot, with the sides of his head shaved. He runs a dirty blond hank of hair through his fingers.

'Looks pretty cool to me,' says Vish.

'He was always taking the piss. Called it a ponytail. Said only girls have ponytails. Said I was a fag. And I just lost it. Grabbed the nearest thing and hit him. I think me fighting back took him by surprise. I was just really angry.'

'What did you hit him with?'

'I can't remember. I just lost it and then I ran out.'

'How many times do you think you hit him?'

'I can't remember.'

'And this thing you hit him with, what did you do with it?'

'I chucked it away. I dunno, it was maybe a hammer or something like that.'

'Do you remember where you chucked it?'

Aidan shakes his head.

'Did you drop it before you left the flat?'

'Probably. Don't remember.'

In the corner of the incident room, Ted Jennings puts his phone down, gets up from his desk and comes over. He hovers at Slater's shoulder.

'Excuse me, ma'am,' he says. He's adopted Collins's habit of calling her ma'am.

Slater turns to face him.

'Think we've got a bit of a problem,' he says. 'Barry Porter, the boy's grandfather, is downstairs. He's brought his lawyer and he's kicking up a rumpus.'

Megan watches the exchange. There's something shifty in Ted's look; he's no good at dissembling. Has Slater noticed? But she says, 'Can't you deal with him?'

'Might be better if you had a word, ma'am. He wants his lawyer to see the boy.'

Slater sighs. 'Okay. He's downstairs?'

Ted nods and retreats.

Megan's hoping she can do the same. But Slater glances at her and says, 'Let's go and see what he's got to say, shall we?'

Megan knows what the boss is up to: trying to reel her in and get her to engage with the case.

They find Barry Porter pacing the foyer like a caged grizzly. His lawyer is small and dapper. He's from a local firm and known to Slater.

'Tim, how are you?' she says. 'What can we do for you?'

Tim Wardell dips his head in acknowledgement.

'My client, Mr Porter, is the grandfather of Aidan Porter,' he says, then turns to Porter. 'This is DCI Slater.' Megan is ignored, which is fine by her.

'And this is bloody ridiculous,' says Porter. 'You do know that, don't you? My grandson did not kill his father. I don't know who says he did.'

Slater remains perfectly still. 'He's telling us that he did.'

'He's a child. You can't drag him in here and intimidate him like this.' Porter glances at his lawyer for support. 'Can they?'

'He came to us voluntarily,' says Slater. 'And he's being interviewed in the presence of his aunt, who is an appropriate adult. And a solicitor.'

'You mean Penny? Well that's bloody absurd! I won't have it. And who's the bloody solicitor? This is his solicitor, chosen by me.'

'Barry—' says the lawyer. But he gets short shrift.

'You think I don't know what's happened here?' Porter wags a forefinger in Slater's face. 'You had a suspect, an open and shut case. Some nasty money-grubbing slut that Greg employed as a cleaner. But now a little bird tells me that she's related to a cop. So you lot are closing ranks and trying to pin this on Aidan. I know how it works.' He looms over Slater.

Slater turns to the lawyer and her voice is icily calm. 'Tim, you need to advise your client that his accusations are entirely unfounded. Moreover, I will not tolerate his aggressive manner. He may be angry and upset but there's no excuse. He needs to go home and calm down. Get him out of here. Now!'

The lawyer grabs Porter's arm. 'Come on, Barry—'

'Don't think you can shut me up, you stupid bitch. You haven't heard the last of this! I'll go to the press,' shouts Porter, as the unfortunate Tim shoves him towards the door.

Slater turns on her heel and walks back up the stairs. Megan follows. She can feel the fury crackling around Slater like static electricity.

When they reach the top of the stairs, Slater says, 'Tell Ted I want to see him in my office.'

Megan nods. She could almost feel sorry for him. But she doesn't.

CHAPTER THIRTY

Saturday, 5.15 p.m.

As Megan drives home, she mulls over the encounter with Barry Porter. She doesn't want to take it personally, although it's hard not to. She reminds herself that he's an angry old man trying to deal with the fact that his grandson may have murdered his son. He's lashing out and looking for someone to blame. His view of her sister is based entirely on hearsay and rumour. Megan is fairly sure he's never met her. But it still rankles.

The conversation Slater had with Ted Jennings happened in the privacy of her office. Slater is not a shouter. Her physical presence is neither large nor imposing; her power resides in the coldness and precision of her voice. The stooped outline of Ted could be glimpsed through the opaque glass as she eviscerated him. In the middle of the process, DI Collins emerged from the interview room. He glanced across at Slater's office and frowned. Megan wondered if he knew of Ted's cosy relationship with Barry Porter. She tended to doubt it.

Brittney was in a corner, filling Vish in on what had been happening. Collins watched them for a moment. He seemed almost forlorn. It was beneath his dignity to ask a DC what was going on. He looked in Megan's direction. This was the point at which she decided to go home.

It seems to her now that given Barry Porter's accusations and threats, the chief super won't allow Slater to put Megan on the murder inquiry. He'll find a DS from Exeter or even Penzance, he'll have to. And that suits Megan down to the ground. As she walked out of the office, she avoided Collins's eye. The whole thing is a shitshow and she wants nothing to do with it.

It's a relief to get home. She steps through the front door and Scout comes trotting down the hall to greet her. She rubs his muzzle and he licks her hand. He follows her into the kitchen.

Debbie is cooking. The aroma of chicken and wine wafts from the pot she's stirring. The prospect of coq au vin, a few glasses of wine and a film on the telly lifts Megan's mood.

'Hiya,' she says. 'That smells great.'

Debbie gives her a sidelong glance but says nothing. She's intent on chopping vegetables for the pot.

'Got my message then?' says Megan.

'Yeah,' says Debbie. 'So I'm off the hook.' There's a surliness in her tone which is impossible to ignore, although Megan tries.

'It's thanks to Brittney,' Megan says. 'She spent hours tracking down and stitching together all the necessary CCTV so we had a map of the route you took from the pub, round the harbour and back, proving your alibi.'

'And what?' says Debbie. 'I'm supposed to be grateful to your fat little friend? Grateful that you lot finally did your job and decided I was telling the truth? Maybe I should send her a box of chocolates? And when do I get my phone back?'

'Deb, I know you're upset,' says Megan.

'Upset?' says Debbie. 'Don't try and pat me on the head and calm me down, big sister. I'm not twelve. And as for those tossers that came round here this morning...'

'There's absolutely no excuse for Collins,' says Megan. 'I do know that. And so does my boss.'

'So why didn't you back me up?'

'I think I did. I told you to stay upstairs while I sorted it out.'

'That's bollocks, Meg. You were just intent on shutting me up. And I get it, he's a DI, you're a sergeant. Can't upset the bosses.'

That's not what happened.

Megan stands stock still. She doesn't trust herself to speak. Debbie is still seething and looking for somewhere to direct her anger. But that doesn't make it any easier.

The front door slams and Mark walks into the room with a hessian bag of shopping. He glances at his wife but ignores Megan.

It feels as if she's being made the fall guy.

But she smiles and says, 'Hi.'

He replies with a curt nod and starts to unpack his shopping on the kitchen table. A bottle of wine, some ice cream, which he puts in the freezer.

There's an uncomfortable silence.

Then Debbie says, 'Amber's going to her mate's for a sleepover. And I'm putting the other two to bed early so that Mark and I can have a quiet dinner together.'

Megan feels as if she's been slapped in the face. She *is* the fall guy. They blame her. They don't want her around.

'I think that's a very good idea,' she says evenly. 'I'll make myself scarce and leave you to it.'

She heads for the door with as much dignity as she can muster.

'Is anybody even going to apologise to us?' says Mark. 'I feel as if we've been completely done over.'

Megan looks at her brother-in-law. There's a hostility in his face that she's never seen before.

'It was a bad mistake,' she says. 'It should never have happened. I expect Superintendent Barker will write to you.'

'I look forward to that,' says Mark sourly.

He turns away from Megan and puts a protective arm round his wife's shoulder and gives her a little squeeze.

Megan watches them. They're battered and angry and they've closed ranks against her. She wants to cry out: *this is not my fault.*

'For what it's worth,' says Megan. 'I am really sorry about this. My boss is really sorry about this. But sometimes situations develop—'

'I don't understand how you can work with people like that,' says Debbie with a tearful crack in her voice. 'It's like the power has just gone to their heads. We were treated like scum. Every financial detail about us, they had it all. Questioned Mark like he'd done something wrong too. It's so unfair. None of this is his fault. Whatever happened to innocent until proved guilty? Isn't that the law?'

Now Megan is beginning to understand. This is also about Mark's pride and the exposure of his debts.

'Yes, it is the law,' says Megan. 'And I don't know why I'm apologising for Collins. The man's an idiot and he got it wrong. What more can I say?'

'We don't blame you,' says Mark stiffly. *He's lying. He does.* 'You did what you could.' She did rather more than that but she says nothing.

She meets his gaze. His look is cold and truculent. And her sister is avoiding eye contact. Debbie has to put her marriage back together; Megan gets it. Choices have to be made. *Closing ranks.*

'Well,' says Megan. 'I'll leave you to your meal.'

Debbie glances tentatively at Mark, then she sighs and says, 'There's plenty. You can eat with us if you like.' She's backtracking now because she can see Megan's upset and she's feeling bad. Megan knows her sister only too well. Debbie's emotions erupt in a cascade, whoosh, then it's over. She's angry, then she's sorry. Her moods flip at lightning speed, they always have.

'No, it's fine,' says Megan. 'I was planning to go out anyway.'

'Okay,' says Debbie. 'Well, if you're sure.' She sounds relieved. Megan can see Debbie's caught between the two of them. But there's nothing she can do.

She walks out of the kitchen and heads upstairs to her room. On the way she glances into the open doorways of the children's bedrooms. Kyle is on his PlayStation. Amber and Ruby are in the bedroom they share, in order that Megan can be accommodated in the attic room. Not a comfortable thought at this moment. Amber has headphones on; she's listening to music and texting. She catches Megan's eye for a second and immediately looks away. *Amber too?* It's like a kick in the gut.

Ruby is sitting on her bed, cross-legged, reading a picture book to herself out loud. *It's not the kids' fault*, Megan has to remind herself. They're all adrift in the backwash of this trauma.

As Megan mounts the final flight of stairs to her room, she realises how desolate she feels. This is her family, her home, and yet she's being given the cold shoulder. It's understandable they're angry. Megan is angry herself. But somehow the blame has shifted onto her shoulders and it's hard not to feel resentful. Why does unfairness always get passed down the line?

She walks into her room and tosses her bag onto the bed. She has a lump in her throat. She's trying to hold it all down, but a sense of choking misery rises up from her guts. She sinks down on the bed, puts her face in her hands and cries. But her tears are silent and private. She doesn't want the children to hear. She certainly doesn't want Debbie and Mark to know. Their rejection of her stings. She sits alone in her tiny attic room and wonders what she's going to do. She feels abandoned. Now she definitely has to get her own place. She should've done it months ago. It was stupid not to. She's not wanted here.

The tears gradually stop.

She wipes her eyes, takes her phone from her bag and calls Danny Ingram.

CHAPTER THIRTY-ONE

Saturday, 6.30 p.m.

Yvonne is sitting at the kitchen table. It feels as if she's been there for a very long time. She's been watching the sun move across the back of the house and sink behind the garden hedge. Her thoughts drift; there's no coherence to any of them. She wonders where the children are. Then she remembers: arrangements have been made. Penny has grasped the reins. When the phone rang this morning, she answered it. She dealt with it. The new nanny arrived from the agency at lunchtime. The awful Christine, with her grubby fingerprints, has been banished. Yvonne's not sure how her sister managed that.

The kitchen is her favourite place in the house. Hand-built, bespoke, unique; the cabinets are faced with brushed steel and the worktops are marble, making it all really easy to keep clean. It has bi-fold doors onto the terrace, which means she can keep an eye on the children when they're playing in the garden. But the new nanny has them safely corralled in the playroom. The situation has been explained to her.

Yvonne thinks about the children. If she's brutally honest, Aidan has always been her favourite. He's her firstborn, so perhaps that's natural even though she always wanted a girl. Imogen is a sweet, pretty little thing, but she's never touched Yvonne's heart in the same way as Aidan. And she's such a nervous child, which is annoying. It's wrong for a mother to have favourites. She knows that. She does try and treat them all the same.

The front door slams. Penny has returned. Her sister walks into the kitchen and plonks her bag down on a chair. Yvonne eyes it enviously. It's Hermès. In her opinion Prada is more classy. But it's still a lovely bag.

'They've arrested him and he's being held for further questioning,' says Penny. 'The lawyer was bloody useless. We'll have to get someone else. Are you listening to me, Yvonne?'

Yvonne drags her eyes from the bag. 'Do you want a glass of wine, darling?' she says.

'You mean you haven't consumed every bottle in the house yet?'

Yvonne meets her sister's gaze. *It's not fair. Why is she being so nasty?*

Penny shakes her head. 'Oh, what the hell,' she says. She goes to the fridge, takes out a fresh bottle of white and unscrews the top.

Yvonne gropes through her fuddled thoughts for the question she was about to ask. *Here it is!*

'Where's Aidan?' she says. 'When's he coming home?'

Penny pours herself a glass of wine. 'I've just told you. He's locked up in a police cell. The lawyer friend I spoke to in London said we should argue for release under investigation. But, as I said, the solicitor they gave us was useless. Aidan's made a detailed confession, that's the problem.'

'Locked in a cell?' says Yvonne. 'He's a child. They can't put a child in a cell, can they?'

'They can hold him for questioning for up to thirty-six hours from his arrest. They told me to come back in the morning.'

Yvonne picks up the new bottle of wine and tops up her own glass.

'Are you just going to keep drinking yourself into oblivion?' says Penny. 'We have to do something. Make a plan. Get a better lawyer.'

Yvonne doesn't reply. She doesn't like it when Penny tries to bully her like this. She takes a large swallow of wine to steady her nerves.

'You think this is all my fault, don't you?' she says.

'Oh for Christ's sake, stop feeling sorry for yourself,' says Penny.

'Maybe, if I'd been a better wife to him—'

'Don't talk nonsense. That wouldn't have made a scrap of difference and you know it.'

'But maybe if I'd—'

Penny grabs her wrist.

'Ouch!' says Yvonne. Her sister's manicured nails are sharp.

'Listen to me and focus,' says Penny. 'Are you listening?'

'Yes!'

'Whatever's happened in the past with Greg, who did what, that's water under the bridge. He's dead. All that's behind us. We forget it. Now we have to think about Aidan. Do you really want him to go to prison for this?'

Penny releases her. Yvonne cradles her wrist.

'No, of course I don't,' she says.

'I'm trying to help you, Yvonne.'

'I know.'

'Then you need to pull yourself together. The police are going to be coming here and asking questions. You need to be able to deal with that.'

Yvonne nods. Tears well in her eyes. 'I'm sorry, Pen. I never meant—'

'You've got to be ready for them. Do you understand me? That means you have to sober up.'

Penny's right of course. *Penny's always right, isn't she?*

Yvonne wipes her face with her palm. She's trembling. But she has to say it. 'Why would Aidan go to the police and say he did this?'

Penny exhales and gives her that long-suffering look. 'You know why.'

'I'm confused.'

'Darling, he thinks it's the only way he can protect you.'

Yvonne's chin quivers. *Her beautiful boy!* She loves him so much.

CHAPTER THIRTY-TWO

Sunday, 9.35 a.m.

Megan didn't expect to be summoned to police HQ in Exeter on a Sunday morning. She was supposed to be going with Ingram to interview Ranim. But an urgent message from Chief Superintendent Rob Barker's office takes precedence. She has no option but to obey. She was told to be there at nine thirty but Barker is running late. She doesn't mind waiting. She has plenty to think about.

When she drove out of Berrycombe the previous evening, she was at her lowest ebb for months. The rift with Debbie and Mark has poleaxed her. Even so, as she headed for Torquay and Ingram's hotel, she couldn't escape the feeling she was making a colossal mistake. Wasn't it sheer desperation, running to a man? There've been times in her life before when she's done this and it's never turned out well. And yet she couldn't seem to stop herself.

Ingram met her in the hotel bar. He bought her a fancy G and T with all the trimmings and listened. She gave him a tightly edited version of her tale of woe. She didn't want to come over as a complete basket case. He didn't say much, he let her talk. *He was probably bored.* After two drinks, he suggested they went for something to eat. That's when she realised he was trying to take care of her and make sure she didn't drown her sorrows in booze. He'd researched some restaurants and gave her a choice: Italian,

Lebanese or steak. She opted for steak. *The bloodier the better*, she thought. Bloody suited her mood.

Over the meal she made an effort to move on to other topics. He told her about his ex-wife. They were far too young when they married, he said. He'd thought she was his dream girl but as the years passed her talent for manipulation emerged. She could be selfish and petty and liked everything her own way. She decided she didn't want to be married to a police officer – not enough money – and he knew that he didn't want to do anything else. They battled it out for a few more years and finally divorced. He has a daughter, now a teenager, who he rarely sees.

Megan told him about her marriage to Paul but she glossed over the part about the children she wanted but never had.

He said, 'Sounds like we both did the same thing: chose the job. Stupid thing is I didn't even realise at the time that's what I was doing. You turn round and suddenly it's all gone. And my daughter's turned into a stroppy teen who doesn't want to know me.'

The hurt of Debbie and Mark's rejection began to fade as they ordered another bottle of wine and laughed about the absurdity of it all.

She wasn't sure whether she wanted to sleep with him again or not. But when it came to it, there was little discussion.

'Do you want this?' he asked and her reply was simply 'yes'.

They were both more tentative than the first time. The impetuousness of a night of sex with a stranger was gone. Now there was a sense that this could become a thing in both their lives. But for her the best part was lying in his arms afterwards. It felt an easy and safe place to be and she needed that as much as she needed raw passion.

The text from Barker demanding her presence the next morning arrived late on Saturday night. She went home at the crack of dawn for fresh clothes. She didn't know where any of this was going with Danny, but that didn't really matter. Two divorced lonely forty-somethings who met on the job? It all felt rather desperate. But, even when he was poncing about in his baseball cap and aviator shades, he made her smile. It was something different, a new chapter, and that had to be a good thing.

She managed to shower and change and get out of the house without bumping into anyone. Only the dog saw her come and go. She slipped him a treat.

Now she sits outside the chief superintendent's office in her best suit. She doesn't know why she's been summoned. It's unusual. Her previous encounters with Barker have always been at the offices of the Major Crime Team. And on a Sunday morning?

The door finally opens and Barker steps out.

'Sorry to have kept you, Megan,' he says. 'A phone call I had to take.'

'Not a problem, sir,' says Megan.

The chief super's office is modern and functional. The bookshelf contains only police manuals and legal tomes. Barker is not a man to display his awards and citations.

He invites Megan to sit down.

'Sorry to drag you up here to Exeter on a Sunday,' he says. 'But getting down to Plymouth wasn't an option. And this whole situation needs sorting out urgently because we're on the clock with this latest suspect.'

Situation. She scans him. It's her default setting to assume that she's done something wrong. Too many childhood visits to the head teacher's office and a residual guilty conscience.

Rob Barker's a burly bloke, a rugby prop forward gone to seed. His ears are mashed and stick out from his balding pate. But appearances can be deceptive. He's a subtle operator. He manages the Major Crime Teams and his officers with the lightest of touches. And he takes chances on difficult individuals like Megan.

'This murder inquiry has got completely out of hand,' he says. 'If I had the resources I would transfer in a new DI and that would be an end to it. Jim Collins has been a good officer in the past, but he's made a complete hash of this. And to have allowed DS Jennings to be feeding back confidential information to the victim's father shows very poor judgement.'

Megan wants to mention what he did to Debbie and Mark but she decides against it. It seems wiser to wait and listen to what he has to say.

As if he's read her mind, Barker says, 'I'm aware that your sister discovered the body and I know that Collins went off at a tangent with that.'

'My sister's alibi was confirmed by CCTV footage,' says Megan.

'And as a result, is there bad blood between you and Collins?' asks Barker.

Bad blood? Megan wonders how she should answer that.

'We've had words, sir,' she says.

'Yes, I heard,' says Barker. 'However, I need to ask you to put that whole situation behind you. I want you to join the murder team as Collins's DS. I'm sure you already know it's what DCI Slater wants.'

Megan sighs. She's been bushwhacked. *Typical Slater move.*

'Are you aware, sir,' she says, 'that Barry Porter, the victim's father, has made certain allegations concerning my sister? And he's threatened to go to the press. I may not be the best choice for this inquiry.'

Barker chuckles. 'I know you don't want to do it. Laura made that clear. But if I listened to every angry blowhard who starts shouting about police corruption, I'd never solve any crimes. The man has lost his son, so he's entitled to let off a bit of steam, but that's as far as it goes. It will not have any bearing on how I run this inquiry.'

Megan wonders what she's doing there. It's clear that Barker has already made up his mind. She's working with Collins. End of story. She didn't need to drive all the way to Exeter to find that out.

'However, I'm not going to force you to do this against your will,' he says. 'That would be counter-productive, wouldn't it?'

Megan says nothing. She thinks about Ranim and Hassan. These are the people she should be helping. She couldn't give a stuff who murdered Greg Porter. He probably deserved it.

Barker laces his chunky fingers and smiles. 'Where do you want to be in five years, Megan?

She shrugs. *Alive? Sane?*

'I really haven't thought about it, sir.'

'When are you planning to take your inspector's exams?' he asks.

'I have no plans to do that,' she replies.

'Why not?' says Barker.

'I don't think I'm ready.'

'Bullshit,' says Barker. 'You need to stop being frightened of your own shadow.'

Megan bites back an angry riposte. She's had it in the neck from Debbie and Mark, now Barker's getting in on the act.

'I'm still seeing Dr Moretti,' she says. 'I've still got a diagnosis of PTSD. I do the job as best I can. But at the moment, living one day at a time is what works for me.'

'Fair enough. You have to take care of yourself. I understand that. Which is why you're the perfect person to teach Jim Collins to do the same.'

Fuck that!

'I'm sorry, sir. But our circumstances are totally different.'

'I don't think so. I've worked with Jim. He's not a bad bloke. And panic attacks come in different forms.'

How the hell does he know about that? Moretti? Vish or Brittney?

'In case you're wondering,' says Barker. 'Your colleagues didn't rat you out.' He laughs. 'Probably not the best turn of phrase. Anyway, the whole incident filtered back to me months ago from someone who knows the contractor who was there that day to fix the septic tank.'

Megan stares down at her hands. She has butterflies in her stomach at the mere thought. The memory of that septic tank, putting her head down the hatch to check out a dead body and seeing the rats, still sends shivers through her. She had thought she was going to die. It had certainly felt like it.

'Look, I'm not trying to embarrass you,' says Barker. 'I'm making the point that you lost your nerve that day. But there's no shame in that. You recovered and you're a better police officer for it.'

What the fuck does he know about shame?

'I don't see how you get to that,' she says.

'Jim Collins has lost his nerve. That's how I read this. He's playing tough as a way to cover just how scared he feels. That's why he's making stupid mistakes.'

Send him to Moretti then!

Barker is staring right at her. 'I need an officer capable of getting this inquiry back on track. Someone who can handle Collins. It's a huge ask. But I think you're up to it. As SIO Laura will support you every inch of the way.'

That'll be a first.

Megan sighs and says, 'What are you saying, sir? You took a chance on me, now you want me to return the favour and babysit Collins?'

Barker opens his palms. 'Ultimately I think you and I care about the same thing, Megan. Getting the job done. This is a murder case and it's our responsibility to bring the culprit or culprits to justice. Of the officers available to me, I think you're the best placed to do that.'

She meets his eye. Cunning old bastard.

Yep, it's payback time.

CHAPTER THIRTY-THREE

Sunday, 11.15 a.m.

The holiday traffic is heavy and it takes Megan ages to get back to Plymouth. The industrial park on the outskirts of the city, where the offices of South Devon's Major Crime Team are located, is choked with lorries and vans, parked up for the weekend. She's forced to do two circuits before she finds a parking space on a side road around the corner. She's checking her phone as she walks towards the MCT building and initially doesn't notice Jim Collins. He's loitering close to the main entrance, smoking a cigarette. *Possibly not the best idea for a man recovering from cancer*, thinks Megan.

As she approaches, he tosses it and grinds it underfoot.

'So are you going to do it?' he says. *Has he been lying in wait? Maybe he saw her drive up?*

'Do what exactly?' says Megan.

'C'mon, you know what I'm talking about,' says Collins. 'Slater is transferring you to the murder team. I've already been informed.'

Megan looks at him more closely. His cheeks are pale and gaunt and there are heavy shadows under his eyes. She needs to find a way to regard him differently. Even to sympathise. But she knows she'd be a fool to forget what a spiteful weasel he can be.

'I don't think it's what either of us wants, Jim,' she says.

'Then tell them no,' says Collins. 'They can't make you if you dig your heels in and refuse.'

There's a whiff of desperation coming off him. His tie may be neatly knotted but his carefully laundered shirt hangs loose on his torso and a fresh notch has been cut on the belt holding up his trousers. He looks as if a strong wind could blow him over.

Megan sighs. 'Don't you think that in the circumstances I've got more reason to be aggrieved about this than you?' she says.

Collins dismisses this with a shrug.

'How the hell was I supposed to know that Ted Jennings was some bloody golfing buddy of the victim's father?' he says. 'Did you know?'

'No, but I don't think Ted was exactly advertising the fact.'

'Try telling that to Slater. He's been shipped out, back to a desk job in CID. And where does that leave me? Makes it look like I'm either a complete fool or bent, doesn't it?'

'I don't want to get into this,' says Megan.

'Why not?' says Collins. 'Everyone knows you're being put in to keep an eye on me. So what's your opinion, bent or stupid?' He seems wired and twitchy.

'I think you should take this up with Barker not with me,' says Megan.

'And what did he promise you? A leg-up to inspector?'

He's standing facing her with hands on hips and blocking her way into the building.

'For your information,' she says, 'I haven't even taken my inspector's exams and nobody has offered me a leg-up to anything. But I don't think they're pissed off with you just because of Ted. You pursued one suspect and didn't consider other lines of inquiry. And I think you know that. You want to save your career? Then stop feeling so bloody sorry for yourself. I'm just here to do my job. And if you do yours we'll get along fine.'

She scoots round him and walks into the building. She takes the stairs two at a time, knowing he won't be able to follow. When she gets to the second floor she glances down the stairwell into the foyer below. He's waiting for the lift.

Megan walks into the incident room to find Laura Slater listening earnestly to the Crime Scene Manager, Hilary Kumar.

'Ah, good,' says Slater. 'You need to hear this, Megan.'

Slater must know she's just driven all the way to Exeter to have her arm twisted by Barker. But it seems she's not going to mention it.

Megan greets Hilary; they know each other, though not well.

'Hey, glad you're going to be on this,' says Kumar with a big smile. Considering the grimness of her job, she has a cheerful disposition.

Not everyone is, thinks Megan, though she refrains from saying so. It's hard not to feel tetchy and put upon. But she has to just get on with it. She has no choice. Out of the corner of her eye she sees Collins following her into the room.

Kumar holds up her iPad. On the screen is a picture of lump hammer. 'We found this in a skip about three hundred metres down the hill from the crime scene. Blood on the head of the hammer will probably match the victim's. Some hair and tissue from the scalp too.'

'This is probably the murder weapon then?' says Megan. She becomes aware of Jim Collins coming up right behind her. He stops inches from her shoulder. She can hear his breathing, shallow and laboured, and smell the tang of his cologne.

'Jim,' says Slater. 'We're just bringing Megan up to speed with the forensics.'

'Excellent,' says Collins. 'As I've just told Megan, I'm really glad she's going to be on the team. She'll be a great asset. I think we're agreed what happened with her sister is water under the bridge.'

Weasel, definitely.

Slater gives him a quizzical look. 'I hope you two will work well together,' she says. She glances at Megan.

Megan says nothing.

'Absolutely, ma'am,' says Collins with a smile. 'It's certainly what I want.' He turns to Kumar. 'So did we get lucky on the fingerprints?'

'There's a couple of fairly clear prints,' says Kumar. 'But I'm afraid they don't belong to Aidan Porter.'

'Okay, well, looks like the lad had an accomplice then,' says Collins. 'Any hits on the database?'

'No,' says Kumar. 'It's extremely difficult to tell but looking at the spacing of the ridge patterns, I'm wondering if they could belong to a woman.'

'A woman?' he says.

'I'm only speculating,' says Kumar. 'It's impossible to tell for certain.'

'But it tells us someone might've helped him,' says Collins. 'He could have a girlfriend, I suppose.'

'Or,' says Megan, 'he's confessing to something he didn't do.'

CHAPTER THIRTY-FOUR

Sunday, 1.30 p.m.

Megan lets her gaze rest on the boy. Aidan Porter sits across the table from her, bony shoulders hunched like angel wings, his eyes downcast. He's next to his solicitor, Tim Wardell, the local lawyer that Megan met previously with the boy's grandfather. His aunt, Penny Reynolds, sits in the corner. Megan concludes that she and the old man have come to some kind of accommodation.

'Tell me about your mum, Aidan,' Megan says.

He's much more sullen than before. The reality and the boredom of incarceration in a cell overnight must be weighing on him; and for a rich kid like him it's probably been a shock. He twists the plaited band on his wrist round and round.

'What d'you want to know about her?' says Aidan.

'What's she like? I've never met her. How would you describe her to me?'

He huffs and thinks for a moment. 'S'pose she's quite particular about the way she dresses. Likes posh stuff.'

Megan notes the regression in his behaviour. He sounds more like a petulant fourteen-year-old than a seventeen-year-old. And his impatience is palpable.

She waits, fiddles with her notes. She's establishing a deliberately sedate pace with the questioning. Slater has made it clear she wants this done with care and Megan has discussed their approach on the phone with a Tier 5 interview adviser.

Aidan shoots a look at his aunt. She smiles back. An anxiously reassuring smile, thinks Megan. Should they read anything into that?

'What sort of relationship do you have?' asks Megan.

He huffs again. 'Well, she's just my mum.'

'Do you get on?' asks Megan.

He shrugs. There's definite tension and resistance. He doesn't want to talk about her.

Megan can see Penny Reynolds fidgeting in her chair. She keeps glancing at her nephew. Megan wonders at her jumpiness. She doesn't come over as a particularly nervous woman. Is she afraid of what the boy might say?

Vish sits next to Megan. He's leaning back in his chair and, following the new brief, watching Aidan with an encouraging smile. Collins's strategy of trying to intimidate has been abandoned and he's been relegated to the back room.

Megan turns to Vish and raises her eyebrows. He smiles and picks up the questioning.

'Yesterday,' he says, 'you spoke to us about your father. You said that he teased you about your hair. Had a go at you and that's what provoked you to attack him.'

Aidan nods, but now he's avoiding eye contact and picking at the edge of the table.

'Did he tease you often?' asks Vish.

'Look, I've said I did it,' says the boy impatiently. 'Why don't you just accept that? I'm fed up of answering all these stupid questions.'

'We're just trying to understand your family situation and the background to what happened,' says Megan.

'Why?' snaps Aidan. 'Why? I killed my father, okay? Now I want to be left alone.'

Tim Wardell clears his throat. 'Perhaps we should take a break?' he says.

'I don't want a break. I just want this to be over!'

'Can you explain to me why, Aidan?' says Megan. 'Because when your case comes to court, understanding the context of how this happened is going to be important in determining how you're treated.'

Aidan gives her a defiant look. 'No it's not,' he says. 'I've been on the net and looked it all up. I'm seventeen, I'll get a few years inside because I'm under age and I was traumatised. He was a vicious bastard and beat the shit out of my mother.' He turns to Wardell. 'Mitigating circumstances, right?'

The lawyer shifts uncomfortably in his chair.

'Did he hit you too?' asks Megan.

The boy swallows hard. 'Occasionally.'

'You wanted to protect her? Did you do this to protect her?'

'I didn't go down there deliberately to do it. It happened how I said.'

'You went down to help him prepare for the launch?'

'Yeah.'

'Seems an odd thing to do,' says Megan. 'You talk of his teasing, which suggests you didn't get on that well. Plus he abused your mother. Yet you wanted to go and help him.'

Aidan sighs. 'He's still my dad.'

She scans the boy. He seems very close to the edge. But the edge of what? She can feel no sense of regret from him, which is unusual. An angry family row leading to violence is usually followed by regret. Megan is beginning to feel that Aidan Porter is playing a part. But who's provided the script? She glances at Penny.

'Okay,' she says. 'Tell us about the weapon you used again?' Megan looks down at her notes, putting on a puzzled frown. 'What was it? Remind me?'

'I dunno. I just grabbed it. Some kind of hammer?'

'What did you do with it afterwards?'

'Can't remember.'

'Did you just drop it there on the floor?'

'Yeah, probably.'

'And you went down there that evening on your own?'

'Yes! I've said. Now can we stop? I've got a headache.'

'Of course,' says Megan. 'Can we get you a drink? And maybe some paracetamol?'

'Thank you,' says Wardell, with relief. The tension in him is unusual too. A lawyer who doesn't like the position he's been put in?

Megan and Vish stand up and she announces, for the benefit of the recording, the time and the fact that they're leaving the room.

Vish holds the door open and follows Megan out into the corridor. They turn the corner and walk upstairs to the incident room.

'What do you make of the aunt's reaction?' asks Megan.

'She's very twitchy. Something's going on,' says Vish.

They arrive at the incident room. Vish keys in the code and opens the door. Laura Slater and Jim Collins are standing in front of the bank of monitors.

Slater turns to face Megan and Vish.

'Nicely done,' says Slater. 'Provoked an interesting little exchange after you left the room. Wind it back, Jim.'

Collins scrolls the recording back to the moment the door shut behind Megan and Vish.

Aidan turns on his aunt. 'You said it'd be all right,' he hisses.

'Not here, darling,' she replies, her gaze flying up towards the camera.

Tim Wardell looks completely ill at ease. Aidan folds his arms and scowls. The three of them lapse into an awkward silence.

'Interesting,' says Megan. 'I'm wondering if maybe he's been persuaded to cover for his mother?'

'I'm thinking exactly the same thing,' says Collins. 'Maybe we'll find her prints on the murder weapon.' He grins at Megan. 'The grieving widow. I guess she's our next port of call.'

Megan returns the smile. There's a smugness about him which irritates her. Aidan Porter may be putting on a performance for them, but Jim Collins is doing exactly the same for Slater.

The DCI sighs. 'I think we've gone as far as we can with this. I know we haven't got DNA confirmation that this is the murder weapon. But it probably is and his prints aren't on it. The confession still sounds dubious. I've spoken to the CPS and they don't think there's enough to charge him. I'm going to release him under investigation. Are we agreed?'

Both Megan and Collins nod.

'Gives us a chance to rattle a few cages,' says Megan.

CHAPTER THIRTY-FIVE

Sunday, 3.05 p.m.

As they walk out of the office and across the pock-marked concrete yard towards the car, Megan is careful to keep Vish between herself and Collins. Out of sight of Slater, Collins's cheeriness has evaporated. He looks washed out and weary, hands in his trouser pockets and a glum expression. The strain of trying to maintain a front is obvious. And this worries Megan. With a DI who's not up to the job, the whole inquiry could go pear-shaped again.

Aidan Porter, his murdered father, his angry grandfather, his squirrelly aunt: there's much more going on than meets the eye. She's been tasked with helping Collins unravel this toxic family. But it's clear that won't be easy.

Vish is the designated driver, a relief to Megan. She doesn't much fancy going out with Collins on her own. Or being driven by him. She exchanges a covert smile with the young DC. Vish has a breeziness and a resilience about him that she knows she's going to need. He's been a detective for less than a year, but he's sharp and a fast learner. He clicks the fob as they approach the car. This is when Megan notices Ted Jennings lurking. Collins is opening the front passenger door, relegating Megan to the back seat as Jennings steps forward.

He ignores Megan.

'Can I just have a quick word, guv,' he says.

His appearance takes Collins by surprise.

'For Christ's sake, Ted!' says Collins, wheeling round and shooting an embarrassed look at Megan and Vish. 'Get in the car, you two,' he says briskly. Vish gets into the driver's seat. But Megan takes her time as Ted Jennings hovers awkwardly.

'Make this quick, mate,' says Collins.

Megan is surprised by the gentleness of his tone, given that Jennings has caused him a ton of trouble.

'I've put you in a tricky position,' says Ted. 'And I'm sorry.'

As she slides into the back seat and slowly closes the door, Megan is well placed to eavesdrop on their conversation.

Ted has a sorrowful look on his face. 'I know I overstepped the mark,' he says. 'But I really didn't think it would do any harm. I thought we had the case pretty much sewn up. Porter just wanted some assurance that we were doing our job and I thought that's what I was giving him. Then when the boy came in...'

Collins sighs. 'Yeah, but you know what it's like nowadays. Rules and box-ticking. But listen, if I get the chance, mate, I'll put in a word for you with Barker.'

'Thanks,' says Ted. 'Really appreciate that.'

Collins turns towards the car.

'But that's not what this is about,' says Ted. 'Remember on Wednesday, the DCI told me to go and pay a visit to Dennis Bridger.'

Dennis Bridger. Megan's ears prick up. With everything else that's been going on she'd almost forgotten about Bridger. A seriously nasty villain, released on licence and back in Devon. But far worse than that, he could be connected to Zac Yilmaz. *Zac Yilmaz!* Even the name sends a chill through her. She strokes the scar on her forearm; the cross he carved in her flesh so she could never forget.

'I did what she said,' says Ted. 'Made sure the little runt got the message that we've got our eye on him. He acted as if butter wouldn't melt. Still, I think we both know what a complete tosser he is.'

'Ted,' says Collins, 'can we wrap this up because I've got things to do.'

'Yeah, right. Sorry,' says Ted. 'After Slater hauled me over the coals yesterday, I wanted to do something to make amends. I know that little toerag must be up to something, so I thought I'd keep an eye on him.'

'I don't see the need for that,' says Collins. 'Barker's got a surveillance team on him 24/7. Whatever he's up to, they'll be on it.'

'Oh come on, guv,' says Ted. 'Standing off? You know what that means. Some idiot sitting in front of a computer screen in Exeter. All this bloody technology can't replace boots on the ground. They do it because it's cheaper. They haven't even got anyone boxing the routes to Bridger's place. I've looked.'

'So what are you telling me?' says Collins. 'You've been keeping him under surveillance too?'

'Nah, he's a professional. Sitting outside his house won't crack it either. So, last night, I climbed over the fence into his back garden.'

'What?' says Collins. 'Are you mad?'

'That's what he's not expecting. And guess what I found?' says Ted. 'He's got a little shed at the bottom of his garden. Tucked away. You'd never know it was there. And that's where he goes to do business. Barker may have his phone tapped and trackers on his car but they're missing the essential thing. He's down in his shed, talking on a burner. He's definitely got something going on. Maybe a deal, I dunno.'

'What sort of deal?' says Collins.

'I couldn't get close enough to hear any details. But the thing is, you know and I know that we're not going to be able to get the likes of Bridger playing by the book.'

Collins huffs. 'Listen, Ted, whatever you're thinking, I don't want to hear it. Okay? Christ, you're already in enough bother.'

'But I thought you said…' Ted lowers his voice. 'Point is, we've both got something to prove, haven't we?'

'I've got a murder inquiry to run. And it takes me all my energy at the moment just to get through the bloody day,' says Collins sourly.

'What if he's talking to this London mob? He's definitely talking to someone. If I can get something concrete, will you take it to Slater?'

'Ted, you've done one daft thing, don't do another. Don't go sticking your neck out. Dennis Bridger is not a fool.'

'But you will go to Slater for me? If I get something? That's all I'm asking.'

Collins exhales, opens the passenger door of the car and gets in.

'Let's go!' he says to Vish.

Vish starts the engine and they drive off, leaving Ted Jennings standing.

Megan says nothing.

Collins cranes round in his seat to glance at her. 'I don't know how much you heard of that. And I don't know what you're thinking' – he looks at Vish – 'either of you. But I'm going to presume that neither of you wants to be known as the sort of officer that goes snitching to the boss.'

'Are you threatening us, Jim?' says Megan coolly.

'I'm just saying.'

The rest of the journey takes place in silence. Megan is grateful.

Her brain's in overdrive. She'd thought Collins was her main problem but that pales into insignificance beside this. She moved to Devon to escape the fallout from her previous life as an undercover officer in London. This place has saved her and become her haven. But perhaps it was too good to last.

Her nemesis may be in jail, serving a life sentence for drug trafficking and multiple homicides. But his gang is still in business and the authorities seem powerless to prevent him running it from his prison cell.

Bridger could be talking to Zac Yilmaz.

Megan reminds herself that she needs to stay calm. Bridger doesn't know her so at present the connection and threat are indirect. And Zac has no reason to suspect she's living in Devon now. But that could all change.

Her chest feels tight and she's finding it hard to get her breath. *This is the last bloody thing she needs. A panic attack!*

She winds down the window and tries to remember what the shrink told her: breathe.

Breathe! Oh fuck!

CHAPTER THIRTY-SIX

Sunday, 4.15 p.m.

The Porters' home looks like something from a glossy design magazine and is set on rising ground overlooking the River Dart. It's approached via a winding drive with high hedges surrounded by farmland. *The location could be peaceful and idyllic or it could be lonely and isolated, depending on your point of view*, thinks Megan.

She's feeling better. The fresh air streaming in through the car window and a tight focus on her breathing helped her avoid a full-blown panic attack. It was touch and go for a while. But she's managed to force her fears back into their box. As she gets out of the car she's still pale and shaky.

'Are you okay?' says Collins with a frown.

'Fine,' Megan replies. 'I get a little carsick in the back.'

'Should've said. I don't mind riding in the back,' he replies.

Megan wonders if this is true. But he's giving her a concerned look, which may or may not be genuine. Perhaps he's nervous. Staying one jump ahead of Collins's mercurial moods takes a lot of energy. And the near panic attack has left her blitzed. But the DCI has been precise in her instructions: a low-key approach. Slater's expecting Megan to take the lead.

The front door is heavy oak and looks like it could've been nicked from a medieval church. Vish presses the bell, which is set below a small electronic screen and keypad. A singsong chime echoes through the large house.

Several moments pass and Penny Reynolds opens the door.

Her lips pursed, she gives them a curt nod. 'Come in.'

'You got home all right, then?' says Collins with a smile. Aidan Porter was released under investigation around two o'clock and his lawyer was advised by the custody sergeant that he should stay close to home.

'Yes,' says Penny. 'Aidan's having a swim in the pool with his brothers and sister. I trust that accords with the conditions of his release.' There's a sneer in her tone. But Jim Collins doesn't react. Megan has to admit that he does seem to have changed his approach.

He smiles and says, 'It's certainly a lovely day for it.'

The three police officers follow Penny through the house. The hallway has a honey-blond wooden floor which stretches into all the other ground floor rooms. They pass through a double-height atrium and Megan is struck by the neatness. For a house with four children it's remarkably tidy.

'Well,' says Penny, 'do you want me to get him?'

'We're here to speak to Mrs Porter, not to Aidan,' says Collins. She merely nods. *This can't be a surprise to her*, thinks Megan. And it isn't.

They find Yvonne Porter waiting for them in the sitting room. She's perched on the edge of one of three huge rose-pink sofas, set at right angles to each other in the middle of the spacious room. She wears a flowery summer dress that wouldn't look out of place at a posh garden party.

Megan's first impression is of a fragile woman. She's extremely skinny. Her hands are clasped in her lap but there's still a visible tremor. She's carefully made up with her hair neatly pinned in a French twist, the style that Laura Slater favours.

'Do please sit down,' says Mrs Porter in a soft voice. 'Can I offer you some tea?'

Collins is about to refuse, but Megan pre-empts him.

'Thank you, that's lovely,' she says. It's the fastest way to get Penny Reynolds out of the room.

Yvonne Porter shoots a nervous glance at her sister.

'Yes, of course, I'll get it,' Penny says. There's irritation in her tone. Then she heads, rather slowly in Megan's opinion, for the kitchen. But at least the first box is ticked; Yvonne is on her own.

Collins and Megan sit down, Vish remains standing. He walks over to the window. Yvonne's gaze follows him anxiously around the room. Another simple technique but effective.

'Things have moved on a little since we came to speak to you last week, Mrs Porter,' says Collins.

Yvonne nods and swallows. She's still distracted by Vish.

He continues, 'I'm sure you know that your son came to talk to us.'

Yvonne's attention shoots back to Collins.

'He didn't do it,' she says abruptly. 'The whole thing's nonsense.'

'You sound very sure of that,' says Megan.

'I know my own son.'

'He did give us a convincing account, Mrs Porter,' says Collins.

She shrugs. 'Well, he was here with me all evening. And in any event, Greg wouldn't have wanted him down there at the flats.'

Collins glances at Megan and she picks up the baton.

'Aidan says he went to help his father prepare for the launch. Why wouldn't your husband have wanted that?' she asks.

Yvonne raises her chin defiantly and says, 'Because in all probability he'd have been fucking some woman down there.'

Is this meant to shock? The meek manner, the flowery dress, then bang, straight into this.

Megan scans her; the bony hands are clasped so tightly that the knuckles are white.

She waits a moment then says, 'You think your son would've known that?'

Yvonne gives a scornful laugh. 'Of course he did. He's seventeen, he's not a child. He's well aware of what his father got up to. Greg used to boast about it to him.'

'That must've been hard for Aidan,' says Megan.

Yvonne shrugs. 'Greg probably thought Aidan would be impressed.'

'But he wasn't?'

'You'd have to ask Aidan.'

'Are you and your son close?' says Megan.

Yvonne frowns as if the question is ridiculous. 'Do you actually have any kids?' she says.

The frigid, childless, middle-aged cop. Is that how she comes over? Megan wonders.

'No,' says Megan. 'I have nieces and a nephew.'

'As soon as they hit puberty, that's it. They turn into this other creature. Aidan's…' She waves her hands around. 'Oh, I don't know. It's hard to explain.'

'Did his father ever hit him?'

'No. Absolutely not. His infidelity I could live with. But Greg knew that if he ever raised his hand to the children, then that would be it.' She juts her chin. She's lying.

Now they're getting to the nub of it.

'Did Greg ever hit you?' says Megan. She tries to hold Yvonne's gaze. But it skitters away.

Yvonne unclasps her hands and places her palms together. She seems to be lining her fingers up and focusing on them. It looks to Megan like a technique she's been taught. A way to control your emotions? But in an odd way she seems as if she's praying.

She sighs, raises her eyes and stares straight at Megan. 'No,' she says. 'I wouldn't have stayed in such a marriage.'

Megan returns her look. 'Aidan says that your husband was violent towards you. Why would he say that if it isn't true?'

'I've no idea.' Now she sounds tetchy and impatient. The soft voice has become louder. She's a woman defending her honour by refusing to admit the truth. It's a reaction Megan can understand. She's been there. She's been too proud to admit that she let a man hurt her and didn't have the strength to walk away. And if Yvonne did finally lose it and attack him, Megan doesn't blame her.

She wants to reach out to Yvonne Porter and say just that. Tell her not to be ashamed.

But Penny Reynolds walks into the room carrying a tray, which she puts down on the glass-topped coffee table, and Megan knows the moment has been lost.

Yvonne flips back to meek housewife mode and busies herself unloading the tray: a tea pot, milk jug, cups and saucers. They all belong to a matching set.

'Darling, get some coasters,' she says to her sister. *Back to the soft voice*. 'They're in the sideboard drawer.'

Collins and Megan exchange covert looks. He appears to be at a loss, which is probably why he's deferring to Megan. Yvonne Porter's behaviour has all the hallmarks of a performance. This is probably what she spends her life doing. Megan watches her pouring the tea like a perfect hostess. She knows her role. But who's the performance for? For them? Or for Penny?

Megan is puzzled; she decides on a change of tack.

'This has obviously been a very stressful time,' she says. 'But can you tell us about the last time you saw your husband?' There's still a chance they can crack this open.

Yvonne's hand freezes mid-air. She nearly spills the tea she's pouring. 'I suppose,' she says with a catch in her voice, 'it was that morning.'

'He went to work? Where did your husband run his business from?' says Megan.

Yvonne waves her hand vaguely towards the window. 'There's an office, out there in the yard.'

'Would it be okay if DC Prasad went to have a look?'

Megan has already come to the conclusion that CSI will need to go through the whole place. It should've been done days ago.

Yvonne sighs and says, 'I don't see why not. Greg's hardly about to object, is he?' She gives a small, tinkling laugh. Now she's playing the mad wife.

Penny steps forward and seizes the wobbling teapot from Yvonne's hand.

'I'm sure you'll appreciate that my sister is not quite herself,' she says. 'She's been prescribed medication by her doctor.'

Yvonne glares at Penny. Now what's going on? Yvonne is the elder of the two but the power seems to reside with Penny. It occurs to Megan that the fragile female act is for her sister's benefit, which is interesting. But does Penny know or suspect what Yvonne's done?

'All this is very difficult, we understand that,' says Megan soothingly. She doesn't have a chance to continue.

Yvonne jumps to her feet. She has a tear welling in her eye. She wipes her face with a shaky hand. 'I'm sorry,' she says. 'You'll have to excuse me.' And she hurries out of the room like a scolded child.

Megan turns to Penny. She's wondering what they've just witnessed. Penny took control and Yvonne reacted by kicking off?

'I'm sorry if we've upset your sister,' Megan says.

'Her husband's dead,' says Penny tartly. 'What do you expect?'

'And who's telling the truth,' says Megan. 'Aidan or his mother? Did Greg hit her?'

'I live in London,' says Penny. 'I'm rarely here. So I really couldn't say.'

CHAPTER THIRTY-SEVEN

Sunday, 5.10 p.m.

When they leave the Porters' house, Jim Collins is as good as his word and gets into the back of the car so Megan can ride in the front. As they drive towards Torquay he's silent and morose, mostly staring out of the window.

Megan finds the tension uncomfortable and also annoying. She catches Vish's eye; he must be thinking the same.

'Well,' says Megan brightly. 'What do we make of Mrs Porter?'

'Something's seriously adrift,' says Vish. 'It obviously wasn't a happy marriage. He was unfaithful. So big row, she clocked him with a hammer? Son knows this and is trying to protect his mother?'

'But what's the role of the aunt in all this?' says Megan.

'The little exchange Aidan had with her in the interview room suggests it was Auntie who persuaded him to confess,' says Vish.

Is Collins even listening?

'Makes sense,' says Megan. 'After we've talked to the grandfather, we need to get CSI and a fingerprint officer over there. If her prints match those on the potential murder weapon, then we're probably on the money. You didn't arrange for Yvonne's prints to be taken before, did you, Jim?'

Collins turns from the window to look at her. He's deathly pale. 'Sorry?' he says. 'No, didn't seem necessary.'

It's standard procedure. Megan decides not to say that.

Vish surveys him in the rear-view mirror, glances at Megan, then says, 'Need a drink of water, boss?' He extracts a plastic bottle from the door pocket, hands it to Megan, who offers it to Collins. She scans him; it's a warm day, but he's shivering.

'Cheers,' says the DI weakly. He unscrews the top and takes a long drink.

Vish and Megan exchange glances. Megan's not sure how to tackle this, but Collins can be so reactive that keeping it light seems the best approach.

'Honestly, Vish,' she says with a grin. 'Your bloody driving's a nightmare! I ride in the back, I feel like I'm on a rollercoaster, now you're doing the same to Jim.' The forced jollity sounds false even to her.

But Vish takes the hint immediately. 'Really sorry, boss,' he says. 'I keep forgetting I'm not on response any more. Truth is I miss the blues and twos.'

Collins drinks some more water. He screws the top back on the bottle and sighs.

Then he says, 'It's not you, mate. It's me. Forget about it. I'll be fine.'

This is ridiculous, thinks Megan. The man's sick. He shouldn't even be at work. Barker should have brought in another DI.

She cranes round in her seat to look straight at him. 'Jim, you're obviously not fine.'

As he meets her gaze, she can see the fear in his eyes. 'It'll pass,' he says. And she knows what's driving him on. The dread of medical retirement. Pensioned off. On the scrapheap. She also knows what the spectre of that feels like, which is why Barker's got her over a barrel.

'It's after five, it's a Sunday,' she says. 'It doesn't need three of us to question Barry Porter. We can easily drop you back at your place.' She smiles, then adds, 'And whatever you might think of me, I'm not going to go running to Slater and use this against you.'

He doesn't say anything for a moment. He drops his gaze, dips his head and pinches his nose. Then he says angrily, 'Bloody treatment! Fucks with your hormones. I end up crying like a girl. I fucking hate it!'

He wipes his face with his palm and adds, 'I'm sorry. What I said before about snitching… sorry.'

Megan looks away; she doesn't want to embarrass him.

They're nearing the turn-off to Torquay. She doesn't even know where he lives.

'Let us take you home,' says Megan in as neutral a tone as she can manage.

'Okay. Thanks,' he replies. 'Need to get my medication changed. Straighten this out. It won't be a problem again. I'll be back tomorrow.'

'Fine,' says Megan. She knows she's treading a fine line between helping him and exploiting his weakness. *Forget that.* After the grief he's caused her, she refuses to feel guilty.

The diversion to Ashburton takes a little over three quarters of an hour. Jim Collins disappears into a neat Victorian terraced house just off the high street after a curt word of thanks and without a backward glance.

On the drive back to Torquay Megan calls Hilary Kumar. Organising CSI to visit the Porters' house, getting the appropriate sign-offs from Slater, takes most of the journey. Megan doesn't mention Collins, as promised. The relief she feels at having him out of her hair, at least temporarily, is enough.

Vish manages to find a slot in a busy car park near the harbour.

The sea is glistening. It's a Sunday evening, a time for pleasure and relaxation. The town is full of tourists and day trippers taking advantage of the spring sunshine. Megan wishes she could join them. But this murder investigation is barely five days old. It's been up one blind alley, thanks to Collins. And Aidan Porter's confession looks like being another. She's not interested in the DI's reasons or excuses; it's clear he's not up to the job. Her task now is to get the investigation on track.

'I phoned Barry Porter earlier,' says Vish. 'Told him we needed to speak to him again. He was a bit surly but said he'd be on his boat all afternoon.'

The harbourside is jam-packed, cafes and pubs overflowing. Kids with ice creams, families with fish and chips, gaggles of hopeful seagulls.

Megan and Vish walk down the hill towards the marina. The short stroll feels like the first opportunity she's had to ease up even a little. She needs to step off the rollercoaster.

Only two days ago she was here with Danny Ingram and his NCA colleagues. But that was before she fell out with her sister and got drafted into this mess.

She has a text on her phone from Ingram, which she hasn't answered. He says that the interview with Ranim confirmed that the men on the video are the smugglers. She could simply acknowledge that. But composing a suitable reply feels too complicated to manage in her present mood. She wants to say more but she can't decide what. She wonders what he's doing. And she can guess. He's like her, he uses work to fill the empty spaces in his life.

The NCA are probably still scouring Dartmoor in the hope of finding the smugglers' bolthole. But that's just guesswork too. Until another load of illegal immigrants turns up on the authorities' radar, it's likely to be a waiting game.

By contrast the murder inquiry is giving Megan something to get her teeth into and she's glad of that. She's had no time to communicate with her sister either. But then Debbie has made no attempt to phone or text her. The raw pain of the rift between them hasn't gone away but, while Megan remains busy, she can ignore it.

'What did Collins ask Barry Porter when he spoke to him before?' she says.

'Not much,' says Vish. 'The old man was in shock. He'd only just been told that his son's death was suspicious. We didn't get much sense out of him.'

'So we're starting from scratch?'

'Pretty much.'

They reach the steps that lead down to the pontoon.

Vish points. 'That's his boat down there.'

Megan says, 'Yeah, I remember. You pointed it out before. The white one. Third along.'

Some of the moorings are empty. Plenty of yachts are out sailing in the bay. But the luxury cruiser is obvious. Larger than most of its fellows, it's one of the more expensive boats moored at the jetty.

On the apron at the back of his boat, Barry Porter, in baggy shorts and a leather bushranger's hat, is talking to a woman standing on the pontoon. Passing the time of day with the owner of a neighbouring boat? That's what it looks like.

Vish is about to head down the steps when Megan puts a hand on his arm.

'Hang on a sec,' she says. 'Let's just watch for a minute.'

Barry removes his hat, runs his hand through his hair. He's a fair distance away but there's some agitation in his stance. He's speaking and gesticulating. *He's angry. A row? They know each other?*

He plonks the hat back on his head. The woman turns abruptly on her heel and walks away from him. Barry appears to shout something after her. It's too far away to hear.

The woman is walking along the pontoon towards them.

'Go round, see if you can get a picture of her,' says Megan rapidly.

Vish runs down the steps two at a time and scoots behind some tourists talking selfies.

Megan walks down the steps slowly in the hope she can look the woman over without being noticed.

The woman wears a tight blue sundress. Her dark hair tumbles onto her bare shoulders. Most of her face is concealed by large Jackie O sunglasses. The bag she carries looks expensive. It seems quite possible that she's come from one of the other millionaire's gin palaces further along the pontoon. Or maybe not?

As Megan passes her, she gets a whiff of perfume. It smells intense and pungent and, Megan guesses, won't be cheap. It matches the clothes and the imperious manner.

Vish re-joins Megan a few metres on from the bottom of the steps. He gives her a smile. The woman has disappeared.

'You get her?'

'Yep,' he says, brandishing his phone. 'Stills and video.'

'Might be nothing, but you never know.'

'Girlfriend, maybe?' says Vish.

'What would a woman like that see in an old geezer like him?'

He stares at her in disbelief. 'Money?'

'Okay,' says Megan doubtfully.

'C'mon,' says Vish. 'Fortyish but nice bum and flash. Right up old Barry's street, I'd say. And they were having words. And she looked pissed off.'

Megan smiles at him. His direct, no bullshit approach is refreshing. She always likes working with Vish.

As they approach Barry Porter's yacht, they find him pouring a large measure of whiskey into a tumbler. He looks pissed off too.

Megan holds up her warrant card and says, 'Good afternoon, Mr Porter. I'm DS Thomas. I believe you spoke to my colleague DC Prasad on the phone.'

He takes a large swallow of whiskey and says, 'What's happened to Ted?'

'He's been transferred to another job.'

Barry Porter sighs and says, 'Come aboard.'

CHAPTER THIRTY-EIGHT

Sunday, 6.15 p.m.

As Megan steps across from the pontoon to the back of the cruiser, Barry Porter reaches out and grasps her elbow to steady her. He reeks of body odour and booze – shirt unbuttoned to reveal a pot belly and a wiry mat of white hair – and she can't help flinching at his touch. Up close there's nothing attractive about him; this makes Vish's suggestion about a girlfriend seem more outlandish.

'Welcome aboard the *Seamew*,' he says, doffing his hat.

Megan can't decide whether to be offended by his patronising attitude or to accept it as old-fashioned gallantry. She finds it hard to detach from the knowledge of what his son did to her sister. How is she ever going to remain objective in her attitude to the Porters? Yet this is what the bosses are demanding of her.

Under her feet she can feel the undulating motion of the boat, gently rising and falling. Vish follows her across. His stride is long, and he's male, so he gets no helping hand.

'You'd better come into the salon,' says Porter, holding out his arm and showing them the way.

'Salon' seems like a fogeyish term to Megan, but what do you call a sitting room on a boat? Her experience of luxury yachts is limited; she has no idea.

Porter ushers them through a sliding door into a spacious area below decks. The sofas are built-in and the coffee table is screwed to the floor, but apart from that it looks much like a conventional sitting room. To Megan's eye this is a masculine room. There's a bar in one corner, a large television screen fixed to the wall and a dartboard. Random items of clothing are tossed around. It looks like his home from home.

She's aware of Porter's beady eye on her. He still has a glass in one hand and a bottle of whiskey in the other. He puts the bottle on the table. 'My wife's not very keen on the sea,' he says. 'So you'll have to excuse the mess. I get a cleaner in once in a while. But things have got a little chaotic recently, as I'm sure you can imagine.' He dips his head and his bristled chin quivers.

This is a man whose son has been murdered, she has to remind herself. Even a sleazebag like Greg Porter has parents.

'I'm very sorry for your loss,' says Megan.

It's formal and a cliché. But he seems to appreciate it.

He wipes his nose with his fingers and says gruffly, 'Hardest thing I've ever faced. No man expects to bury his own son.'

'Thank you for agreeing to speak to us again,' says Megan. 'I know you were upset when your grandson was arrested.'

He nods and tension ripples through his jaw. 'I shouldn't have blown my stack at your boss,' he says. 'No way to speak to a lady. I did ask Wardell to pass on my apologies. I hope he did that.' There's a gruffness about him. He's over seventy and a different generation. It's part of his mindset to conceal his vulnerability. But Megan notices him eyeing the whiskey bottle he's just put down. Booze is his coping strategy. And that spans every generation.

'I believe he did,' says Megan politely. She wants to get the formalities out of the way so they can press on.

But he rakes his hand through his shaggy grey locks and says, 'Bloody awful business, but Wardell says you've released my grandson under investigation. What does that mean exactly?'

'That's the reason we're here,' says Megan. 'Aidan tells us he attacked his father. But we're looking into that further.'

'You mean you don't think he did it either?'

'It's a confession by a seventeen-year-old. We don't just take it at face value.'

'Okay,' says Porter. 'Mind if I have another drink? You're welcome to join me. Or is it that *on duty* thing?'

'It's that on duty thing,' she replies. 'But please feel free.'

Barry Porter picks up the bottle of single malt and sloshes another hefty measure into his glass.

Vish and Megan exchange glances. She waits. It's hardly by the book, but if getting pissed loosens his tongue that might prove useful.

Porter takes a large swallow, plonks down on one of the sofas and invites them to sit too.

Megan perches on the opposite sofa. Vish remains standing.

Porter gives him a surly look. 'What's he? Your punkah wallah?'

'I beg your pardon,' says Megan. 'DC Prasad is my colleague.'

'Take no notice,' says Porter, with a dismissive wave of the hand. 'I was just joking.'

'As you can see, I have no fan, Mr Porter,' says Vish evenly. 'So the answer to your question must be no.'

Barry Porter glares at him for a moment from under his bushy brows. Then he cracks a smile. This turns into a loud guffawing laugh and ends in a fit of coughing. 'Yeah,' he says, 'very smart. No offence, lad.'

'None taken,' Vish replies. He holds the old man's gaze with a steady stare and a polite smile.

Porter breaks eye contact first.

'Do you mind talking about your son?' says Megan. 'I realise it must be difficult.'

'Ask away,' says Porter.

'What can you tell us about his marriage?'

He sips his drink and glances at Vish. 'If a man plays away, there's a reason, right?'

Vish folds his arm and listens.

'I don't say that my son was a saint, because he wasn't. But he loved his kids and he did his level best to keep that family together.'

He also blackmailed women into having sex with him.

'Were your son and his wife contemplating a divorce then?' says Megan.

'She probably was,' says Porter. 'It was her bloody sister pushing her to it. She's a cold fish, that woman.'

'We're talking about Penny Reynolds here?' says Megan.

'I do my best to keep it civil, but she can be bloody difficult at times.'

'Still, she agreed to Mr Wardell, your choice of lawyer, representing your grandson. I presume you talked to her about that?' says Megan.

Barry Porter shrugs and says, 'Well, she phoned me. I recommended Wardell. She agreed. We both wanted what was best for the boy, obviously.'

Megan finds herself wondering if this is true. Penny Reynolds works in the City, surely she knows some London heavyweight she could call upon. Perhaps she agreed because she wanted his confession accepted.

'Tell us more about your son's marriage,' she says.

Porter sighs. 'Yvonne's an odd sort of female. I've never really made head nor tail of her. As a girl she was very pretty, turned a lot of heads including my son's. But if you ask me, she's got a screw loose.' He raises his glass and chuckles. 'Drinks like a fish too.'

'Has she ever received any treatment for mental health issues or an alcohol problem?' says Megan.

'Treatment! In and out of various posh rehab places for years. Cost Greg a fortune. Not that it did any good. She was depressed apparently. Beats me what she had to be depressed about. Greg gave her everything. Four lovely children. Cupboards full of clothes. More bloody shoes than Imelda Marcos.'

Megan doubts that *having everything* worked for Yvonne. In her own marriage she wasn't short of stuff; it was love and attention that she was missing.

'Tell us about your grandson,' she says.

Porter sighs. 'Aidan's always been under his mother's thumb. When he was a little lad, she would never let him out of her sight. She was always fussing over him. As he got older it got worse. She wouldn't let him play rugby at school, said it was too dangerous. But how's the boy going to grow into a man if he's wrapped in cotton wool?'

'What was Greg's view of this?' asks Megan.

'Oh, he fought her every inch of the way,' says Porter. 'I think that's probably where it all started to go downhill for them. Arguing about Aidan. Just last year, lad wanted to go skiing with the school. She wouldn't have it. But Greg did put his foot down. Aidan was so pleased, because he was desperate to go.'

'So Aidan did feel supported by his dad?'

'Course he did. I always thought they got on pretty well.'

Megan glances at Vish.

He chips in. 'Do you know what Greg thought about Aidan's hair? The topknot?'

Barry Porter shrugs, then he smiles wistfully. 'When he was fourteen he shaved it all off. Bald as a coot. But I think that was to piss his mother off. Kids do stuff with their hair, don't they? I don't think it bothered Greg.'

Megan picks up the thread again. 'As far as you know, did Greg ever hit his wife or children?'

Porter shakes his head vehemently. 'No. You youngsters, you probably think I'm an old fart. But I'll tell you this, I brought my son up never to raise his hand to a woman. Only a coward hits a woman. I don't believe Greg ever hit her. Though she certainly gave him provocation.'

'What sort of provocation?' says Megan.

He takes another slug of whiskey. Megan can see he's on the cusp of becoming maudlin drunk.

'Okay,' he says. 'Look at me, some would say I'm a wealthy man. But I can tell you I've earned every brass farthing. I started out working for my father. He was a builder. I worked on the site, hod carrier for a brickie, that's what I was doing when I was Aidan's age, up and down a bloody ladder all day.' He throws out his arms. 'Now I'm not a hypocrite. There's nothing wrong with enjoying the good things in life. But Yvonne was never satisfied. She was always pushing Greg to earn more. The avarice of that woman knows no bounds.'

'You don't seem to have a very high opinion of your daughter-in-law, Mr Porter,' says Megan.

'Too bloody right,' says Porter. 'For years she led my son a right bloody dance and then she thought she was going to divorce him and take half his money. His money! He earned it, not her. That's what she and her bloody sister were planning. Greg knew it and I knew it.'

'Do you think Greg confronted his wife about this? Could they have rowed about it?'

'I wouldn't know.'

'Would you say that Yvonne and her sister are very close?' says Megan.

'Close,' says Porter. 'But in a pretty messed up way, if you ask me.'

'Messed up how?' says Megan.

'They're all about money too. The fact Penny earns her own living, that's always bothered Yvonne. She's jealous. My wife used to say if Yvonne saw Penny with a new handbag, a week later Yvonne'd have a new bag worth twice as much.'

Porter drains his glass and pours himself yet another drink.

'You're convinced that Aidan didn't kill his father?' says Megan.

'I don't believe it for one moment,' says Porter. 'Bloody ridiculous.'

'Then why would Aidan say he did?' says Megan.

The question hangs in the air for a moment. Porter sighs again. He seems about to speak, then he hesitates. *He knows something.*

Porter frowns, takes another slug of his drink and says, 'Part of me keeps thinking, how can he be dead? It's not real. He's my son. He's just going to turn up with a cooler of beer and off we'll go. Out there into the bay, maybe down the coast. But you never understand how things really are until it's too late, do you? Or maybe I'm just getting old.'

It feels as if he's deliberately changed the subject. *Was he about to accuse Yvonne? Why didn't he?*

Maybe he's just too pissed. By Megan's calculation he's drunk nearly half a bottle of whiskey since they've been there. He's becoming bleary-eyed and his face is beaded in sweat. She knows it's time to wind this up.

'Thank you, Mr Porter,' she says. 'You've been extremely helpful. This must be a very painful subject.'

He shrugs. 'My grandson is innocent,' he says.

Megan stands up. 'We'll do our level best to get to the truth,' she says.

As they leave the salon and walk out onto the deck of the boat, Megan turns to him and says, 'Oh, just one last thing, the lady in a blue dress that you were speaking to earlier, does she own one of these boats?'

Porter frowns. 'What lady?' he says. He's swaying and has to grasp the bulkhead for support.

'I think you were speaking to her earlier,' says Megan.

Porter shrugs. 'I don't remember that,' he says. 'But I quite often have a chat with other boat owners as they pass by.'

'Blue dress? Attractive. You don't remember her?' says Megan.

Porter shakes his head. He smiles sadly and holds up his glass. 'To be quite honest with you,' he says, 'I've had quite a few of these today. Think I'm pissed.'

Megan scans him. His gaze is fixed firmly on her and it's steady. The old man has a harder head than he pretends and he's certainly sober enough to lie.

She smiles. 'Thank you for your help, Mr Porter,' she says.

CHAPTER THIRTY-NINE

Monday, 6.35 a.m.

Megan ploughs her way slowly through the gentle grey swell. Raindrops plip onto the surface in front of her, creating tiny ripples as they melt into the sea. The first time she swam in the rain it seemed like a mad thing to do but she loved it. The wetsuit keeps her warm and the orange marker float bobs along behind her. It makes her feel like a sea creature, solitary and safe under the waves, protected in her watery domain from the winds that strafe the air above and a more spiteful world onshore.

A sunny Sunday has given way to a rain-soaked Monday morning; a shroud of mist hangs over the bay. An Atlantic low has swept in. Still, Megan was out of the house by six.

Unfortunately, as she was about to leave, she met Mark in the kitchen; he was off to catch an early train to return to his job in the North Sea. She hadn't spoken to him since Saturday evening. He was packing some sandwiches and a banana in his kitbag.

He gave her a tentative smile.

'Morning,' she said.

'Morning.' He hesitated then he said, 'Listen, Meg—'

She raised her palm. 'You don't have to say anything. It's fine. I get it.'

'I doubt that you do,' he said. 'I know it wasn't your fault. Any of it.'

'I should've been able to stop it. And if I'd known sooner what Collins was up to—'

'And Saturday night, we were both still really wound up. It was shitty and I'm sorry.'

'I get it.'

And she did. A bottle of wine or two, some hot kiss-and-make-up sex, followed by a quiet Sunday with their children. The cracks had been papered over, they wanted everything back to normal.

'Deb feels really bad now,' he said.

She would, thought Megan. *So now I have to make it all right?* But she wasn't ready, not yet.

Mark smiled sadly. 'You've spent your whole life taking care of her, rescuing her. You passed the job on to me and I'm the one who's made a hash of it.'

'That's not true. You're the best thing that's ever happened to my sister.' He probably wouldn't have been so flattered if he'd seen the competition.

His face softened. 'But I should've been here. Not five hundred miles away in the middle of the bloody North Sea. We both know she doesn't cope well on her own.'

'I was here,' said Megan. 'And she didn't tell me what was going on. On top of which, Greg Porter would still have been a scumbag.'

'Well, I'm sorry,' he said. 'I suppose it was the shock, when your lot came stomping in here like the bloody Gestapo. But I shouldn't have blamed you. It wasn't fair.'

Megan shrugged. 'I'm a cop,' she said. 'I'm used to people hating me for something I haven't done.'

'If we upset you, that's really bad. Did we upset you?' He gazed anxiously at her.

She wasn't about to go into any of that. Why couldn't he just leave it, she thought, and go and get his bloody train?

'It's no big deal,' she said. 'I've got a tough hide.' *That's a lie.*

He smiled. 'I'm glad I saw you this morning. We're family and I want to make this right with you.'

He stepped towards her and opened his arms. It felt awkward but she allowed him to give her a hug.

As she swims across the bay, she thinks about her brother-in-law. Is it that easy, you say sorry and move on? Perhaps it has to be if you want to stay sane. But what about the pain and the damage? It doesn't just disappear. And what if a line has been crossed? What if a woman like Yvonne Porter has a row with her husband and picks up a hammer and hits him? There's no way back over that line. We all have murderous impulses at times. Megan has seen plenty of homicides where things just got out of hand. Barry Porter reckoned his son faced provocation, but what kind of provocation did Yvonne face?

Megan turns and starts to swim back to shore. It's her job to make a woman confess to murder. *A screw loose?* Is that what propels you over the line? The inside of any marriage is a deeply private place, where small cruelties and betrayals can gradually snowball. Her own was certainly like that. Once trust is broken is there ever a way back? How many years did it take from the moment of thinking 'this was a mistake' to the divorce?

At a distance, through her misted goggles, the beach seems deserted, but as she gets closer a black smudge morphs into a definite shape. An umbrella? Someone sitting on the sea wall under an umbrella? Reaching the shallows, her toes touch the bottom. She wades out of the water with her float tucked under her arm and lifts the goggles up onto her forehead. The figure under the umbrella waves. A jolt of surprise shoots through her. It's Danny Ingram.

Megan's first impulse is annoyance; her private realm has been invaded. How did he even know where to find her? Could he have tracked her car? Using official databases for personal reasons is a disciplinary offence. But perhaps in the NCA you can get away with such things? It wouldn't surprise her.

She walks up the beach, picking her way round the rocks and mounds of seaweed. He stands up and he's grinning. He's pleased to see her. She feels a sudden constriction in her throat, an instant welling up of tears. This man has come looking for her! He wants to see her! Her stomach flips. She puts a hand up to her cheek and finds a wet, briny mix of tears and seawater. She's seized with an impulse to run into his arms. *Don't be ridiculous.*

When she first bought the wetsuit she paraded in front of the mirror in it, so she knows what she looks like. The tight skull cap biting into her forehead completes the picture. She's hardly rising romantically from the waves like a mermaid, more crawling out of the sea like a wrinkled, rubbery slug. But he's still smiling.

'Morning,' he calls cheerfully.

'How did you find me?' she says.

He shrugs. 'What can I tell you? I'm a detective.'

'The car? Surely not?'

He laughs. 'I'm really appreciating the wetsuit. But I've never met anyone who goes swimming in the rain.'

'It's great,' she says. 'You should try it.'

Her towel is in a plastic bag on the wall beside him. He tosses it to her. The rest of her kit she leaves in the car.

She pulls off the skull cap and shakes out her hair. She must look a fright. Ordinarily she wouldn't care but now she does. She can feel his eyes upon her.

'Okay,' he says. 'I'll fess up. You didn't answer my texts yesterday. I hoped you might come over last night. You didn't. So this morning I went to your house.'

'You woke my sister up?'

'Nope. I was lurking outside because it was very early. She saw me out of the window. I explained who I was. She invited me in for a coffee. Then she told me this is where you usually swim.'

It takes Megan a moment to process all this. Danny Ingram and Debbie drinking coffee. *No!*

'You explained who you were?'

He grins. 'Yeah, a colleague from the National Crime Agency, who you've been working with. Said I needed to update you. And I showed her my ID.'

'Right.' Her lover and her sister. *Her lover?* It feels surreal. She climbs the concrete steps up to the sea wall and says, 'I need to get changed. I'm getting cold.'

He falls into step beside her and they walk across a patch of wet grass towards the car park.

'She really looks like you,' he says. He's grinning like a schoolboy.

Megan frowns. 'She does not! I'm about a foot taller.'

'Sorry.' He pulls a face.

They walk on in silence. The rain is falling in a light drizzle. He holds the umbrella over them both and she finds herself enjoying the physical proximity. Is it just a basic pheromonal buzz? Or is there more to it? Being with him, walking side by side, is so natural. It feels as though she's known him for months not days.

She turns to him. 'You really had coffee with my sister? In the kitchen?'

'Yeah. Met Scout. Lovely dog. We had a chat. She said you were angry with her.'

'Me angry with her?' *Typical bloody Debbie. Has to be the victim.*

'I obviously didn't let on that I knew about the murder investigation and her being arrested,' he adds.

When Mark left the house to catch his train, there was no sign of Debbie. Megan has hardly exchanged a word with her sister for the last thirty-six hours. Until she spoke with Mark this morning, she'd had a clear feeling that she was no longer a welcome guest in their home.

'Me angry with her?' she repeats. 'That's rich. I don't know how she's arrived at that. Well, I do and it's just annoying.'

'She seemed quite upset. Said you'd been hiding away in your room and avoiding her. Asked me to tell you that she's really sorry. She just wants to talk to you.'

'You know what,' says Megan. 'I think I might just go home and kick her head in!'

He laughs. 'How about I buy you breakfast instead?'

CHAPTER FORTY

Monday, 7.30 a.m.

Danny Ingram's surprise appearance left Megan feeling skittish and excited, like being a teenager again. It was a long time since anyone had tried to woo her. His offer of breakfast was carefully researched. A small beachside cafe serving doorstep-sized bacon sarnies and whopping mugs of coffee and all with a sea view. Megan knew the place and applauded the choice. Unfortunately she had to turn him down because she has another appointment. Dr Diane Moretti, her annoying shrink, is back from holiday and expecting her.

As Megan settles herself in the familiar armchair, she wishes she'd blown Moretti off. She was sorely tempted. A flirtatious breakfast and an escape from her problems feels much more like the kind of therapy she needs. But Moretti is a stickler and cancelling at the last minute is not acceptable in her book. She and Megan have already had a couple of run-ins over this kind of behaviour and Megan has given an undertaking to keep her appointments in future.

Moretti's smile is as enigmatic as ever. She looks relaxed and slightly tanned. She's wearing one of her five professional outfits. These are all in shades of beige or, as she would probably say, taupe, and worn in strict rotation. Her grey hair is less prim than usual but the biggest change is a rather impressive rock on her usually naked left ring finger.

'Nice holiday?' asks Megan. She doesn't expect a reply. Moretti's mantra is: this is not about me, Megan, this is about you.

However, the good doctor smiles and says, 'Yes, thank you for asking. It was lovely. I do enjoy Italy at this time of the year.'

In the fifteen months that Megan has been a patient of Dr Moretti, this is the most personal information she has ever revealed. She must be in a mellow mood. The clue is the stonking diamond on her finger. Who would want to marry Moretti? Is there a man out there with that kind of courage? Or perhaps it's a woman and the conservative façade conceals a more unexpected private life?

Megan glances at it and says, 'Looks like congratulations are in order.'

Moretti gives Megan her fey, one-sided lip curl. *Her version of 'fuck off'.*

'Thank you,' she says. 'And how have you been in my absence?'

Megan shrugs. 'Oh, you know,' she says.

'No, I don't know,' says Moretti. 'That's why you're here. To tell me.'

The familiar, acidic tone is oddly comforting. Down to business. Moretti has her under the microscope. The least ambivalence, the least hesitation, she'll be on it.

Megan decides to come clean.

'Okay,' she says, 'well, the thing is, I nearly had a panic attack.'

'Nearly?' says Moretti. 'How nearly?'

'I was out on a job.' Megan sighs. She hates this process. Ripping the dressing off the wound. Anticipating the embarrassment then feeling the shame of her weakness.

'Like before?'

'Not quite. I was riding in the back of a car,' says Megan. 'I felt it coming on, but I wound down the window and really focused on my breathing. And I managed to stave it off.'

'That's good,' says Moretti. 'But the back of a car? That's a very different situation to before, isn't it?' *The rats with their swishing tails and scratchy claws.*

'Well, it was sort of related to my experience in the cellar. I overheard some information. About him.' She doesn't even want to say the name.

'You heard something about Zac Yilmaz and it frightened you?' says Moretti.

'Yeah,' says Megan. 'Unnerved as much as frightened. It was a shock.'

It's been nattering away in the back of her brain ever since the briefing nearly a week ago. The possible connection between Yilmaz and local villain Dennis Bridger. But when she overheard Ted Jennings talking to Collins about it, somehow it tipped her over the edge. And down she went. A vertiginous drop. Fear and panic combined. The shadow of him, the threat of him stalks her in her dreams. But she's learnt to deal with that. This is different because it's concrete. The stark truth that this man, this dangerous killer, will hunt her down and he's getting closer.

'So was this panic attack anxiety-driven?' says Moretti.

'You mean is this me being paranoid?' says Megan.

'I'm not saying it's paranoid,' says Moretti. 'I'm asking if you think it's paranoia?'

'I think a stone-cold psychopath has just taken one step closer to me,' says Megan.

'If this is a real threat,' says Moretti, 'then you should certainly be talking to Superintendent Barker and your colleagues. But I thought he was in prison and likely to stay there.'

'He is,' says Megan. 'But that's not going to stop him.'

'You seem to be according him a lot of power,' says Moretti. 'If he's securely behind bars, then surely his capacity to do you any actual harm is limited. So, is this paranoia?'

Megan looks at her. They live on different planets. To smug, middle-class professionals like Moretti, justice is done and the system works. Criminals are put away and become harmless. This is her belief because it's what most people believe. You have to live in Megan's world to know how naive that is.

She considers explaining the far-reaching tentacles of organised crime, which enable a gangster like Yilmaz to continue to operate from within prison. But she decides against it.

She sighs and says, 'Maybe you're right. Also I've fallen out with my sister.'

Moretti smiles. 'It all seems to kick off when I go away, doesn't it?'

Megan smiles back. Now they're on safer ground, the nitty-gritty of family life. This is Moretti's stock in trade. Sibling rivalry she can sort out, no problem.

Megan knows that when it comes to dealing with Yilmaz, she's on her own. And she always will be.

CHAPTER FORTY-ONE

Monday, 9.50 a.m.

After her session with Moretti, Megan walks into the office in a sombre mood. They spent half an hour chewing over the workings of her little sister's psyche.

Megan already knows that Debbie's default setting is to play the victim. Even though she got angry and blamed Megan for what happened, she's never going to recognise that. Debbie will have a different story; she reacts to unfair treatment and it's never her fault. The fact this left Megan feeling used and rejected will not be acknowledged. But this morning Megan has a job to do. For the time being her sister will have to stew.

As she walks past the DCI's office, Slater beckons her in.

'Morning, boss,' says Megan. She tries to inject a little cheeriness into her tone.

'Can you shut the door?' says Slater. *Sounds ominous.*

Megan braces herself.

'So how are things going with Jim?' says Slater.

'Okay, I think,' Megan replies.

Slater nods and sighs. Megan scans her. Her face is tight and she's fiddling with her pen, turning it over end to end. Not good signs.

'I've had him in here this morning,' says Slater, 'and he is not happy.'

'Not happy how?' says Megan.

'He says you're making things difficult for him. Undermining his authority with the team. Is this true?'

It's tempting to laugh and Megan would, if it weren't so annoying. She really should have predicted this. *No good deed goes unpunished.* Collins's ego is dented so he's on the attack.

'I don't know what to say, boss,' says Megan. 'I'm doing my best.'

'For Chrissake, Megan, the man's had cancer. Surely it's not too much to ask that you just tread a little softly round him.'

'I have been trying to do that.'

'Well, clearly it's not working. I know you didn't want to work with him. Okay, he got it wrong with your sister. All I'm asking is that you act like a professional and put personal resentments aside.'

Megan fixes Slater with a steely gaze. 'I have been doing that,' she says. 'Perhaps you shouldn't just take what he says at face value?'

Challenging Slater? Wrong move!

'Don't tell me how to manage the team,' says the boss tartly. 'It strikes me that you're being difficult because you'd prefer to be swanning round with Danny Ingram instead of doing this. I gather you and he get on rather well.'

So that's how it is. The gossip mill has been busy. Megan bites her tongue and waits for Slater to say more. But she huffs and backtracks. 'Anyway,' she says, 'that's none of my business. Just see if you can't focus on the matter in hand.'

'I'll certainly try,' says Megan drily.

Megan walks out of Slater's office and crosses the room to her desk. She plonks her bag down. She's cursing her own stupidity. You think you're being discreet but these things always get out. *Sex with a colleague, always a bad idea.* She feels tacky.

Vish is at the adjacent desk. 'You don't look very happy,' he says.

'Where's Collins?' she asks.

'In the incident room preparing for the briefing, I think,' says Vish. 'You okay?'

He's smiling at her with concern. He's a nice guy and, she'd like to think, a mate. It's tempting to have a rant and garner some sympathy. But she reins herself in. Complaining to Vish about Collins may make her feel better, but it will probably make the whole situation worse. She just has to suck it up.

Megan's phone buzzes with an incoming call. She glances at it, expecting it to be Debbie and another hassle she can do without. It surprises her when Ted Jennings's name pops up.

What the hell does he want? She clicks the phone off. He can certainly take a hike.

Megan needs to distract herself, so she goes to the coffee station and pours herself a large mug of black coffee before heading for the incident room.

The briefing is scheduled for ten o'clock. She taps the security code into the keypad and opens the door.

Jim Collins is carefully arranging Post-it notes on the large whiteboard, which has been set against one wall. His shirt is crisp, silk tie, crease in his trousers. Megan finds herself wondering if he needs the uniform to hold himself together. What's wrong with Slater? Why can't she see how physically fragile he is? But perhaps she can.

He has a red marker pen in his hand and is drawing careful lines linking one section of notes on the board to another. Megan watches him for a moment. He ignores her, pretending to be engrossed in what he's doing. She came into the room with the intention of challenging him but, watching him for a moment, she changes her mind. What good would it do?

There are several other officers in the room already, gathering for the briefing. Megan nods to Kitty, the civilian analyst. She's perched on the corner of a desk, arms folded. She raises her eyebrows in Collins's direction and goes boss-eyed deliberately. Megan smiles. Some of the team have Collins's number, which is a small comfort.

Slater enters, the door held open for her by Vish, who follows her in. No sign of Brittney. Slater has obviously followed through on her plan to send Brittney to replace Megan as liaison officer with the NCA. Megan sighs. Perhaps it's for the best. Slater's got a point, when she's with Danny Ingram her mind is definitely not on the job.

'Morning, everyone,' says the DCI. 'Let's get started. Jim, would you like to bring us up to speed?' She gives him an encouraging smile.

Laura Slater's approach is to continue to placate his ego and Megan finds herself resenting this. Be nice to Jim because he's been ill. But having cancer doesn't turn you into a suffering angel overnight. Collins's illness hasn't improved him. Try and help him and he goes for the jugular. Megan won't make that mistake again.

Collins stands at the front of the room next to the whiteboard, hands on hips in his habitual I'm-the-bloke-in-charge stance. He's written up the names of all the relevant parties in the murder investigation on the board in a neat, rounded hand. Some also have mugshots.

'Morning, everyone,' he says brightly. 'We have an important new piece of intel that's come to light. We've had a chance to look in some detail at the contents of Aidan Porter's phone. And it contains some interesting video footage.' He glances across the room. 'Kitty, you discovered this, perhaps you'd talk us through it.'

Kitty is a small bundle of repressed energy in leggings and Lycra. She bounces off the desk where she's perching, seizes the handset for the TV monitor, clicks through the controls at lightning speed.

A frozen pixelated image appears on the screen next to the whiteboard.

'Okay,' she says briskly. 'We found a lot of footage of a similar nature. Adds up to nearly an hour of it, shot on different occasions. These are just a few edited highlights. But you'll get the gist.'

She presses play.

The image on the screen comes to life. The camera is eavesdropping, peering through the narrow gap in a partially open doorway. And a woman can be heard sobbing. A slow steady keening as the camera creeps forward and the woman comes into view. She's lying prone on the floor, her arms are clutched tightly around her head to protect it. A man is standing over her.

'Get up, you stupid bitch!' he growls. He grabs her arm and tries to haul her to her feet. She remains limp, like a rag doll. He drags her across the floor and her face comes into view. Blurred at first and contorted but Megan recognises Yvonne Porter. The whimpering continues in short, pitiful bursts as he drags her. First by the wrist, then by the hair. He pulls back his arm and whacks her across the face with the back of his hand. Only his profile is visible. But Megan can recognise him. It's Greg Porter.

'Thanks, Kitty,' says Collins. 'I think we've seen enough.'

Kitty clicks the video off. There's a heavy silence in the room.

Megan can feel tension in her chest as the anger bubbles up. She never listened to the recording of Porter abusing her sister. Slater wouldn't let her. Seeing him beat his wife sickens her. It also makes clear the kind of monster Debbie had to deal with.

'So there we have it,' says Collins. 'Conclusive proof that Yvonne Porter was violently abused by her husband. Filmed by their seventeen-year-old son. Any thoughts or ideas on this?'

'I think,' says Slater, 'that this can be read in one of two ways. First, as motive for Aidan Porter's attack on his father. He filmed the domestic abuse in his home and we already know he was disturbed by it. However, his fingerprints are not on the potential murder weapon and his account of what actually happened lacks convincing detail. So, an alternative way to look at this is that Yvonne Porter was the victim of violent abuse, who finally got to the end of her tether and attacked her abuser.'

Good for her!

'Can I just say, boss,' says Vish, 'that when Megan and I interviewed Aidan Porter, Megan said that Aidan's confession could well be his attempt to protect his mother. Filming his mother being beaten and not being able to intervene must've been really hard for him. So he probably felt really guilty. Lying to protect her is maybe his way of making up for that.'

'Very good point, Vish,' says Slater. 'Do we assume he knew what she'd done?'

'Or he thought he knew,' says Megan. 'Unless Aidan was a witness – and the fact his account of the murder is vague suggests he wasn't – Yvonne's guilt is not proved by this.'

Megan wants to protect her. It's a gut reaction.

'I think we're splitting hairs,' says Collins. 'The important point here is that it establishes motive and puts Yvonne Porter squarely in the frame.'

'Domestic abuse is a complicated motive, it produces different reactions,' says Megan.

'Which is what I'm saying,' says Collins peevishly.

'Well, she should certainly be questioned again under caution,' says Slater.

'Exactly, because she's lied,' says Collins. 'Horrible, abusive marriage, yet when questioned she denied vehemently that her husband ever hit her. Why would she do that unless she wanted to conceal the fact she had a motive to kill him?'

'I think the reason for that is fairly obvious,' says Megan. 'It's a pride thing. She doesn't want to appear weak, she was ashamed of the state of her marriage, maybe even blamed herself. So she lied. That's what people do when they're in denial: lie to cover up weakness.'

Megan stares at Collins. He meets her gaze and looks away.

'Yes, well, good point,' he says. 'Shall we move on?'

CHAPTER FORTY-TWO

Monday, 12.30 p.m.

Yvonne Porter sits at the table in the police interview room. She's pale and composed, hands neatly folded in her lap. She's doing this for Aidan. A mother must protect her son. Of course she must. Yvonne has always put her children first. She wanted to come to the police voluntarily but Penny said that wasn't a good idea. She's been thinking about it since yesterday morning when she stopped drinking. In the end they came knocking on her door again, said all this you-don't-have-to-say-anything business and put her in the back of a police car.

The woman detective has kind eyes. Quite serious. The same woman who came to the house yesterday afternoon. She's the sergeant but she does seem like the sort of person that Yvonne could talk to. The young man sitting next to her is Asian and extremely handsome. He could be a male model or an actor. With looks like that, why would he want to be a policeman? It makes no sense to Yvonne.

The room is small and rather smelly. These institutional places are never clean. The police sit across the table from her, arranging papers in front of them. They offer her a plastic bottle of water. She refuses. You can't rely on these sort of bottles being BPA-free.

She waits. Penny's instructions have been clear: don't say anything. The lawyer sitting beside her is a funny little man. Yvonne is not quite sure what to make of him. His suit looks cheap and she can't remember his name. Wood? Ward? That's always the problem in the first twenty-four hours of being sober. Her head's like a sieve. She can't remember a thing. Penny has given her some tramadol that she got on prescription and that's muted the headache a little. But it leaves her feeling spacey. She finds it hard to concentrate.

The lawyer has repeated to her several times what Penny told her: when the police ask you a question, you simply reply 'no comment'. If they want to accuse her of a crime, he said, it's up to them to prove the case. Her most sensible course of action is to admit nothing.

Yvonne wonders if she is a bad person. Greg certainly thought so. That's what he used to tell her. She was a bad wife, a bad mother, a drunk, a disgusting slut that no man could bear to fuck. When he got in one of his rages, it all came out. Yvonne is not stupid, she knows what they all think. They think that she killed her husband. That's why she's here. And if that's the case then she certainly is a bad woman. But she doesn't care what anyone thinks, she'll do whatever she has to in order to protect Aidan. He's a good boy and whatever he did, he was trying to protect her.

The woman detective is smiling at her. With a decent haircut and some make-up, she could almost be attractive.

She's saying all this legal stuff again. The same rigmarole they went through when they came to the house this morning. It seems stupid to Yvonne that they keep repeating it.

'Do you understand what that means?' says the woman detective. 'That you're still under caution.'

Yvonne nods. She doesn't. Not exactly. But you can't let these people think you're stupid.

The woman detective is still looking at her.

'Yes,' she says. 'Of course I understand.' She turns to the lawyer. 'Or is this where I'm supposed to say "no comment"?'

He shifts in his chair. 'Once they actually ask you a question,' he mumbles.

'But surely that was a question.'

She shrugs and looks at the handsome young man. He grins. He has lovely teeth.

'Would you like me to call you Mrs Porter?' says the woman detective. 'Or can I call you Yvonne?' She laces her fingers as she speaks. Her nails are short but well manicured and clean. Yvonne knows that personal grooming and hygiene are important indicators of the nature of a person. Someone with clean fingernails is someone you can trust. Perhaps she can relax just a little. Penny is not right about everything. Far from it. And she lies. Probably best not to think about that just now.

'Now Greg's dead,' she says with a smile, 'I might even go back to my maiden name, but, yes, I'm happy for you to call me Yvonne.'

Making a joke helps; she doesn't want them to know how much she misses him. How she wishes it could all have been different. If she could've just been the kind of wife he wanted. Why couldn't she?

'Well, Yvonne,' says the woman detective. 'We just want to find out what really happened on the night that your husband died. Keeping secrets can be a terrible burden. People have fights, sometimes things just get out of hand. If you talk about this, you may be surprised to find that you feel much better.'

Yvonne glances at the lawyer. He'll rat on her to Penny if she doesn't do what she's told. But what the hell? At this point she could really do with a glass of wine. *Don't think about that.*

She huffs. 'I've already told you it wasn't Aidan.'

'And you know this how?'

'He's saying that because he thinks it was me. And he's trying to protect me.'

'Was it you, Yvonne?' The woman detective is smiling but her gaze is unnervingly direct.

Yvonne sighs. 'I want to tell the truth,' she says.

'I know you do,' says the woman detective.

'Okay,' she says, 'thing is, I don't actually remember what happened that night and the reason I don't remember is because I was drunk. Greg went out shortly after supper, and I knew he was going to see her. So that's when I started to drink. I think I passed out. Later on I woke up on the floor.'

'Who do you mean when you say *her*?' says the woman detective.

'His mistress,' says Yvonne. 'Everyone thinks I didn't know what was going on. He thought I was too stupid to work it out.'

'To work out that he had a mistress?'

'Greg said she was his business partner. She even came for drinks with her husband. But I suppose, over there, they have a more permissive attitude.'

'Over there?'

'Spain. I suppose it's the climate. Fewer clothes, more fucking.'

'And you think Greg was having sex with this Spanish woman?'

'Of course he was. I'm not stupid. I knew he was seeing someone.'

'Were you jealous?'

Yvonne considers this. It's a question she can't answer. The lawyer shifts in his chair; he's trying to catch her eye.

Jealous? How can she even begin to explain? Sex is one thing. She didn't care who he had sex with. But he liked spending time with her, thought she was clever. Yvonne had always tried to do everything he wanted. The house, the garden. She'd kept it all looking perfect. And herself. She tried to look perfect too. But it was never enough. Why didn't anyone ever see that she was clever too? But they didn't.

She realises Penny and the lawyer were right, she should just say 'no comment'.

'No comment,' she says.

'Okay,' says the woman detective. 'Let's go back a bit. You can't remember much about that night because you were drinking. Are you still drinking?'

'No. I'm back on the twelve steps,' says Yvonne. 'I've done it before. In rehab. I know I have to for the children's sake.'

The woman detective glances at her gorgeous sidekick. *They're up to something.* He gets out his phone and starts scrolling.

'Are you attending AA meetings?' asks the woman detective.

'Oh, those things are just ridiculous,' says Yvonne. 'Stupid people talking about their stupid personal problems. I can't be bothered with any of that. There's only one way to stop drinking. You just stop drinking.'

Of course, she did talk to Dr Davenport about her private life. Sometimes. But he was paid handsomely not to blab. That was the whole point.

The hunky cop hands the woman detective his phone. She holds it up and shows Yvonne a picture.

'Do you know who this is?' asks the woman detective.

Yvonne looks and it's like a kick in the gut. And she knows what that feels like, courtesy of her dead husband. *It doesn't make sense. It's her!* But why does the gorgeous young cop have her picture on his phone? Surely her tentacles can't extend that far?

She looks at him and mutters, 'You know her?'

'Can you tell us who she is?' says the woman detective gently.

'It's her!' says Megan. The pain inside just explodes. Tears are welling up and she can't stop them. 'It's bloody well her!'

'The woman you were talking about, who you suspect was your husband's mistress? What's her name, Yvonne?'

'Elena. Bloody Elena!'

'And she's Spanish?'

'Yes.'

'Do you know her second name?'

Yvonne is sobbing. 'That bitch stole my husband! If I was going to kill anyone, I'd kill her!'

CHAPTER FORTY-THREE

Monday, 12.46 p.m.

The simmering anger in the room makes the narrow confines of Slater's office feel claustrophobic. Slater is standing behind her desk, which takes up most of the floor space. She has her arms folded and a frown on her face. Megan is in one corner facing off against Collins in the other. He's deadly pale, hands on hips and a bullish expression.

'It makes this woman Elena a viable alternative suspect,' says Megan. This is so blindingly obvious to her. Why can't he see it?

'You didn't even show her the phone footage of her husband beating her and ask her about that,' says Collins. 'That was the strategy we agreed. It clearly establishes motive.' He's quietly seething. Megan can feel it.

'Jim's got a point,' says Slater.

'Oh for Chrissake,' says Megan. 'It was obvious that wouldn't work. She's not going to confess to murder. Why? Because she's an alkie who hardly knew what fucking day it was.'

'We don't know that,' says Collins. 'She could just be making all this up.'

Megan knows she isn't. She only had to look at Yvonne Porter and she knew. The fact he beat her was irrelevant because Yvonne blamed herself for it. And Megan knows exactly what that's like:

loving a man who hurts you. She can still feel the pain and shame of her relationship with Zac Yilmaz.

'Look,' says Megan. She glances at Slater for support. How the hell can she explain this? If you've never been in that mindset, how would you know? 'I think the abuse is beside the point. You heard what she said. She blames the other woman. Why? Because she still loves him in spite of what he did to her. If she'd gone down there on Tuesday night, even supposing she was capable of getting there, she'd've bashed Elena's brains in, not Greg's.'

Collins is not listening. He's just waiting to make his next point.

'And on top of this,' he says. 'You videoed this woman talking to Barry Porter yesterday. I don't understand why you've been keeping that secret.'

That's the problem. He thinks he's been kept out of the loop.

'We weren't keeping it secret. We just didn't know if it was relevant. What crossed my mind at the time was that it might be useful for the NCA inquiry. Lateral thinking, Jim? Ever hear of that?'

Collins just glares at her. *If looks could kill.*

'Okay,' says Slater. 'This isn't getting us anywhere.'

'There has to be proper respect for the chain of command, ma'am,' says Collins. 'Otherwise how do we proceed efficiently?'

'Oh fuck that!' says Megan. *They're wasting time.*

'Megan, enough!' says Slater.

'I think, ma'am, that DS Thomas should be taken off this case. As SIO I think you should recognise how inappropriate her approach and attitude is.'

Me, inappropriate?

Now Megan is spitting mad; the sheer hypocrisy of the man coupled with his arrogance makes her see red.

'And what's your approach, Jim?' she says. 'Try and fit up Yvonne Porter, like you tried to fit up my sister?'

'You need to control your temper, Megan,' says Slater. 'This kind of behaviour is not acceptable on my team.'

'And what is acceptable?' says Megan. 'Is it all about results? Doesn't matter if we get the right person, just so long as we get someone. So we intimidate a vulnerable, mixed up alcoholic into confessing to something she didn't do. And that's justice?'

Slater's lips are pursed. She's standing very still. Megan knows she's blown it.

'Jim, give us a minute,' says Slater.

Megan catches his eye. He's smirking. *He thinks he's won.*

'Certainly, ma'am,' he says.

He goes out of the office and closes the door carefully behind him.

Laura Slater shakes her head wearily and plonks down in her chair. Then she sighs.

'Why do you have to be such a fucking headbanger, Megan?' she says bitterly. 'I hate bad language. But, by God, you make me swear.'

'I'm sorry, boss.' Megan wants to feel contrite but, truth is, she doesn't.

'No, you're not.' Slater huffs again. 'You're an intelligent woman. Has it never occurred to you that, in certain circumstances, being right is not necessarily an advantage?'

'I'm not sure what you mean.'

'Oh, don't try and be cute! You've been married and you've been in this job long enough to know that, unfair as it might seem, it's down to us to manage the male ego. You do not get a man who feels weak to agree with you by telling him how weak he is.'

'I know that,' says Megan with a sigh. 'But don't you get bored with always having to make it all right for the Collinses of this world?'

'Of course I do. But this is my job. That's why it's called management. It's a sexist world. Get over it!'

'You may not believe this,' says Megan. 'But I have been trying to get on with him. I do have some sympathy for him. He's had cancer; I know it's tough.'

'The other problem,' says Slater, 'is that if he feels you're pitying him, you're going to get an even worse reaction. Surely you can relate to that.'

Megan nods. She meets Slater's eye. 'I am sorry,' she says. 'Truly. Maybe you should take me off the case.'

'Oh yeah, you'd love that, wouldn't you?' says Slater with a cynical sigh. 'A moment ago you were shouting about justice for Yvonne Porter. You really want to abandon her to DI Collins's approach?'

Megan smiles to herself. Slater is spot on. She knows exactly which buttons to press.

'No, boss,' she says. 'So what do you want me to do?'

'Take Vish and see what more you can find out about this Elena. And stay out of Collins's way.'

'What are you going to do with Yvonne Porter?'

'I'm going to release her under investigation. We've got her fingerprints. But we're still waiting for DNA on the hammer. Until we get that, we can't confirm it's the murder weapon. Plus CSI have also downloaded a huge amount of material from the Porters' home security cameras. It seems Greg Porter had quite an elaborate system. Cameras all over the house, which he accessed from his phone. He certainly liked to keep tabs on them all. Once we break that down I hope we can establish who came and went from the house at the relevant times.'

'Do you think the prints on the potential murder weapon will belong to Yvonne Porter?'

'Probably not. I'll know in about half an hour. But they may well belong to Elena. So you'd better get on and find her.'

CHAPTER FORTY-FOUR

Monday, 2.05 p.m.

They drive to Torquay in silence. Their hope is that Barry may shed some light on Elena's whereabouts. Vish shoots a concerned glance at Megan from time to time; he's well aware of the row that took place in Slater's office. Everyone is. But he has the good sense to keep quiet.

Megan walked straight out of the building and phoned Vish from the car park, where he joined her. She found her hands were trembling and she felt sick. At first she couldn't work out why she was so badly affected. She'd done her job, interviewed a suspect. There was a disagreement over the approach. Nothing that out of the ordinary. Collins was being an arse. Nothing out of the ordinary there either. Then she simply lost it. She kicked off big time and she didn't care. *It was stupid stupid stupid!*

The anger has receded and in the backwash she feels shaky and drained. She needs time to recover. She gazes out of the car window at the greening countryside. The southern flank of Dartmoor rises up and dominates the skyline. A few days of bright sunshine and the hedgerows are bursting with white splashes of hawthorn blossom. Megan wishes she could put names to the magnificent trees that sweep by, fringing the road. She feels edgy and out of place in this flourishing landscape and also in herself. But in the murky recesses of her mind, she knows what's going on. Moretti would have a field day.

On the surface she and Yvonne Porter couldn't be more different. And yet deep down there's a connection and Megan wants to protect her. Why does any woman love a man who beats her? For the money and the posh house? Out of a lack of self-worth? Or for a completely different reason.

When Megan went undercover she knew what she was getting into. She came into his world pretending to be an agency temp; that was her cover, working in one of the businesses that Zac Yilmaz used as a front. She was there to quietly gather intel. She didn't expect to catch his eye. She didn't think she was attractive enough. But he took one look at her and knew what he wanted. The excitement of it took her breath away. The charisma and sexual energy that he focused on her was something she'd never experienced before. He wasn't conventionally good-looking. Balding, shorter than her and at least fifteen years older, but he had a presence that was electric. Raw power. She always knew that if he found out who she really was, he'd kill her. But did fear fuel the intensity of the passion? Knowing the smallest slip could spell disaster?

As Vish turns into the car park above the harbour, Megan's phone buzzes. She glances at it. It takes a moment to register. Ted Jennings. Again? Why is he calling her? It doesn't make sense. He told Collins that he planned to redeem himself by chasing Bridger. And he wanted Collins's help. So why's he hassling her? The call goes to voicemail then a text pops up from him. 'Please call me' is the gist. Written in upper case with exclamation marks. Then a second text arrives: *I don't know who else I can trust.*

Megan gets out of the car. On top of everything else she can't get entangled in some stupid melodrama that Ted Jennings is trying to engineer in order to prove what a good cop he is. They've never got on that well and are certainly not mates.

She has to clear her head and focus. Elena. Finding the Spanish woman is the priority.

Vish walks ahead of her. He remembers the access code to the pontoon. But even before they get there he notices.

'Think we've got a problem,' he says.

'What?' says Megan. She's still struggling to get her head in gear.

'Looks like Barry isn't here. His boat's gone.'

'Shit,' says Megan. She was hoping to take him by surprise. 'Okay, try ringing him.'

Vish gets out his phone. 'Do you still want to go on the pontoon?' he asks.

'Yeah, let's take a look.'

Vish keys in the code and opens the gate for Megan. They walk down onto the pontoon. Quite a few boats are absent from their moorings. It's turned into a lovely afternoon, calm sea, perfect weather for a cruise.

Vish clicks on Barry Porter's number and lets it ring. 'Depends how far out he is. Phone might not work but he'll have a radio.'

Megan wanders along the pontoon. If Elena had come from a neighbouring boat, which one could it be? Is it too much to hope that she could still be around?

Suddenly Vish comes rushing past her. 'Bloody hell!' he says. 'Listen!'

The faint sound of a phone ringing?

He kneels down and reaches his arm underneath the pontoon. The structure is made of steel struts and floats up and down with the tide. There's a gap of about half a meter between the wooden decking on the top and the surface of the water. Vish lies on his stomach so he can reach further.

'I think it's down here on the float,' he says.

'Don't fall in!' says Megan.

He stretches a little further. 'Gotcha!'

Vish's arm comes up and he rolls onto his back. In his hand he has a ringing phone.

'Barry's phone,' says Vish, holding it up. 'He must've dropped it over the side but it landed on the buoyancy float.'

Megan stares at it. 'You know what,' she says. 'I think we've been looking at this case all wrong.'

CHAPTER FORTY-FIVE

Monday, 3.10 p.m.

Megan stares up at the crossbeams in the vaulted ceiling of the Porters' huge hallway. They've been stripped and treated with a light stain to match the blond wood floor. The overall effect is to lift and lighten. She finds herself wondering what it's like living in an enormous house like this. The luxury of such space. Her entire life, until moving into her sister's terraced house in Devon, has been lived in flats. Most of them small and pokey, from dark basements to a dingy tower block.

Vish has his hands in his pockets. She wonders what he's thinking, possibly something similar. He's still living with his parents and commuting.

The nanny greeted them at the door and has gone to fetch Penny Reynolds.

As her eye roves around Megan notices Imogen peeping at them from the kitchen doorway. She's wearing a bikini and pink heart-shaped sunglasses.

'Hello,' says Megan. 'Are you Imogen?'

The little girl nods but remains half concealed behind the door jamb.

'You know what we did yesterday,' says Megan. 'We went on your granddad's boat. Do you like boats?'

The little girl nods again.

'What do you like best about them?'

Imogen ventures half a step forward. 'The jet ski,' she says, almost in a whisper.

'Wow!' says Megan. 'You've got a jet ski. That's amazing! I'm so envious. Who do you go on the jet ski with?'

'With me,' says Aidan, appearing in the doorway behind his sister. He wears a checked pair of baggy swim shorts, which are dripping water onto the polished floor. 'My aunt's on the phone. She'll be with you in a minute.' He turns to go.

'Well,' says Megan with a smile. 'It was just a quick question really: does your dad have a boat?'

'Not any more, 'cause he's dead.' The tone is surly. 'So technically I suppose they belong to my mum.'

They? So more than one boat.

'Of course,' says Megan maintaining the smile. 'Jet ski, several boats. Wow! Most kids'd envy that.'

'I would've,' says Vish.

Aidan bristles, which is her intention.

'It's not like that,' he says in a tetchy tone. 'My dad and my granddad have got this company, it owns luxury yachts that they rent out. It's a proper business not a plaything.'

Megan nods, glances at Vish.

'Still, you get to go on them,' he says. 'Your granddad's boat, that's amazing. I bet it goes fast.'

'The *Seamew* isn't my granddad's, it belongs to the company. I've just told you.'

Penny Reynolds comes striding out of the kitchen towards them. 'Sorry to keep you,' she says briskly. 'I've been speaking to my sister's lawyer. I gather you're releasing her under investigation.'

'Yes,' says Megan.

'Then I don't understand why you're here.'

'Under investigation means we're continuing with our inquiries. And we'd like to take another look at your brother-in-law's office.'

'Thought you said you just wanted to ask about the boats?' says Aidan.

Penny shoots him a warning look.

'Darling,' she says sharply, 'I'll deal with this. You and Imo go back to the pool.'

Aidan looks like he's about to argue then he turns, puts a hand on Imogen's shoulder and shepherds her away.

'This must be really hard for them,' says Megan. 'How are they holding up?'

Penny shrugs. 'They're okay I suppose. I'm not much of an expert on children. They'll be glad to have their mum back.'

'I'm sure.'

Megan fixes the other woman with a steady gaze. Penny stands stiffly, clutching one hand with the other. She's rippling with tension.

'Well, you'd better come this way,' she says.

'Thanks,' says Megan. 'By the way, you haven't spoken to Barry today, have you?'

As soon as they found the phone, Megan called Slater. Uniformed officers were despatched to Barry Porter's home but his wife hasn't seen him. He does appear to be missing.

'Why would I?' says Penny. 'He tolerates me but we don't exactly get on.'

Penny leads them through the kitchen and out onto the terrace. Below it the twins, Harry and Lucas, are splashing around on a huge inflatable dinosaur in what Megan judges must be at least a twenty-metre pool. Aidan has retreated to a lounger and headphones. His sister watches them pass like a nervous mouse keeping an eye out for cats.

They cross the terrace and take a small gravel path, which weaves across the lawn to a long, low building. It's brick-built, probably once a cow shed or stable block.

There's a digital keypad on the door overlooked by a security camera. Slater's right about the security system. High end, cameras everywhere. Megan's beginning to wonder why Greg Porter felt the need to take such precautions. But it will definitely help them once they've broken all the data down.

'So why are you interested in boats?' says Penny Reynolds, a little too casually.

'It's just one line of inquiry,' says Megan. 'Your brother-in-law was in the business of renting out luxury yachts. Has he been doing that long?'

Penny taps in four digits, but one of them is wrong. She huffs and tries again. 'These bloody things, they're so annoying.' Megan watches her hand, which is visibly shaking.

'What's wrong with an old-fashioned key?' Megan says jovially.

On her third attempt, Penny succeeds in unlocking the door.

Megan is monitoring her escalating stress; she goes in for the kill.

'We were also wondering,' she says. 'Do you know where we can find Elena?'

This stops Penny in her tracks. 'Sorry? Who?'

'Just wondered if you knew her?' says Megan. *Clearly she does.*

'No. I'm only here to support my sister. I know next to nothing about Greg's business interests or who he dealt with. He was a property developer. That's all I know really.'

But she knows the code to his office.

'You never went on one of his boats?' says Megan.

Penny hesitates. She's calculating how likely it is her lie will be found out, that's Megan's guess. 'I get seasick really easily,' she says.

'Did Yvonne ever mention she thought he had a mistress?'

'Well, Yvonne's always felt insecure in her marriage. I don't think you can read that much into some of the things she says.' *A diversionary tactic?* But why does Penny Reynolds want to protect Elena? What's their connection?

They step into the office, an airy space with a picture window at the far end, which overlooks a field of spring barley. The bare brick walls are hung with photographs and plans of various property developments. Megan and Vish wander around, leaving Penny hovering by the door.

A large glass desk sits under the window. Next to it on the wall is a small framed photo of a sleek yacht, newer and bigger than the *Seamew*. Megan gets out her phone and uses the magnifier to read the name on the prow: *Seahawk*. Then she snaps a picture of it.

Over her shoulder she's aware of Penny Reynolds nervously watching her.

CHAPTER FORTY-SIX

Monday, 5.30 p.m.

Megan is running on adrenaline but the feeling that they could be close to a breakthrough is spurring her on. The twitchiness of Penny Reynolds, the disappearance of Barry Porter and his boat. A much larger puzzle seems to be emerging and, for Megan, it's what makes being a detective exciting.

She and Vish stride down the hotel corridor side by side. The once palatial establishment has seen better days. Built to serve wealthy Victorians, it now relies on coach parties of elderly tourists and bevvies of Chinese language students. They reach the end of the corridor and a door marked 'The Gladstone Suite'. Vish raps on it.

A moment passes and it's opened by Brittney. She's grinning from ear to ear.

'Hey, welcome to the A team,' she says.

'Yeah, you wish,' says Vish. 'This place looks more like somewhere doddering OAPs come to die.'

Brittney tilts her chin upwards. 'You're just jealous 'cause you're not working with the NCA.'

'True,' he replies, following her in.

Megan brings up the rear. They follow Brittney down a short corridor into the drawing room. It's full of mock Louis Quinze furniture, which has been rearranged to accommodate an array of computers with extra monitors. Wires snake across the floor connecting to blocks of surge protectors. The NCA has set up a rapid response incident room of its own.

Danny Ingram is leaning against the heavy brocade curtain and talking on his phone. He raises a hand in salute.

'Danny's talking to Slater,' Brittney explains. 'And I think you know the others.'

Garcia, Rodney and Bibi are at their respective computers.

Garcia jumps up and gives Megan a quick hug. But her gaze strays immediately to Vish.

'Hey, Vish the dish,' she says. 'Welcome to the gang.'

He returns the look. Ingram was obviously right; she's catholic in her tastes.

Bibi smiles and Rodney remains glued to his screen, oblivious to their arrival.

Megan does a circuit of the huge patterned carpet. She's feeling too wired to just be still. There's an energising buzz in the room, a sense of purpose and competence. If it's a choice between this and arguing with Collins, Megan knows where she'd rather be. But Brittney has taken her place as liaison officer and is in her element. Megan watches her teasing Vish.

Ingram hangs up the phone and gives her a smile. She catches the look in his eyes but only for an instant. He flips straight into professional mode.

'Right,' he says. 'DCI Slater is asking for our help with some specific lines of inquiry. Could the murder of Greg Porter be related to a wider conspiracy to traffic illegal migrants into the UK? Was Porter part of this conspiracy? Let's start with the boats.'

He glances round the room expectantly.

'Okay,' says Garcia. 'Well, we've checked and they are gone. The one you sent us a picture of, Megan, is the *Seahawk*. The other boat you've told us about is the *Seamew*. We've been in touch with the company that owns the marina. Greg Porter rents moorings for two boats from them. The company he uses to do this is interesting though. Registered offshore, beneficial owner concealed behind a series of shell companies.'

'Is this about tax avoidance?' asks Vish.

Garcia gives him a smile. 'Good question. That could be one reason. But the *Seahawk* looks new, the *Seamew*, from your description, is maybe only six months old. And these are expensive boats. Each one three or four hundred grand minimum. So the shell companies could also disguise the source of the financing.'

'Dirty money?' says Vish.

'Could be,' says Garcia.

'But how does a man like Porter get into this?' says Megan. 'He's a property developer, his dad's a builder. How do they decide to rent luxury yachts?'

'They know someone who knows about money,' says Ingram. 'Either legitimate business loans – because Greg Porter would have collateral – or more dubious sources.'

'So it would help if your sister-in-law worked for an investment bank?' says Megan.

'Certainly would,' says Garcia. 'Do we have a name?'

'Penny Reynolds,' says Megan. 'Works in Canary Wharf somewhere I think. And as soon as she found out we knew about the boats, she looked ready to shit a brick.'

Garcia's fingers fly across her keyboard. 'Here we go,' she says. 'I'll put it up on the monitor. Is this her?'

They all turn to one of the screens. A slick, professional shot of Penny Reynolds, carefully coiffed and looking younger, pops up on the screen. Garcia reads from the text appearing beneath the photo. 'LSE, MBA at Stanford Business School, which got her into an American investment bank. She's a high flier, now a senior VP in their London office.'

'It's definitely her,' says Megan.

'And this particular bank is also interesting,' says Garcia. 'They have been accused on several occasions of having some very dodgy clients. We've had run-ins with them before. And money laundering does go on there.'

'Okay, let's play devil's advocate,' says Ingram. 'Why does Penny decide to give her brother-in-law a shedload of money to buy boats he can rent out? What's in it for her?'

Brittney raises her finger nervously. 'Can I say something?' she says.

'Go for it,' says Ingram.

'Maybe she's not doing it for him. It's the other way round. She's using him as a front. He's a local businessman, if he wants to rent moorings in the marina, who's going to find that suspicious? Him and his dad belong here, probably know the local bigwigs. They're ultra respectable.'

'I'll buy that,' says Ingram. 'They're the front. But who's Penny doing all this for then?'

'Elena,' says Megan. 'What if Greg wasn't lying to his wife? She is actually his business partner and provides the dosh. Based in Spain. Upmarket people smuggling. Posh boats.'

Ingram nods. 'Which is exactly who we've been looking for.'

CHAPTER FORTY-SEVEN

Monday, 8.30 p.m.

By the time Megan gets home she's ready to crash. Danny Ingram tried to inveigle her into going for a drink. But she refused. She was spent, emotionally and physically. Switching from professional mode back to something more intimate was too taxing a prospect. All she wants is her own bed and sleep.

She lets herself into the house. It's quiet and calming, her haven. Scout comes trotting down the hall, tail wagging, to greet her. She can hear the sound of nebulous voices accompanied by a tinny laughter track: the television. She passes the open sitting room door. Kyle is curled up at one end of the sofa, Ruby, in pyjamas, with cuddly elephant at the other.

She wanders into the kitchen to find her sister sitting at the kitchen table, peering through her reading glasses and writing a list.

'Hiya,' says Megan casually, plonking her bag on a chair.

'There's some moussaka in the fridge,' says Debbie, without looking up. 'If you're interested.'

Megan remembers that she missed lunch.

'Yeah, if it's going spare,' she says.

Debbie takes off her glasses and gets up. 'Do you want a bit of salad with it?' she asks. She's maintaining a cool distance.

'It's okay. I can get it myself,' says Megan.

'I don't mind,' says Debbie. Megan notices the tone: neutral bordering on irritated. She knows her sister has been brooding. Probably for most of the day.

'You look completely knackered,' says Debbie, opening the fridge.

'Long day,' says Megan. She's glad to sit down.

Debbie takes a Pyrex dish from the fridge, gets a plate from the cupboard and spoons a generous portion of moussaka onto it.

'Did the bloke from the NCA find you this morning?' she asks.

'Yeah. Thanks,' says Megan.

'You didn't mind me telling him where to go?'

Megan scans her sister. She's wearing her sorrowful face. It hasn't really changed since she was about seven. Megan wants to say: can't we skip this bit and go back to normal? But Debbie likes to play out the drama. Moretti says it's the only way her sister can feel better.

Megan sighs. 'No, I didn't mind,' she says. 'He brought his umbrella.' Her encounter with Ingram on the beach feels like an eternity ago, although it was just this morning.

Debbie puts the plate in the microwave and sets the timer.

'Did he tell you I wanted to talk?' says Debbie.

'Yeah,' says Megan, 'and I've been meaning to ring you, but things have been a bit mad.'

Debbie shrugs. 'Doesn't matter,' she says in a martyred voice. 'Have you found out who did it yet?'

This is all starting to grate on Megan's nerves. She looks at the dog, snug in his corner basket but keeping a beady eye on things. She knows she must keep her temper.

'Things are moving on a bit,' she says evenly. 'But no, we haven't nailed anyone yet.'

Megan gets up, goes to the sink and pours herself a glass of water. Besides being tired, she realises how dehydrated she is, which probably explains the niggling headache.

Then she says, 'When you were cleaning at the flats, I don't suppose you ever saw Greg with a Spanish woman, about forty, attractive, quite posh.'

'You think Greg was screwing her?' says Debbie. 'Sounds a bit out of his league.'

'Maybe. Or perhaps they were connected through some kind of business deal.'

'I never saw a woman,' says Debbie, 'but there was a Spanish bloke.'

'A bloke?' says Megan.

'Yes, big tough-looking bloke, about fifty-odd, with a beard. I'm sure he was Spanish because I heard him talking to the two lads that came with him.'

'When was this?' says Megan. *The CCTV from the harbour office. Three men in the middle of the night: one older, with a beard, two much younger.*

'A week or so ago. Greg was furnishing the show flat. Three of them came with a van-load of furniture. Fancy stuff too. I watched them unload it. Must've cost Greg a mint.'

'Did you see Greg with them at all?' asks Megan.

'Yeah, he let them into the show flat and I heard them talking.'

'Talking in English?' says Megan.

'They were laughing. The big Spanish guy said something like, "Hey, don't ask me. I just do what she tells me. She's the boss."' *Greg Porter knew the smugglers!*

'Do you think they were just delivery guys?'

Debbie shakes her head. 'No, they seemed more like mates doing him a favour. He helped them carry stuff in. Greg would've never helped a delivery guy.'

'Any names?'

'Not that I can remember.'

The microwave pings. Debbie lifts out the plate of moussaka and puts it on the table for Megan.

'Aww, that smells great,' says Megan. 'But hey, don't bother with salad. This will be fine.' She wants to eat and she wants to think, to process this new information.

But Debbie sits down opposite her sister. 'Meg, I wanted to say... oh, shit, I don't really know what I want to say. Sorry, I suppose.'

'It doesn't matter, Deb,' says Megan tucking in with her fork.

'Yeah it does,' says Debbie. 'I spoke to Mark on the phone earlier. He said he saw you this morning before he left. He thought you looked quite down in the mouth. You have to understand, this whole thing really did my head in. And I hate it when you're angry with me.'

Megan puts her fork down. Do they have to do this now? She appears to have no choice.

'I'm not angry with you,' she says, 'but I was hurt and upset. That's different.'

'Feels to me like you're angry,' says Debbie. 'But whatever. What can I do to make it up to you?'

'Two things,' says Megan. 'Number one: I want you to admit that you were angry with me. It wasn't the other way round. You were angry and you lashed out. I got hurt. That's what actually happened. You can't always play the little sister card and be the victim.'

Debbie sighs and looks sheepish. 'Is that what I'm doing?'

'Yes,' says Megan. 'Second thing. I'm going to make you and Mark an interest-free loan to pay off your credit cards.'

'No, I couldn't possibly accept that,' says Debbie.

'Yes you can. I got a lump sum from my divorce settlement. It's just sitting there in the bloody bank earning bugger all interest. You've given me a home, somewhere to belong and the chance to put my life back together. Let me do this. Please.'

Debbie walks round the table and flings her arms around Megan. There are tears in her eyes.

'Thank you,' she whispers.

'And in future talk to me, Deb,' says, Megan. 'Doesn't matter what you've done, I'm not going to judge you. Believe me, I'm in no position to judge anyone.'

'Okay,' says Debbie. Her chin is quivering but she's smiling. 'Shall we seal the deal with a glass of wine?'

'Oh, absolutely,' says Megan. 'And this moussaka is great.'

Debbie goes to the fridge and takes out a bottle of white wine. She unscrews the top and pours two glasses.

They raise their glasses in a toast.

'What shall we drink to?' says Debbie.

'I dunno,' says Megan. 'Don't let the bastards grind you down?'

They clink glasses and drink. The phone in Megan's bag buzzes. She picks it up and looks at it. An incoming call from Vish.

She sighs. 'I should probably take this.'

She clicks to answer and says, 'I thought Sasha Garcia had persuaded you to go for a meal and who knows what.'

'My virtue is intact,' says Vish. 'But we just got a call from comms. Uniforms have found Barry Porter's four-by-four parked up a farm track. There's a body stuffed in the boot and a lot of blood.'

'Shit,' says Megan. 'Who's duty DI?'

'Collins. But they can't raise him. Slater told me to call you.'

'Okay,' she says. 'Text me the postcode, I'll meet you there.'

She gazes at her half-eaten moussaka and the wine and sighs.

CHAPTER FORTY-EIGHT

Monday, 9.44 p.m.

The blue lights guide Megan for the last quarter of a mile. She glimpses them intermittently through the high hedgerows. The narrow lane rises steeply. Even the edge of the moors at night can be a spooky place. The car clatters over a cattle grid and she has to brake sharply to avoid two Greyface Dartmoor sheep. They stand frozen in the headlights for a second before skipping away.

As she approaches the farm, a uniformed officer flags her down with his torch. She shows her ID and he points to where she can park. She finds Vish leaning on the open door of his car and talking to the other response officer.

Megan parks and walks towards them. They're illuminated by the interior light from his car.

The PC with Vish is female and upset. She's blowing her nose on a tissue Vish has just provided.

'Sorry,' she says. 'Don't mean to be such a wuss.'

'Hey,' he says. 'First time is always a shock. You don't need to apologise.'

Megan joins them.

'This is DS Thomas,' says Vish. 'PC Harrison found the body in the boot.'

Harrison stands up straight. 'Sorry, ma'am,' she says. She looks extremely young, probably a probationer.

'It's Megan. What's your first name?'

'Sonia.'

'Okay, Sonia,' says Megan. 'I'm guessing it was grim. Talk me through what you did.'

'It's just that I wasn't expecting it. The blood and the smell. Comms just told us they'd had a call from the farmer because this vehicle was blocking the track and it's the only access route in and out of his farm. He was stroppy and threatening to shunt it with his tractor. Oli, my partner, started looking inside and he said check the back and—'

'Keys in it?'

'Yes,' says Sonia. 'Key fob was on the dash.'

'So you opened the back?'

'Yeah. At first I didn't really know... I thought maybe a dog. But the smell...'

'Is it wrapped in anything?'

'No. I think it's a man. Khaki shorts and sandals. The head's just all bloody.'

'You've done really well, Sonia,' says Megan. 'Because I'm going to go and look at it now and I'll know what to expect. So you've done your job. Have you talked to the farmer?'

'Yeah, him and his son came out when we arrived. The farm's just over the field there.'

Megan glances in the direction she's pointing. The shadowy outlines of the building are visible with a few splashes of light.

'Go up to the farmhouse. Don't give them any details. Just say I'll be up shortly to speak to them. Okay?'

Sonia nods, relieved to have something to do. She disappears across the field into the darkness.

Megan turns to Vish and says, 'Got any gloves?'

He pulls some blue vinyls out of his pocket. She puts them on as they walk up the track towards the four-by-four.

'We're sure this is Porter's car?' she says.

'Yeah, they called in the registration when they got here and it came up as his and that he was reported missing.'

The lane is single track, grass in the middle, and the grey Toyota RAV4 effectively blocks it. The open front doors touch the hedgerows either side. The courtesy light is on, casting a ghostly glow over the interior. Vish switches his torch on. The beam dances over the back of the vehicle. The tailgate is open a few inches. Megan lifts it up.

The stench of blood and faeces and puke hits, reminding her of every post mortem she's attended; it's not a smell you forget. In the luggage compartment behind the back seats, the body lies on its side in the foetal position. The knees are curled up pointing towards them, the arms crossed over the chest. The mouth is open, the tongue lolls and the eyes are open and staring. The entry wound in the middle of the forehead is comparatively small but the whole of the back of the head has been blown off. Still the face is recognisable enough. Barry Porter.

Megan and Vish stare at the corpse for several moments.

Then she sighs and says, 'Looks to me like they put him in the back of the car alive. He curled up, clutching his arms round his torso to protect himself. Then later they opened the back and shot him through the head. Poor old Barry.'

Vish exhales. 'Bloody hell, the look on his face – that is scary. No wonder the PC freaked. I've not seen a gunshot like that before. It is a gunshot?'

'I'm no expert but I'm guessing it's a nine millimetre. You can get some nasty types of bullets.'

Vish glances at her. 'You seem to know quite a lot about this stuff.'

Unfortunately he's right. 'Whoever did this is a professional criminal,' she says. 'Up close, no emotion. It's an execution.'

'Do you think they're still around?'

'Highly unlikely. They came here to dump the body. They will have needed a second vehicle. So with any luck there'll be some tyre tracks and footprints. We'll need CSI up here pronto. Be careful where you step, we don't want to contaminate the scene any more than we have already.'

'Phone signal's crap. We may need to use the landline at the farm,' says Vish.

'I'll go and talk to the farmer. You and the other PC get a secure cordon round this. Ten feet in front and behind the vehicle. Then post the PC down the hill there, tell everyone to park up there. Let's retrace our steps back to the cars exactly the way we came.'

Vish sighs. 'Right.' He swallows hard.

'You all right?' says Megan. She can't really see his face.

'Yeah,' he says. 'I don't get it though. Why would anyone do this to a stupid old fart like Barry Porter?'

'Good question,' says Megan. 'He obviously knew some unsavoury people.'

She sets out across the field towards the farmhouse. The torch on her phone casts a spectral light across the grass.

Why would anyone do this to Barry Porter? She shouldn't even be here. But yet again she's doing Collins's job.

Less than a week ago this saga began with the murder of Greg Porter. Debbie discovered the body and thanks to Collins's stupidity, she ended up in the frame. From there the inquiry veered off into the Porter family when his son Aidan confessed. The boy thought his mother did it. He'd filmed her being beaten up by his father. It looked like Yvonne Porter was an abused wife who finally snapped. But now they're in vastly different territory. Greg Porter and his father seem unlikely criminals but it appears they were running a front operation for a gang of people smugglers. What puzzles Megan is the shock in Barry Porter's eyes. It suggests a man who had no idea what was happening or why.

CHAPTER FORTY-NINE

Tuesday, 10 a.m.

It was a long night. Megan stayed at the farm until she could hand the crime scene over securely to Hilary Kumar and her team. Megan took a statement from the farmer. But he and his family saw and heard nothing, which was what Megan expected. She went home but couldn't sleep. Barry Porter's ghoulish face, frozen in horror at his own fate, haunted her. His death and his son's might well be connected, but to Megan they seem to be very different sorts of murders: a frenzied attack with a hammer, a pre-meditated execution with a gun.

The incident room is full to capacity. Chief Superintendent Rob Barker is at the front to lead the morning briefing with Laura Slater at his side. Megan notices Jim Collins tucked away hoping to look inconspicuous. She tries not to feel resentful even though she's lost a night's sleep covering for him. He was the DI on call.

Danny Ingram and Sasha Garcia arrive with Brittney. He catches her eye and gives her the briefest smile. Brittney is joking with them, enjoying her new role as part of the gang. Megan feels a pang of envy.

'Morning, everyone,' says Barker. 'And a special welcome to our colleagues from the National Crime Agency, who will be working alongside us on this joint operation. We now have two murders: father and son. And we have a connection with a human trafficking gang known to be operating on our patch. Danny, I know your team's been busy. Perhaps you could kick off with an update?'

Ingram edges towards the front. 'Thank you, sir,' he says. 'To start with, our operation was based on intelligence received from European partners that an organised criminal gang was running an upmarket service to smuggle illegal migrants into the UK. Their presence in this area was confirmed last Thursday when we detained an illegal Syrian migrant and her child at Blackpool Sands. After interviewing her we suspected that the boat or boats being used by the smugglers were being hidden in a local marina, in plain sight, so to speak. CCTV from Torquay marina led us to suspect a man in his fifties, two much younger men and a woman. We tracked them through ANPR up onto the moors, where we lost them. Yesterday DS Thomas and DC Prasad pointed us in the direction of two boats owned by a company run by our murder victims. I'll let my colleague Sasha Garcia pick up the story.'

Garcia gets up and carries her laptop to the front. She takes her time, no nerves. Seems to love the attention. Megan wonders how you get that kind of confidence. Garcia hands a cable to Kitty, who plugs it into the monitor. Megan's gaze skips round the room and meets Ingram's eye. He smiles at her. Is he reading her thoughts? Is she that transparent?

'Hi, everyone,' says Garcia. 'We've been doing some in-depth analysis into the digital record. There are a lot of expensive boats in the marina and a network of high-end CCTV cameras to protect them and record their comings and goings. The two boats in question disappeared from the marina, probably on Sunday night, and they've gone off the grid. There's a Border Force vessel patrolling in the Channel which is on the lookout for them and the coastguard has been alerted. Problem is they could be tucked away either side of the Channel. A small cove, an estuary? Plenty of places to hide.'

'And all the relevant agencies have been provided with a detailed description?' asks Barker.

'Yes, sir,' says Garcia. 'Turning to the owners. Company data we've collected suggests Greg and Barry Porter were the front. But as yet the connection between them and our potential smugglers is hard to prove. This woman is a link.'

She taps the keyboard and the pictures Vish took of the woman in blue appear on the monitor.

'We think she's called Elena. We think she's Spanish. And we're using some facial recognition software to see if we can find out who she is. But she is wearing sunglasses, which makes it more difficult.'

'In any event that's a long shot,' says Ingram. 'Unless she's got a criminal record. We've put in a special request for information to our colleagues in Spain. Sent them the images. But the murders, particularly the second one, are probably the key to this. She had some kind of row with Barry Porter shortly before his disappearance. Are these two things connected?'

'Thanks, Danny,' says Barker. 'Megan, you were the officer on the scene last night. What do we know so far?'

Megan stands up. A knot in her stomach tightens as all eyes turn to her.

'Okay,' she says. 'The post mortem on Barry Porter is scheduled for later today. But I spoke to Hilary Kumar this morning and we're fairly convinced this is a gunshot wound to the head at close quarters. Looks like someone got hold of Barry Porter, shoved him in the boot of his own car, drove him to a secluded track on Dartmoor and shot him. After the PM we'll have a better idea of the time of death.'

Barker nods and turns to Slater. 'Laura, you're SIO. Talk us through what we think all this means.'

'Well, first of all,' says Slater, 'let's go back to the murder of Greg Porter. Bludgeoned to death with a hammer. It has all the appearance of a loss of control in an angry and personal attack. However, now we have DNA confirmation of Porter's blood on the hammer it's clear that it was the murder weapon, and since their fingerprints aren't on it, we can exclude both his son and his wife from suspicion. And Kitty's been through all the footage from security cameras at the Porters' home for the night of the murder. Neither of them left the house. You want to add to this, Kitty?'

'Just to say, boss, the boy was online playing *Call of Duty: Black Ops* until two a.m. His mother watched television in the sitting room and drank until she passed out.'

'As a result,' says Slater, 'they're no longer suspects. But Yvonne Porter, though not a reliable witness, claims her husband was with his mistress, Elena, that night. If this is true, we still may be looking at a personal attack. So she's now our prime suspect. The question is, who is she? Yvonne confirmed when interviewed that this is the same woman seen arguing with Barry Porter. But the other potential link between the two murders is Yvonne's sister, Penny Reynolds. We want to talk to her about where the money for the boats came from. She'll be brought in later this morning and interviewed under caution. Megan and Sasha, I'd like you to tackle her. You may want to put your heads together and work out an approach. I think that brings us up to speed unless anyone has anything to add.'

Megan raises her hand. 'I did discover yesterday, boss, some evidence that three Spanish guys, matching the men in the video from the marina, delivered furniture to Greg Porter for his show flat and appeared to be his friends. If they are the smugglers, then he knew them. It even raises the possibility of some kind of business connection with the flats he was building, which would explain why they were bringing him furniture.'

'Right, that needs to be followed up. Let's see if there's any CCTV footage of them. DI Collins will be issuing actions.' She turns to Barker. 'That's all for the moment.'

'Thanks,' says Barker. 'Unfortunately, I have to end on a very sad note. A number of you will know Ted Jennings. He was a DS and a longstanding member of this team. Many of you will have worked with him. I just heard this morning that he's died. Apparently, he took his own life.'

Surprise and dismay ripple round the room.

Megan's gaze shoots across to where Collins is standing. He's turned away and is pouring himself a coffee.

Megan can't quite take this in. As she watches, Collins picks up his coffee and walks out of the room.

'Funeral details will be posted in due course for anyone who wishes to attend,' Barker adds.

'Can I ask, sir,' says Megan. 'Took his own life how?'

'I believe his body was recovered from rocks below Berry Head early this morning,' says Barker. 'He jumped. It looks like suicide.'

CHAPTER FIFTY

Tuesday, 10.15 a.m.

As the incident room empties out after the briefing, Megan stands rooted to the spot. *I don't know who else I can trust.* Those words were in the text Ted Jennings sent her after she'd ignored two of his calls. She pulls out her phone and scrolls but she's deleted the thread.

Sasha Garcia comes bouncing up to her. 'So,' she says. 'I've dug up some pretty interesting background on Ms Reynolds and—'

Megan swallows hard. 'Sasha,' she says. 'Can you just bear with me a minute? There's something I need to sort out.'

'No problem,' Garcia replies.

'Vish'll show you where the interview room is.'

Garcia beams. 'Okay. Take your time.'

Megan heads out into the corridor. Danny Ingram is outside the door talking to Barker; she slips past them, deliberately avoiding Ingram's eye. She catches up with Jim Collins in the main office, where he's sitting at his desk staring into space and sipping his coffee.

As she approaches, he gives her a baleful look.

'Last night,' she says. 'I covered your shout. Aren't you even going to thank me?'

He stares at her; there's a blankness in his eyes. 'Yeah, thank you,' he says coldly. 'Took some sleeping pills. I was out for the count. Didn't hear the phone.'

She nods. 'Okay. Did you know Ted Jennings was dead?'

He sighs. 'Yeah, I heard from Barker when he arrived this morning. Very sad.'

Megan studies him. Something about him is off kilter. He's deathly pale, more than usual. He tends to be wired, even when he's knackered. But this morning he's calm and detached.

'Sad?' she says. 'Why do you think he did it?'

Collins huffs. 'What do you care? You're rapidly becoming the squad's blue-eyed girl. Right about Yvonne Porter. Right about everything really. Don't know why the rest of us bother,' he adds sourly.

This is closer to his usual style.

Megan shakes her head, 'Do I really piss you off that much, Jim?'

He sips his coffee. 'I don't think about you that much.'

'Well think about this,' she says. 'On Sunday, when we were leaving the office to go and question Yvonne Porter, Ted came up to you as we were getting in the car.'

'Did he? I don't recall.'

'Yeah you do. What did he want?'

'Oh for Chrissake, Megan. Some nonsense. The bloke was upset. He'd been chucked off the team. And quite right too. He'd been bloody stupid.'

'I heard what he said to you. He was going after Dennis Bridger.'

'I think you have to take that with a pinch of salt.'

Megan sighs. 'Listen, I worked with Ted for long enough to know him a bit. I don't think he'd go and chuck himself off Berry Head because he'd got a rap over the knuckles and a demotion to CID.'

Collins frowns. Now it feels like he'd love to shove her away. 'You are so arrogant, y'know,' he snaps. 'What the hell do you know about Ted's state of mind? Or anyone's? You don't know what was going on with him. Maybe his wife left him.'

'Did she?'

Collins reins himself in. He shakes his hand dismissively. But it feels to Megan that something inside him is close to snapping.

'Who knows?' he says. 'Anyway, haven't you got an interview to prepare? You and that dyke from the NCA that's so full of herself.'

Garcia is currently chasing Vish; Megan wonders what Collins would make of that.

But she says, 'Ted tried to phone me twice. Sent me a text. What if he did go after Bridger? At the very least, I think the DCI should be made aware of what he was up to, don't you?'

Collins stares at her; his forehead is damp, his jaw clenched. Megan has the sudden impression that he might burst into tears.

'Actually,' he says, 'it's my wife who's left me. She saw me through all the cancer treatment. Said she wanted to get me back on my feet and back to work. Now, out of the blue, she says she wants a divorce. She feels trapped. She wants to be free to find out what she wants from life before she's too old. What do you make of that?'

Megan stares at him. She doesn't know what to make of it or what to say. Collins's behaviour seems bizarre on a number of levels and a sudden personal confidence from him is the last thing she'd have expected. He looks broken and forlorn. She notices that his shirt has not been pristinely ironed and a button is missing halfway down. He's coming apart – literally.

She sighs. 'I'm sorry, Jim, truly I am. I know you've had a tough time.'

'Maybe it's what I deserve,' he says. 'Maybe I'm a selfish shit and I took her for granted.'

'I suppose if you were struggling to get well... I dunno.'

They lapse into silence.

He exhales, glances up at her awkwardly. Now the embarrassment is kicking in. After all his manipulative games and what he did to her sister, Megan didn't think she had any sympathy left for Collins. But she does.

'Are you married?' he asks.

'Divorced.'

'Did you want to be free of your husband so you could find out what you wanted?'

'No, he dumped me for a younger woman.' She could've added, *and now they have a baby, which he couldn't have with me.* But she doesn't.

Collins nods. 'That's tough too.'

Megan says nothing. She has no intention of making Collins her new best friend.

He sighs again. 'You're probably right. Slater should know what Ted was up to. Then it's up to the bosses to decide whether to investigate, isn't it?'

'Yes,' says Megan.

'Okay. Is it all right with you if I tell her?'

'Fine. I've got no problem with that. Just so long as she knows.'

He wipes his nose with the back of his hand. 'Thanks.'

Megan is about to walk away. But a conversation with Vish suddenly springs to mind.

'Oh and you should probably have a word with Vish,' she says. 'He reckons Ted told him some story about a murder charge against Bridger being dropped because of lost forensics. Maybe that's why Ted was on a mission?'

Collins nods. 'Okay, I'll look into it. Thanks, Megan.'

Megan smiles and walks away. She's not sure she understands what that was about. Perhaps his wife leaving is the straw that broke the camel's back? All she knows is she has other more pressing problems.

CHAPTER FIFTY-ONE

Tuesday, 11 a.m.

Penny Reynolds turns up for her interview with a new lawyer in tow. He's corporate and expensive, a totally different proposition to Tim Wardell, the local guy who represented Yvonne and Aidan. Slater, Garcia and Megan watch them arrive on the monitor in the incident room.

'She whistled him up pretty quickly,' says Slater.

'Helicopter,' says Garcia.

Megan and Slater turn to look at her. She's not kidding. And she's beaming from ear to ear.

'What are you looking so pleased about?' asks Megan.

'I think we've hit pay-dirt,' says Garcia. 'I've just looked him up. The firm he's from specialises in money-laundering cases. They call it financial regulation. But that's what it means.'

Slater sighs. 'Do you think she's just going to go "no comment"?'

Garcia shrugs. 'She must've been talking to her bosses at the bank. I doubt they'd fly in a heavy hitter like him just to do that. It's obviously important to them to seem innocent and to make Penny seem innocent. I think they're going to try and be super helpful and charming and feed us a line in the hope we're stupid country plods who don't know which way is up.'

Slater gives Garcia an acerbic look. 'And is that what you think we are?'

'No, of course not, ma'am,' says Garcia. *She's lying.*

Megan suppresses a smile. 'Let's not keep them waiting.'

Megan and Garcia enter the interview room. The lawyer jumps to his feet and offers his hand to shake.

'Craig Henderson,' he says. He can't be more than thirty, his suit fits like a glove and he sounds like a preppy American.

Megan introduces herself and then adds, 'And my colleague Sasha Garcia is from the National Crime Agency.'

His eyes barely flicker. But it's enough to reveal it's not what he was expecting.

'This is a murder inquiry,' says Garcia. 'I went on your firm's website. Surely you're a commercial lawyer, Mr Henderson?'

'Penny is a dear friend and the untimely death of her brother-in-law has upset her deeply, as you can imagine,' he says. 'She wants to help you and I want to give her as much support as I can.'

Megan watches Penny as this little charade is played out. The nervousness she displayed yesterday when she showed them Greg's home office has disappeared or been suppressed. She appears composed, ready with a polite smile but completely professional in her manner. It occurs to Megan that, as a senior investment banker, she's used to taking difficult meetings with a lawyer at her elbow. The fact this one is with the police in a dingy interview room doesn't seem to faze her.

Yesterday Megan had the element of surprise. But not now. Reynolds is prepared.

Megan recites the caution and adds, 'Your brother-in-law had a number of business interests and that's what we want to ask you about. In particular he had a boat rental business. Yesterday I asked you about this and you denied any knowledge of it. Is this true?'

Penny smiles and tilts her head. 'The truth is you caught me off guard, sergeant.'

'You were lying then?'

'I think if I'm going to be entirely honest, and Craig has advised me I should be, then I'd say I was playing for time. I knew we'd be having this conversation and I needed time to think.'

'Think about what?' says Megan.

'How best to protect my sister, of course. When we spoke before she was still under investigation for her husband's murder. But I understand that all charges against her have been dropped, so I feel I can be candid.'

'She was arrested but not charged. She was helping with our inquiries.'

'And that's what I want to do,' says Penny.

'So you do know about your late brother-in-law's boat business?' says Megan.

'He came to me for a loan. Greg was basically a builder but sailing was his hobby. Barry, his father, taught him. They had various dinghies they mucked about in. The rental idea was really just a way of paying for a much bigger boat. Barry is quite a character. He always fancied himself on a luxury yacht. I looked at their business plan and there was no way the bank would back it. They had some vague idea of who their clients would be; rich tourists wanting to cruise the south-west coast. The problem for me was, if I said no and refused to help, then I suspected Greg might take it out on my sister.'

'You thought he'd be violent towards her?' says Megan.

'Frankly, yes. He had a nasty temper. That's why I didn't want to talk about this before. You thought she was an abused wife who finally snapped, didn't you?'

She fixes Megan with a steely look. Megan doesn't reply. She suspects Penny thought that too, which is why she encouraged Aidan to confess.

'Anyway,' says Penny. 'The bank has certain clients, mainly from abroad, who wish to invest in the UK and, shall we say, have a more tolerant attitude to risk.'

Garcia grins. 'Clients you launder money for, you mean?'

'We do not launder money,' says Penny Reynolds primly. 'As Craig will confirm, we comply with all UK laws and regulations to the letter. But if you understand anything about these matters, Ms Garcia, you will know that the world is awash with cash, whose provenance cannot always be established. I put my brother-in-law in touch with an intermediary who could help him access a loan. The amount was relatively small. This agent, who is based in the Middle East, was doing me a favour.'

'What's his name?' says Garcia.

'He's a confidential contact of the bank,' says Craig Henderson, 'and unless you can produce any evidence that he was involved in Greg Porter's murder, which I don't think you can, then we can't help you.'

Penny Reynolds smiles. 'Believe me, if I thought this had any bearing on Greg's death, I would tell you.'

'You're saying the boats were really just toys for Greg and his father?' says Megan.

'Yes,' says Penny.

'How much was the loan for?' says Garcia.

'I didn't involve myself in the details. But less than half a million I think. Which is actually next to nothing,' says Penny. 'It was a small favour.' Her expression borders on the smug.

'To keep Greg happy and protect your sister?' says Megan.

'Exactly.'

Megan smiles. 'Okay, Ms Reynolds. Thank you for your co-operation. But you should know that we'll be looking into this further because we now have two murders, which may be related.'

'Two murders?' says the lawyer.

Megan fixes Penny with a penetrating stare. 'Oh, I'm sorry to be the bearer of bad news. You obviously haven't heard. Barry Porter has been found dead.'

Penny looks confused. This doesn't compute for her.

'Barry?' she says, as if it's some kind of story. 'Dead?'

'And both boats are missing,' says Megan. 'Perhaps they've been stolen. Barry was found in his car last night, shot through the head.'

Megan has the satisfaction of seeing that she's hit the mark as the colour drains from Penny Reynolds's face.

CHAPTER FIFTY-TWO

'That was a cool trick,' says Garcia. She and Megan are walking down the corridor towards the incident room. 'I don't say the smug bitch didn't deserve it.'

Megan glances at her. To Garcia it's all a game, an elaborate puzzle to be solved. And she's a young woman having fun. Megan can recall a time when being a detective felt like that to her. An interesting challenge. An exciting job. She wonders what changed.

Somewhere along the line other people's pain started to get under her skin. Too many missing children, beaten wives, kids in gangs caught up in random violence. Then she went undercover and realised the everyday world she thought she knew was a fragile web. Things are always going wrong. Her job is picking up the pieces. It's what drives her anxiety and gives her sleepless nights.

The panicked look on Penny Reynolds's face is still rattling round in her head. Yes, freaking her out was justified. But it was also cruel. Fear is the one thing guaranteed to change people's attitudes. And if Penny Reynolds didn't know what Elena and co were capable of, she does now.

'What they just told us in there is a load of hogwash, isn't it?' says Megan.

'Oh yeah, absolutely,' says Garcia. 'But interesting hogwash.'

'How?'

'Damage limitation. Henderson's here to assess if it's going to work and to report back to his bosses at the bank. From our point of view this confirms that dirty money is involved.'

Dirty money. A second brutal murder. Suddenly the process of connecting them feels glacially slow to Megan. She thinks of Ranim on the beach, desperately looking for her son. And Hassan's body, washed up like a sack of rubbish. Just collateral damage in a business deal?

'What do we do now though?' she says. 'The boats are gone. Elena's probably gone. How are we ever going to nail these people?'

She's feeling tetchy but maybe it's lack of sleep.

Garcia shrugs. 'It's a game of patience.'

Megan sighs. She needs a cup of coffee. She can't get Barry Porter's shocked face out of her head either. This is what happens when serious criminals don't get what they want. She wonders if Barry was simply naive. He didn't understand who he was dealing with either.

In the incident room Slater turns to greet them. 'Nice piece of cage rattling,' she says.

Megan just nods and moves on. Her focus is on coffee. She heads for the machine, pours herself a mug and scans the room.

The team is busy. They have a huge amount of material to sift through. CCTV footage from the harbour office at the marina. Acres of it. Reports on forensic evidence coming in from the CSI lab.

Brittney is leaning over Kitty's shoulder. Kitty has one eye on her own screens and she's also supervising the efforts of two new recruits next to her. To Megan the screens look dark and pixelated. Staring at them for hours is like staring into a black hole. She knows, she's done it.

'No!' says Kitty to one of her charges. 'Slower. You're not searching for a bloody film you fancy on Netflix. You're gonna miss something. Every movement could be a clue.'

Megan feels restless. The slow accumulation of evidence has always frustrated her. She needs to keep moving.

She turns to Brittney.

'How's it going?' she asks.

'We've got the last known sighting of Barry Porter,' Brittney replies. 'He left the *Seamew* at 7.34 p.m. on Sunday night. He was pretty drunk, which may explain why he dropped his phone. But he was on his own. No kidnapper.'

'That's annoying,' says Megan. 'No sign yet of who took the boats?'

'Nope. It was probably later that night so it's a way down our timeline yet.'

'What about the phone?' says Megan. 'Anything useful on that?'

'It's still being analysed,' says Brittney.

'Lots of anonymous random numbers,' says Kitty over her shoulder.

'Are you trying to be cute?' says Megan.

'No, I'm analysing, because that's my job,' says Kitty. 'The numbers will all need to be traced, but I think it'll just confirm that an array of different numbers with no ID suggests the use of burners. Look at your own phone. Most of the calls are to numbers with names attached. Barry's phone is atypical. He was in communication with someone who uses burners. Such people are usually criminals.'

Megan has to smile. Kitty can be bolshie but she's meticulous at her job.

'Point taken,' says Megan.

'Doughnuts,' Kitty replies. 'That's the penalty for dissing my efforts.'

'Duly noted,' says Megan.

She wanders round the room sipping her coffee. No sign of Ingram. Garcia is talking to Slater.

Megan checks her watch. Barry Porter's post mortem is scheduled for noon. That's next on her agenda. But she's not looking forward to it. Blood, viscera, the stench. She tries not to think about it.

Garcia leaves and Slater heads purposefully in Megan's direction.

'Megan,' she says. 'If you don't mind, I want you to leave the PM to Vish. It'll fill in the details but probably confirm our assumption he was shot. Instead I want you to go and talk to Marion Porter, Barry's widow.'

'Okay,' says Megan. Deliverance comes in unexpected guises.

'She's been informed. Family liaison are with her.'

'Any particular line of questioning?' says Megan.

'Follow your nose,' says Slater. 'That's what you're good at.'

CHAPTER FIFTY-THREE

Tuesday, 1.30 p.m.

After Greg Porter's impressive rural barn conversion, Megan is surprised by his parents' home. A modest bungalow with a front garden bursting with spring flowers on a hillside overlooking Torbay. The only flowers Megan can name are the bluebells and tulips. But it's clear the garden is someone's pride and joy, and she doubts that person was Barry.

The family liaison officer lets her in and explains that Marion is with her daughter-in-law in the conservatory.

A visit from Yvonne? *Could prove interesting.*

'How's she holding up?' asks Megan.

Christine sighs. 'Well, I was at the daughter-in-law's house previously,' she says. 'She's a drinker, as you probably know. Marion's got a bathroom cabinet full of antidepressants and sleeping pills.'

'Should we be worried?' says Megan.

Christine shrugs. 'The GP's been round. I mentioned it, so it's up to him. He gave her a sedative. She was all over the place. It has calmed her down.'

Megan inspects the neat hallway: a shiny parquet floor with an old-fashioned rug, a smell of wax polish and floral air freshener. The whole place has a well-kept but elderly feel, a complete contrast with Barry Porter's floating gin palace.

Suddenly there's a loud roar from the back of the house. Is it a howl of distress? Megan and Christine exchange looks as it becomes apparent that it's laughter – hysterical laughter. *This is calm?*

Christine leads Megan through the sitting room to where French windows open into a large conservatory.

Yvonne Porter is rocking a small, dumpy woman in her arms; they're both crying with laughter.

Megan waits for them to notice her.

Yvonne does. She frowns in embarrassment and releases her mother-in-law. For a moment Marion Porter looks like a startled pixie. Her face is round and her large eyes blotchy with crying. Her grey hair is flecked with white, cropped short and sticking out at zany angles. She wipes under her eyes with her fingers. Yvonne hands her a tissue.

'Hello, Mrs Porter,' says Megan, holding up her warrant card. 'I'm DS Thomas. Your daughter-in-law and I have already met. I'm really sorry for your loss. I was wondering if you feel able to answer a few questions?'

'Well,' says Marion belligerently. 'I didn't kill him, if that's what you want to know.'

This is not quite what Megan was expecting but she's been a detective long enough not to be surprised. Go with the emotional flow, that was a piece of advice given to her years ago by her old DI. People in shock can have weird reactions, particularly when they've been medicated.

'That wasn't going to be my first question,' she says. 'But do you know who did?'

Marion's chin trembles. She swallows down a tear. *Maybe she does.*

'I told him no good would come of it,' she says. 'But he wouldn't listen.' She shakes her head. 'God knows I shall miss the stupid old bugger.'

She clutches her daughter-in-law's hand fiercely.

Megan waits.

Then she says, 'No good would come of what, Mrs Porter?'

Marion doesn't answer immediately. She needs time to process. *Zoned out but not completely.*

Megan waits. *Be patient.*

Marion smiles wistfully. 'Greg was so like his father,' she says. 'Well, it's to be expected, isn't it? But much smarter. He was such a perfect little boy.' She turns to Yvonne. 'Just like Aidan.'

Yvonne smiles and squeezes her mother-in-law's hand. The two women are holding on to each other as if their lives depended on it. Perhaps they do.

Megan wonders what the hell they were laughing about. She decides not to ask.

Marion frowns. She seems to be following a rambling thread of her own. 'But men can be so silly sometimes. They both thought they were such clever clogs. Barry, I can understand. No fool like an old fool. When something's too good to be true, it's too good to be true, isn't it? Greg should've known that.'

'What are we talking about here, Mrs Porter?' says Megan.

'I'm talking about those bloody Spaniards,' says Marion angrily. 'Her in particular.'

'Tell me more about that,' says Megan.

Marion seems to drift again. 'Well, she's lovely-looking, I'll give her that. People my age would call her a vamp. As soon as Penny brought her down here and introduced her, it was obvious how it was going to go. You know what men are like.'

Megan glances at Yvonne. 'We're talking about your sister Penny?'

Yvonne nods. 'She was only trying to be helpful.'

'No she wasn't!' says Marion indignantly. 'I don't want to upset you, lovey, but that sister of yours helps nobody but herself. You should keep your eye on her.'

Yvonne doesn't look offended; she shrugs and says, 'It is all very confusing.'

'Do you mind if I sit?' says Megan. 'And make a few notes?' She gets out her pocket book.

'Do you want a cup of tea?' asks Marion brightly. 'Christine's very helpful. It's like having a maid.'

'I'm fine,' says Megan. She sits on a basket chair opposite the two women. 'So, these Spaniards. A woman and who else? And do you know their names?'

'Oh yes,' says Marion. This seems to be something she's been brooding about. Rehearsing the details so she won't forget? 'Lopez. Elena and his name's odd, you write it with a J but say it with an H. Javier?'

Megan notes it down. 'Elena and Javier Lopez. Were they a couple?'

Marion nods. 'They seemed quite nice to start with.'

'You met them both?'

'Oh yes,' says Marion again. 'They took Barry and me out to dinner once. Very fancy.'

Yvonne chips in. 'But it was clear she targeted Greg.'

This irritates Marion. 'She knew what she was doing. But sex makes men stupid, doesn't it? It wasn't Greg's fault. She played him and his dad off against each other.'

'But she slept with Greg,' says Yvonne.

Marion shakes her head. 'No no! Greg would never have done that,' she says. 'I think it was a game.'

Yvonne seems about to disagree.

Megan jumps in. 'And what was the purpose of this game, do you think?' she says.

'I suppose to keep them off their guard,' says Marion. 'Make them both besotted with her so they didn't ask questions. Barry was easy to fool, poor old bugger. I mean, as if…'

A ghostly smile comes across Marion's features as she mentions her husband. 'He was a fool,' she says. 'But not Greg.'

'Okay,' says Megan. 'Just explain to me what the Lopezes wanted. What was it all about?'

Marion Porter has detached herself from Yvonne. She laces her fingers and frowns as she struggles to concentrate.

'They said they wanted to buy some boats,' she says. 'They'd provide the money. Penny would arrange it. But for tax reasons to do with some EU regulations a company run by Greg and Barry would be the official owners and rent the moorings. Barry knew people at the marina. He's belonged to the yacht club for years.'

'What did they want these boats for?'

'Just as an investment, they said. Greg and Barry could use them. But occasionally they might borrow them back for a day or two.'

'You didn't think this was odd?'

Marion gives a hollow laugh.

'I thought it was bloody suspicious,' she says. 'I told Barry, they're up to something. Drugs, I don't know. But he believed the tax thing. I think because he wanted to. Bit dodgy but not too dodgy. And of course Greg told him not to worry.'

She seems to be vacillating between two positions: Greg's fault, not Greg's fault.

Megan turns to Yvonne. 'What about Greg? Did he think this was a tax thing?'

Yvonne hunches her shoulders and stares at her hands. She doesn't answer.

'No,' says Marion. Her chin trembles again as she struggles with this. 'My son was clever. He must've known more.'

She's staring at her daughter-in-law. Yvonne starts to cry.

'Oh come on, lovey,' says Marion. 'They're… gone. We must tell the police what we know.'

'I don't know anything,' whines Yvonne. 'He never told me anything.'

Marion sighs. 'Somehow Greg and Penny cooked this up. They've always been close.'

'That's not true,' says Yvonne emphatically, through her tears. 'He chose me.'

Marion takes her daughter-in-law's hand and pats it.

'Penny was his first love. She turned him down. So he married you instead. He told me that on your wedding day.'

Yvonne pulls her hand away. 'That's simply not true,' she says. 'He chose me. He loved me.'

Megan watches the two women. There's nothing fake about their distress and both are resolute in their beliefs. Yvonne has built her life around a bad marriage. But that doesn't make the pain of her loss any the less. Marion Porter wants justice but is clinging desperately to a rosy image of her son. *Does she suspect the kind of man he really was?*

Marion stands up, walks to the window and gazes out at her immaculate garden. Her steps are shaky and she leans on the back of a chair for support.

'Barry phoned me on Sunday, about seven,' she says. 'Silly old sod was drunk. Told me some tale about telling her straight. He was so upset about Greg, well… obviously. He ranted on, said he was keeping the boats. I didn't take much notice. He wasn't really making sense. I told him to come home. He didn't.'

'What do you think he meant by "telling her straight"?' says Megan.

'I reckon he told Elena he was keeping the boats. I think that's what he always wanted.' More tears erupt from Marion and course down her cheeks. 'Stupid bloody fool! That's what's got him killed, isn't it? Those bloody Spaniards! They're bloody criminals and they killed my husband and my boy!'

She sinks to her knees. Yvonne rushes over to her.

They both end up kneeling on the floor, Yvonne rocking the old lady.

'Sssh,' says Yvonne. 'Sssh.'

CHAPTER FIFTY-FOUR

Tuesday, 4.15 p.m.

Megan sent the names to Ingram by text. By the time she walks into the Major Crime Team incident room, they already have Javier Lopez's mugshot on the screen.

The beard is black and bushy, the eyes fierce. A people smuggler who looks like a pirate? Megan's first impulse is to laugh. A night without sleep followed by a rollercoaster day has left her frazzled. Or perhaps she's been infected with Marion and Yvonne's hysteria.

Her encounter with Marion Porter has left her wondering how many women remain in marriages that disappoint them. Out of laziness? Out of fear of being alone? She seemed fond of Barry in the way you might love an old dog; her only real affection was for her son. Perhaps it explains why Barry preferred life on his boat and was determined to hang on to it.

Slater and Ingram are standing in front of the screen. Collins is standing apart. The presence of the NCA seems to be pushing him out of the loop even more. He stands, arms folded, a blank expression.

Megan joins them.

'Is he our people smuggler then?' she asks.

'He's a good candidate,' says Ingram. 'Got out of jail in Spain eighteen months ago after serving time for drug smuggling. He's got form going back twenty years. Maybe he was looking for an easier career. Dealing with the drug cartels can be rough. He does have a wife and two sons who fit the age profile. Sasha's talking to the Spanish police.'

Across the room Garcia is on a Skype call. Rodney and Bibi have joined the techie corner, presided over by Kitty.

'Let me guess,' says Megan with a smile. 'In Spanish?'

Ingram grins back. Megan is still getting used to the warmth and openness of his smile.

Slater shoots them a look, shifts uncomfortably. The boss is never at ease around intimacy. Especially other people's.

'We're trying to see if we can match him with the first lot of CCTV from Torquay harbour,' she says briskly.

Megan catches Ingram's eye. *Back to business.*

'The other part of this equation,' Megan says, 'is that Penny Reynolds brought the Lopezes down here and introduced them. And whatever her scheme was, Marion reckons Greg was complicit. We need to talk to Reynolds again.'

'So what are we looking at?' says Collins. 'Barry rows with Elena Lopez, so they kidnap him and shoot him?'

'Probably,' says Megan.

'What about Greg?' says Slater. 'Elena whacks him too? We haven't yet identified the prints on the murder weapon. Are they going to be hers if we can ever get hold of her?'

'But why?' says Ingram. 'If Greg was part of the scheme and it was running smoothly, why would she do that? This was a very lucrative business for them. They'd gone to a lot of trouble to set it all up. Arguably it's Greg's death that put a spanner in the works. Barry got difficult. Then they had to deal with him, take the boats and make a run for it. The last bit makes sense but not Elena and Greg.'

'Villains fall out,' says Slater. 'Perhaps Greg started to demand a bigger slice of the profits?'

'Yeah,' says Ingram. 'That's certainly another way to look at it.'

'Perhaps the argument wasn't about the boats, it was about the flats,' says Megan.

Slater frowns. 'Okay, go on.'

'Well,' says Megan. 'If Lopez and his sons brought furniture for the show flat, maybe they had money in that business too?'

'I'll buy that,' says Ingram. 'If the Lopezes had put money into the flats and Greg was trying to screw them, that could've precipitated a row.'

Brittney comes over. She hovers, waiting for Slater's attention.

'I think we've got a possible match, boss,' she says to Slater. 'We've slowed down the first lot of footage from the harbour on Wednesday night, early hours of Thursday morning We're fairly sure the older bloke who walked down the pontoon is Javier Lopez. You see him walk past the *Seamew*—'

'So he was coming from the other boat, the *Seahawk*?' says Slater.

'That's the assumption,' says Brittney. 'But the camera doesn't cover the far end of the pontoon, so it's still an assumption.'

'What about Sunday night? Did they come for the boats? Do we know that yet?' says Megan. She's aware of the impatience in her own voice. Her colleagues are working flat out. She knows this but it doesn't help. The window of opportunity to arrest these people is closing fast.

'You want us to go back to the Sunday night footage now?' says Brittney to Slater. She sounds weary.

'Yeah, but take a break first,' says Slater. 'You must all be getting square-eyed.'

Brittney nods and retreats to the techies' corner.

Slater turns to Megan. 'And you take a break too. Go home. Get some sleep.' She looks at Ingram. 'It's going to take time to crack through all the material we've got.'

'Okay,' says Ingram. 'What do you want from me?'

Slater's lips are pursed, she glances at Megan then back to him. 'Make sure she gets something to eat.'

Megan smiles to herself. Even when she means well Slater can come over like a prissy headteacher.

CHAPTER FIFTY-FIVE

Tuesday, 7.45 p.m.

Megan lounges full length in the sunken bath. Ingram's hotel bathroom is huge and faced with marble. The taps are chrome and chunky. It all dates from another era. The nearest thing Megan has ever seen to it was an old-fashioned Turkish bathhouse in London.

Ingram connected his phone to the sound system, selected some mellow music and left her to it. There's even a dimmer switch on the recessed lighting. Megan isn't used to the luxury of hotel living or any luxury really. About ten years ago she treated her sister to a spa weekend. But apart from that she has nothing to compare it with.

On the drive from Plymouth they spoke little. They shared a wry chuckle over Slater's awkward manner. But Ingram pointed out she was being kind and acknowledging Megan's important contribution to the inquiry. A good manager takes care of their staff.

Megan tops up the hot water and lets the tension seep out of her. It's not an easy task. Her brain is still nattering with questions she feels she has to answer. She's finding it hard to adjust to being a team player. But maybe that takes time. She always feels burdened by the responsibility of getting the job done, or taking care of others. She finds it hard to remember a time when her life wasn't like this. After her father left and her mother started to crumble, Megan stepped up to the plate. And it's been her default setting ever since.

When she finally climbs out of the tub her whole body, from the pores of her skin to the soles of her feet, feels warm and open. Ingram is sitting at his laptop. He turns and smiles at her.

'You look more comfortable,' he says.

'I can't remember the last time I had a bath,' she replies. 'Well, I have a shower every day to keep clean…'

He laughs. 'And you swim in the sea.'

She looks at him. The thought she can't get out of her head is, *Why is this man being so nice to me? What does he want? Sex? Probably.* She remembers her mother saying, in one of her rare lucid phases, 'When you meet a bloke always ask yourself this: what's it going to cost me?'

Megan's father cost her mother everything. Her health, her sanity, her happiness. Then years later he turned up with another family, behaving like a responsible adult instead of the selfish arsehole he was. Megan thought about it but decided not to forgive him. They haven't spoken since.

She scans Danny Ingram. Divorced, but then so is she. Left his wife and child. Does that automatically make him an arsehole?

'What are you thinking?' he asks.

'You don't want to know,' she replies.

'Well, Slater told me to feed you, so I've ordered room service. It's nothing fancy. But I'm reliably informed that the hotel dining room is like an episode of *Fawlty Towers*.'

'Probably best to give it a miss then. Also means I don't have to dress for dinner.'

A waiter wheels in dinner on a trolley and leaves them to it. It's locally caught sea bass, salad and a bottle of white wine. Megan finds she's surprisingly hungry.

After a couple of attempts at other topics they drift back to discussing the case.

'What do you think the chances are of nicking the Lopezes?' says Megan.

'Slim,' he replies.

'Why?'

'This is a slick operation. They've thought it all through. They don't strike me as stupid people.'

'Pretty stupid to fall out with Greg,' says Megan.

'If in fact they did.'

'What if Greg was having a thing with Elena?' she says. 'Lovers' tiff. She simply lost it and brained him with a hammer.'

Ingram chuckles. 'Remind me not to fall out with you.'

'Come on, Danny, smart people don't always do the smart thing. Emotions become involved. Anger being the one that most often leads to murder.'

'I liked your idea about the flats,' he replies. 'I gather it's a very upmarket development so he would've needed investors. He could've taken the unwise decision to try and shaft them. But what would Penny have said about that?'

'Penny's the one I can't make sense of,' says Megan. 'She knew her sister had a crappy marriage and she does seem to be trying to protect her. But then she does all this stuff with Greg.'

He smiles. 'You've got a sister,' he says. 'You know what a tangled web it can be.'

They drink the wine and once the bottle is empty, they make love in its afterglow. Megan is extremely tired and, sinking into the opulence of the king-sized bed, she's soon asleep.

It's still dark when she wakes abruptly. Ingram has switched on the torch on his phone so he can see to get dressed.

'I was hoping not to disturb you,' he says.

She peers at him. 'What's going on?'

'Garcia called me. Some kind of incident in the Channel last night. I don't know the details. But a fishing trawler pulled two half drowned illegal migrants out of the water. They're bringing them into Berrycombe.'

Megan throws back the covers. 'Wait for me. I'm coming too.'

CHAPTER FIFTY-SIX

Wednesday, 5.50 a.m.

Megan and Ingram are on the quayside in Berrycombe when the trawler comes in. Dawn is leaching into the eastern sky. Vish is directing the paramedics, who've just arrived in an ambulance. Garcia is talking to the coastguard beside their Mitsubishi Land Cruiser.

Even though it's early, the port is bustling. It's the busiest part of the day. Refrigerated lorries are arriving and manoeuvring to load up. Boats small and large are landing their catch and white-coated owners, agents and fish merchants are milling around waiting for the fish market auction to start at six a.m.

The police presence attracts a few curious glances but no more than that.

As the trawler edges alongside the dock to tie up, Megan sees the two forlorn figures crouched on the deck, wrapped in yellow oilskins. Two males. They both look young and scared. Vish jumps aboard and starts to talk to the skipper. The gangplank is slotted into place by the trawler crew. Vish beckons the paramedics who follow him on board.

Megan and Ingram watch and wait while they all do their jobs. Garcia joins them.

'Coastguard were contacted by Border Force,' she says. "I'm trying to get a patch through to the captain of HMC *Fleetwood*, the coastal patrol vessel in the Channel last night. At the moment we've only got a rough idea of what might have happened.'

'Were they in a dinghy?' says Ingram.

'No,' says Garcia. 'The trawler crew pulled them out of the water. All they had were life jackets. They were lucky. It was a relatively calm sea. The story seems to be *Fleetwood* had two unidentified boats come up on its radar. It tried to contact them and get them to heave to.'

'Heave to?' says Megan.

'I've got an uncle who sails,' says Garcia. 'Basically in boat terms *Fleetwood* tried to pull them over. But they were quite a distance away and they made a run for it. Back towards the French coast.'

'And we think these two came from those boats?' says Ingram.

'Yeah,' says Garcia. 'Unless they were trying to swim the Channel.'

The paramedics have replaced the oilskins with silver space blankets. They are helping their charges ashore.

'Let's go and talk to them,' says Ingram.

As Megan, Ingram and Garcia approach, the young men turn to face them. Their heads are bowed, their eyes full of fear.

'Are they all right to talk to us?' Ingram asks one of the paramedics.

'Bit hypothermic,' she replies. 'But they seem fine.'

One of the young men steps forward. He's a teenager; wispy traces of beard, wild, dark eyes.

'Are you police?' he says. There's a tremor in his voice but his English is good. 'We are Kurds. From Syria. We wish for asylum.'

'What's your name?' says Ingram.

'I am Adnan Ghazi, sir.' The boy dips his head in deference. 'My cousin is Omar Ghazi.'

'How old are you, Adnan?' says Ingram.

'I am seventeen, sir. Omar is sixteen.'

'Well, Adnan, we have a process for asylum claims and you will be able to apply for that. But we are the police and we need you to tell us what happened last night on your journey here.'

Adnan shoots a nervous glance at his cousin. The other boy stares down at his feet. He has one sock on, his other foot is bare. They both seem reluctant to speak. Megan wonders at the desperation that has forced them to make such a trip. They're in shock. Who wouldn't be? And hardly more than children.

'Whatever you tell us about how you came here will not affect your asylum claim,' she says. 'We just want to know how you ended up in the water.'

The boys exchange looks again. The younger, Omar, seems close to tears. He meets Megan's gaze nervously. She smiles and says, 'Do you speak English too, Omar?'

The boy nods. 'My father say we must learn. We must come here. He pay extra to keep us safe.'

'But it all went wrong, didn't it? Tell us what happened.'

Omar's lip trembles.

'It'll be okay,' says Megan.

'They have gun,' he blurts it out. 'They shout. And shout. Everyone panic. One woman they shoot, push over side. Shout more. So then we all jump. People so frightened, they jump. We swim.'

'How many boats?' says Ingram.

'Two,' says Adnan.

'And how many people in each boat?'

'Maybe ten adults. In our boat four, five children.'

Megan feels a lump in her throat. Two survivors from more than twenty people forced into the sea? The horror of the whole thing is hard to imagine but it's beginning to dawn on her.

'And they threw everyone over the side?' she says. *Like pirates.*

Adnan nods, wipes his nose with the back of his fist.

'Do you know why they did this?' says Ingram. His tone is tight and professional. He's holding it together. But Megan can feel the anger fizzing off him.

'They see the patrol boat,' says the boy. 'They don't want to be caught.'

Ingram turns to Garcia.

'Show him the picture.'

Garcia pulls out her phone, clicks through to Javier Lopez's mugshot. She holds it out.

'You know this man?'

Adnan nods. He dips his head to hide his tears.

CHAPTER FIFTY-SEVEN

Wednesday, 7.15 a.m.

Megan drives back to Plymouth with Vish. She remains in a daze. Two murders have suddenly escalated to possibly two dozen. The casual brutality of it is something she's finding hard to get her head around.

She watches Vish; he grips the steering wheel, his jaw rippling with tension. Anger is something they're all feeling. But for Danny Ingram it was also an explosion of guilt.

Just before they parted company in Berrycombe he turned to her and said, 'I should've stopped these people, Megan. That's my job. It's why I'm here. But I took my eye off the fucking ball because I was having too good a time with you.'

She watched him and Garcia walk away. She wanted to argue with his conclusion but he gave her no opportunity.

As they pull into a parking space outside the MCT office, they see Slater locking her car. She waits for them by the main door. There's no preamble.

'You spoke to these two boys?'

'Yes,' says Megan. 'They've been taken to A & E to be checked over by a doctor but the NCA's bringing in a special interviewer to debrief them properly.'

'Any idea how many bodies we should be looking for?'

'Could be over twenty, boss. Including some children.'

'For Chrissake!' says Slater. 'What is wrong with these people? They just tossed them all overboard?'

'They got spotted by HMC *Fleetwood*, decided to dump their cargo and make a run for it. That's the theory.'

'Did *Fleetwood* pick up any survivors?'

'NCA did have a conversation with the captain over the radio,' says Vish. 'They weren't aware of what happened. They were too far off.'

Slater sighs. 'And this was Lopez?'

'One of the boys ID'd him,' says Megan.

Slater heads into the building. 'Superintendent Barker will be here at nine,' she says briskly over her shoulder. 'He's already initiated a search and rescue operation liaising with the coastguard.'

Megan and Vish follow Slater up the stairs.

'I want every trace we can find of these people,' she adds. 'Every scrap of evidence against them.'

In the incident room, there are discarded coffee cups and pizza boxes, the evidence of an all-nighter. But Brittney and Kitty are the only ones left in the techie corner. Most of the other desks are empty. Across the room by the window Jim Collins is sitting in one of two battered armchairs, drinking coffee and reading the *Daily Mail*. He ignores Megan and Vish when they walk in.

Vish wanders over to join Brittney and Kitty.

Megan heads for the coffee station. Yet she finds herself eavesdropping on their conversation.

'How was it?' Brittney asks Vish.

'To tell you the truth,' he says wearily, 'it was fucked.'

He towers over Brittney by more than six inches. But he leans forward and lays his head on her shoulder. She strokes his hair to comfort him.

Kitty rummages under her desk and comes up with a cardboard box. 'We saved you a doughnut,' she says. 'It's the one with peanut butter filling.'

He raises his head and smiles. 'Awesome.'

He takes the doughnut from the box and demolishes it in three bites.

Megan sips her coffee and watches. She's reluctant to gatecrash their circle. She knows she doesn't belong. She glances across the room at Collins. His face is completely concealed by the newspaper. His hand reaches out to lift his coffee mug. She wonders why he's even there. He doesn't appear to be doing anything.

Megan thinks about the two Kurdish boys; an example of the advantages of being young and strong and lucky. They may find other survivors but she doubts it.

It's about to become a day of bodies and media and mayhem.

The door opens and Slater strides into the room. 'Right,' she says. 'Let's have a review of what we've got.'

Brittney hands Vish a tissue to wipe cream from his mouth. Collins folds his paper and regards the room with a jaundiced eye.

Brittney steps forward and says, 'We've got a timeline for Sunday evening, boss.'

'Okay, let's hear it,' says Slater.

'Barry Porter left the *Seamew* at 7.34 p.m. Nothing happened for three quarters of an hour, then at 8.14 p.m. the Lopezes turned up. Javier and his two sons. The sons took the *Seamew*. That left its moorings first. We got some additional footage from the outer harbour. The *Seamew* and the *Seahawk* passed the outer wall at 8.31 p.m. and 8.34 p.m. respectively.'

'No sign of Elena?' says Slater.

'She didn't come down to the marina,' says Kitty. 'But we figured if they arrived at 8.14 she may have dropped them off.'

'Surely there was an information marker on their vehicle to track it on ANPR,' says Slater. 'Didn't it ping in the control room?'

'Well, yes,' says Brittney. 'It was logged but they were short-handed so there was no follow-up.'

Slater huffs. 'You mean we could've stopped these people?'

Megan watches Slater's face. *A window of opportunity. Missed.* The realisation they could've stopped this is searing.

'As soon as we realised she dropped them off at 8.14, we went to the ANPR and tracked it back,' says Kitty. 'We took it back through Torquay and up towards Dartmoor, a similar route to the one they took before. Which suggests they came from the same place.'

'And that's the problem,' says Brittney. 'The timelines do and don't fit.'

Slater sighs. Megan can feel her confusion and annoyance. 'You need to explain that,' she says.

'The Lopezes took the boats on Sunday night, that's clear,' she says. 'Ample time to cross the Channel, make a fresh pick-up and return last night. That's the bit that does work.'

'Is the bit that doesn't work them kidnapping and killing Barry Porter?' says Megan.

'Yeah,' says Brittney. 'They didn't have time. Barry left. We don't know where his car was parked and we don't know where he went.'

'You couldn't track it back from where it ended up with him dead in the back?' says Slater.

'We might eventually. But it ended up completely off the grid,' says Kitty. 'So we've got a gap. Tracking back how it got on the moors is guesswork.'

'Okay,' says Slater. 'Carry on.'

'The thing we do know,' says Brittney, 'is where the Lopezes were. At 7.30 they were clocked on the A38. And they just continued towards Torquay.'

'So someone else got hold of Barry Porter?' says Slater.

'Elena was still around after she dropped them off,' says Megan. 'Where did she go?'

'He was a big bloke,' says Vish. 'It's hard to imagine her doing it on her own.'

'I don't know,' says Megan. 'She lures him somewhere, pulls a gun on him, makes him get in the back of his own car, drives it up onto the moors, shoots him. It's doable.'

'How does she get away though?' says Collins. 'She's up on the moors with a dead body and no vehicle to escape in?'

Megan meets his eye; he gives her a sour grin. He's right.

Slater's phone buzzes. She checks it and sighs. 'Three bodies washed up at Broadsands Bay. It won't be long before the media gets hold of this, so please be aware.'

'What do you want us to prioritise, ma'am?' says Collins.

'I should've thought that's obvious,' says Slater. 'Find this bloody woman!'

CHAPTER FIFTY-EIGHT

Wednesday, 8.05 a.m.

Megan wants to go alone with Vish but Collins is adamant, he's coming with them. Penny Reynolds needs to understand they mean business. Much as she dislikes his bullishness, Megan has to admit to herself that, in this situation, arriving mob-handed might work. They take uniformed back-up in a separate squad car and let them lead with blues and twos. The squad car snakes its way through the morning traffic; Vish follows, Megan is relegated to the back seat again.

As they turn into the driveway of the Porters' house, Collins glances over his shoulder and says, 'You've dealt with this woman, Megan, you take the lead.'

'Fine,' she replies in a neutral tone. She doesn't want any more aggro.

Throughout the journey Brittney has been updating her with the body count. The initial three have turned into five more, including a child, all carried in on the morning's high tide. She checks her phone one last time before getting out of the car. Brittney's latest text reads: *TV vans outside. Shit and fan connecting!*

One of the uniformed officers is hammering on the Porters' front door. It's opened by Aidan.

Collins presents his ID and is first into the house. They find Yvonne and Penny in the kitchen having breakfast with the other three children.

Megan watches as they absorb the effect of having five cops, two in uniform, three in plain clothes, stomp into their kitchen.

'Mrs Porter,' says Collins. 'Perhaps you could take your children into another room while we speak to your sister?' No conciliation. The subtext is: follow instructions now. It has the desired effect. Penny Reynolds is rattled. She puts down her coffee cup and her hand is shaking.

'The children are having their breakfast. Is this necessary?' she says. But there's little conviction in her voice.

'If you wouldn't mind,' says Collins politely. But the point is already made.

Yvonne gathers up the twins, Aidan takes Imogen's hand and they disappear.

It gives Penny time to adjust. She's wearing a silk dressing gown, pale peach. It looks expensive. She draws it across her chest and tightens the belt.

'This is really outrageous,' she says. 'I think I'm going to call my lawyer.'

Megan steps forward. 'Which you're entitled to do, of course,' she says. 'But first you might like to pick up that remote and turn on the television news.' Megan points to the screen mounted on a wall bracket next to the fridge. 'Because how helpful you are to us now,' she adds, 'will probably determine whether or not you go to prison.'

Penny stares at her for a moment then grabs the handset.

She clicks onto the BBC's rolling news channel, where the inset behind the newsreader is a panning shot of Broadsands Bay.

'—our reporter, Clare Carter, is live in South Devon,' says the newsreader. 'Clare, can you tell us more?'

On screen the reporter holds a microphone in front of her. In the background flashing lights, ambulances and police cars are visible.

'The first bodies were discovered by an early morning dog walker,' says Clare Carter. 'But they were just a hint of the terrible tragedy now unfolding here on these beautiful Devon beaches. Details are still being pieced together by the police. But we understand an incident took place in the Channel last night. Two luxury yachts, each believed to be carrying around a dozen illegal migrants, many of them women and children, were involved. They were spotted by a Border Force vessel and, fearing they would be apprehended, the smugglers forced all the migrants overboard into the water in order to escape.'

The reporter turns and behind her, on screen, Megan gets a glimpse of Danny Ingram, wearing blue vinyls, talking to a senior uniformed officer. The reporter pushes forward against the police cordon and shoves her microphone at Ingram. 'Can you give us any more details about the bodies you've found so far?'

Ingram waves her away with a hand. 'No, sorry.' Megan catches a glimpse of his face. Frowning, severe, dismissive. There's no trace of the pain she knows is there.

She turns her attention back to Penny Reynolds. Reynolds's gaze is fixed on the screen. She's standing very still, her face a blank mask. She seems to recollect herself and clicks the television off.

'Quite awful,' she says. 'Though I'm unsure what this has to do with me.'

'The boats involved,' says Megan, 'were the *Seamew* and the *Seahawk*, owned by the company that you set up using Greg and Barry Porter as a front and cash from Javier and Elena Lopez. Officers from the National Crime Agency are already accessing company records and tracing the offshore accounts used to channel the funds. My guess is that Mr Henderson's firm will be advising your employers to co-operate fully because once they see what the Lopezes have done, they will throw you under the bus.'

Reynolds reaches out and places a hand on the kitchen counter to steady herself. Megan takes her by the elbow and guides her to one of the high stools. 'Sit down, Penny,' she says.

Penny sits down.

'Now,' says Megan. 'We know Elena Lopez is still in this country. Where is she?'

Penny shakes her head. 'I never thought,' she says, 'I never imagined—'

'Look at me, Penny. Where is she? You're smart enough to know that you have a choice here. You protect these people now and you become an accessory to murder.'

Penny swallows hard and looks at Megan. 'I don't know where she is this minute. But they've been renting a holiday cottage on Dartmoor.'

'The address?' says Megan.

'I'll need my phone to look it up. It's in my bedroom. I put it on to charge.'

'We'll fetch it,' says Megan. She nods to Vish.

'Top of the stairs, second room,' says Penny.

Vish goes to get the phone. Jim Collins walks round the kitchen counter and stands directly in front of Penny.

'Holiday cottage?' he says sarcastically. 'You sure about that?'

Penny's gaze flickers. 'I don't know what you mean.'

'Who owns it?' says Collins.

'I don't know,' she replies. 'Some company, I suppose.'

She's leaning back in her stool, trying to edge away from Collins. He's certainly intimidating her. Why? Megan has an uncanny sense that he knows something. He's working to an agenda of his own.

'I think you're lying,' says Collins.

Megan is about to intervene. But Penny starts to cry. They've witnessed enough tears from Yvonne. But from Penny it seems unexpected.

'Okay,' Penny says, wiping the tears away with her hand. 'It's someone the Lopezes know. Her name is Sally Doyle. She arranged it for them. That's the truth, I swear.'

Collins's smile is ghostly but smug. He just nods and says, 'You were cautioned when you spoke to us before. That still applies. You need to put some clothes on and come with us.'

CHAPTER FIFTY-NINE

Wednesday, 8.30 a.m.

Megan follows Collins out of the house. He walks across the drive, takes out a packet of cigarettes and lights up.

'Hang on, Jim,' she says. 'Am I missing something here?'

He inhales, turns and looks at her. 'Sally Doyle. AKA Mrs Dennis Bridger. I know you're not keen on my hunches, but try this one for size. The Lopezes didn't kill Barry Porter, they contracted it out to someone with local knowledge. Loads easier.'

'How do the Lopezes know Bridger?'

Collins takes a long drag, blows a plume of smoke.

'I know you don't think I'm much of a detective,' he says. 'Nowadays it's all high-tech gadgets, face recognition software and drones. But I can still do my job.'

'I know,' says Megan. *Jennings was right, they both have something to prove.*

'Last night I went digging in the archives,' says Collins. 'Read up on the life and times of Dennis Bridger. Few years ago, before his last stretch inside, Dennis went on the lam down on the Spanish Costas. Used to be a popular hideaway for his class of villain. To make ends meet he did some work for a local drug gang. Run by guess who? Javier Lopez.'

'What made you look at Bridger?'

'Brittney told me about the problems with timings. They were trying to figure it out, make it fit and they couldn't. She's like a little terrier, that lass. She's turning into a bloody good cop.'

'I know that too,' says Megan.

'It was clear to me the Lopezes needed help. Had to be someone local.' He gives her a wary look, then he says, 'And then I thought about Ted.'

'Did Ted try and get in touch with you too?'

Collins sighs, grinds his cigarette underfoot.

'You were right to be concerned. He sent me quite a desperate email on Monday, which I ignored. Then, after he turned up dead, I looked at it again and discovered an attachment, a video. Bridger's place was supposed to be under surveillance. What the dozy sods didn't realise was that Dennis was climbing over the back wall. Ted realised and he filmed it. He filmed a woman picking Bridger up in a Mini Cooper on Sunday morning and again on Monday.'

'You think it was Elena using a different vehicle?'

'Think about it,' says Collins. 'Once he was on the loose he was free to go after Barry on Sunday evening. Monday night, I think he probably went after Ted. Somehow he must've clocked him.'

'He did this on his own?'

'No. He's got plenty of contacts round here. Thugs he can call on. His problem was just getting in and out of his place without being seen and moving around without being tracked. So, ditch the phone and use a different vehicle. Easy.'

Megan finds she's playing catch-up but it does all make sense. The drug-smuggling business runs on cross-border connections and hook-ups. It's not that surprising that criminals like Lopez and Bridger know each other.

'You sure it was Elena?' she says.

He pulls out his phone. 'Take a look at the video. You tell me.'

He finds the clip and hands Megan the phone. Ted must have filmed it through the hedge of an adjacent garden. The wall at the back of Bridger's house is made of rough stone. It's high but he's over it in a trice. Ted pans across to the car and through the driver's window a woman's face is visible.

Megan scrutinises it carefully.

'Shit,' she says. 'It is her. Did you speak to Slater about any of this?'

'Haven't had the chance,' he replies.

But he did have the chance.

Megan wonders whether to call him on this. He gives her a surly look. He must've guessed what she's thinking but he's a man on a mission. He wants to be the one to crack the case and after his earlier mistakes Megan can see why.

Vish comes out of the house to join them.

'I've got the address, boss,' he says to Collins. 'You want me to call for back-up?'

Collins chuckles. 'What?' he says. 'The three of us can't arrest one woman?'

Yep, this will be his vindication.

'We don't know what we're walking into,' says Megan. 'And given what you've just told me, I think we should request armed back-up.'

'And how long's that going to take? Bloody ages,' says Collins. He grins at Megan. 'Thought you were the one who gets impatient with proper procedure. Don't be such a wuss. We'll call it in on the way.' He turns to Vish. 'Tell the two PCs to take Reynolds in, then let's get cracking. We don't want to get there and find her gone, do we?'

Megan has to admit he's got a point. This could be their one chance to get Elena Lopez. Even half an hour's delay could risk losing her. *The window of opportunity. Missed.*

CHAPTER SIXTY

Wednesday, 9.15 a.m.

Vish is following the satnav but Collins lives in Ashburton and knows the southern part of Dartmoor well. He starts to direct Vish. Megan checks her watch. She's feeling nervous. Their armed back-up is at least forty-five minutes away. On the phone Laura Slater has been precise in her instructions. Once they get there, they should remain concealed and wait. This should be a firearms arrest.

Jim Collins seems to be in a strange, elegiac mood. As they drive up onto the moors he points out landmarks. He sounds weirdly like a guide on a tour bus.

'I used to walk here all the time with my wife,' he says. 'We'd tramp for miles, all weathers, she loved it.'

Megan catches Vish's eye in the rear-view mirror. He's finding the DI's manner odd too.

The road winds across treeless upland then gradually narrows to a track and Collins says, 'Slow down. I think there's a turn-off coming up on the right. It dips right down into quite a hidden little valley. I'm pretty certain that's where this place is.'

Vish looks at the sat nav. 'I can't tell a bloody thing from this,' he says.

'I think we should leave the car here,' says Collins. 'Approach on foot. She'll hear us otherwise.'

'Slater said to wait,' says Megan.

'We haven't even confirmed she's here,' says Collins. 'You want the cavalry to come thundering in and we find the place empty? Slater's not going to thank you for that. Let's just do a recce.'

Megan wants to argue. The problem is he's right. They get out of the car. Collins leads the way.

The path down into the wooded valley is steep and rutted, more of a cart track just wide enough for a single vehicle. There's a sound of rushing water at the bottom of the ravine but its source is invisible behind the trees. The further down the hill they go, the denser the woods become. Sunlight dapples down on them through the canopy of the trees.

'This is such a cool place,' whispers Vish.

Megan nods. It's idyllic and secluded. It's no wonder that the NCA's search drew a blank and even the drones couldn't find it.

A long stone building comes into view between the trees. As they get closer they see that an old terrace of three workmen's cottages has been knocked into one. It sits next to a rushing stream, water bouncing over boulders. Megan pictures the image in the holiday brochures; the perfect romantic retreat.

Next to the main house is an open-sided carport. A black Range Rover Discovery is parked under it and next to it, a Mini Cooper S.

'I'll check the reg of the Discovery,' says Megan. She pulls out her phone, clicks it on and sighs. 'No signal,' she says.

'There won't be down here,' says Collins. He points through the trees. 'Let's do a loop. We should be able to get down and across the stream and along the side of the property without being seen from the house.'

'Unless someone comes out,' says Vish.

'What if there's a dog?' says Megan.

It seems unlikely there would be. But something in Collins's whole manner is making her extremely nervous. He'd made the connection between Bridger and Lopez last night but failed to tell Slater. Why would he keep such information to himself? Megan wonders what his agenda is. Is he hoping to come out of this the hero? Ted Jennings went after Bridger in a bid to redeem himself. Is Collins hoping to do something similar? Is this all about male ego? Proving he can still cut it. Or something else? *A corrupt cop covering his tracks?*

Collins scrabbles down the steep slope, weaving between the trees. It's easy to lose your footing and a couple of times he slides and ends up on his backside. His face is pale and sweaty. Vish follows, more agile.

He turns to Megan, bringing up the rear, and whispers, 'Is our back-up even going to find this fucking place?'

'Probably not,' Megan replies.

They reach the stream. An old stone bridge with a single arch takes the track across it to the front of the property. But Collins crosses twenty metres upstream using the boulders as stepping stones. At one point he slips and Vish grabs his arm to steady him. Megan follows, wondering at the craziness of the whole escapade. All they really needed to do was block the access, make sure no one could leave and wait for support to arrive. She feels she should do something. But what? Collins is the DI and therefore in charge. And they still don't know that Elena is definitely here.

The trees overhanging the stream are willow and alder, their barks overspread with lichen. The valley bottom is a glossy carpet of green. As Megan climbs up from the stream she reaches for handholds and feels the soft dampness of the moss on the rocks.

Collins pushes stealthily through a sea of ferns to the side of the carport. They stop and listen: birdsong and water. He points to the carport and they creep into it.

Vish pulls on his blue vinyls, slips down one side of it to the door of the Discovery. He tries it. It's unlocked. He opens it carefully, scans inside, clicks open the glove compartment, opens the central console. He lifts out a phone, holds it up for the others to see. He puts it in a plastic evidence bag.

Collins and Megan are the other side, next to the Mini. She hands him a pair of blue vinyls from her pocket. He pulls them on, opens the passenger door of the Mini. He searches the glove compartment, then reaches under the front seat. He smiles and lifts out a nine-millimetre Glock handgun. *Could it be the gun that killed Barry Porter?*

'Bingo,' he mouths. 'Got an evidence bag?'

Megan hesitates. They should leave it for a firearms officer and CSI to recover it properly.

'C'mon,' whispers Collins. 'Could be vital evidence. We can't risk leaving it.'

He's right. Megan holds open a plastic evidence bag. Collins puts the gun into it then takes the bag and stows it in his jacket pocket.

Next to the carport is a small space then the side of the building with a half-glazed door. It looks as if it goes into the kitchen.

Collins points to Megan and mouths 'back' then to himself and Vish. They'll take the front.

Megan steels herself. They're relying on the element of surprise.

CHAPTER SIXTY-ONE

Wednesday, 9.32 a.m.

Megan peers through the glass door. Shaker-style units, a butler's sink, a ceramic hob and a microwave. The door of the microwave is open and next to it is a plate of sizzling, freshly cooked bacon. Megan can smell the delicious aroma. Her stomach growls. She turns the door handle slowly. It opens and she steps quickly into the room.

A woman is standing with her back to the door, buttering a plate of toast. She turns abruptly.

'*Que mierda?*' she exclaims.

Megan gets her first sight of Elena Lopez close up. She's a little faded at the edges but still a classic beauty. A mane of dark hair flecked with grey, perfect cheekbones, luminous eyes. The snatched pictures of her don't do her justice. It's easy to see how Greg Porter could've fallen for her.

Megan pulls out her warrant card. 'I'm Detective Sergeant Thomas and, Elena Lopez, you're under arrest.'

Elena raises her eyebrows and sighs. 'Really?' she says. 'You mind if I finish my breakfast?' Her accent is hardly noticeable and the tone full of disdain.

'Are you alone in the house?' says Megan.

Elena tilts her head and takes a bite out of a slice of toast. 'Come and see for yourself,' she says, beckoning.

Megan follows her down a short passageway to the sitting room.

Two men are in the process of carrying several large suitcases towards the front door.

'Look,' says Elena. 'We have a visitor.'

The younger of the two men is scrawny with a pock-marked face and a vacant expression. *A local lowlife being paid by the hour?* The other is Dennis Bridger.

Bridger is a small man but he stands squarely like a fighting cock, glares at Megan and cracks his knuckles.

'A fucking copper?' says Bridger scornfully. 'You lose your way, love?'

'I think at the very least you're in breach of your licence, Mr Bridger.'

'Yeah? And what you gonna do about it?'

'I suggest you open the front door.'

Bridger opens the door. Vish is standing there, arms folded, waiting. He marches straight in followed by Collins. It's a standard plan of attack and, with luck, Bridger will assume that they're not alone.

'Morning, Mr Bridger,' says Collins. 'What are you up to?'

Bridger smirks and raises his palms in surrender. 'I'm released on licence,' he says. 'But I'm doing nothing wrong. This place is a holiday let that belongs to my wife and we're just helping this lady with her bags 'cause she's off home today.'

Collins nods. 'Okay. What if I ask where were you on Sunday evening and did you shoot Barry Porter in the head and leave him in the back of his car?'

Megan is keeping her eye on Elena. She's finished her toast and is dusting the crumbs off her fingertips. She's hyper vigilant but the sudden arrival of the police doesn't seem to have fazed her.

Bridger guffaws, 'Oh what? Is that why you're here, to fit me up with some random murder? Well, all I've got to say to you, mate, is no fucking comment. And I want my lawyer.' He folds his arms.

'Yeah, I thought you might say that,' Collins replies. He takes the Glock out of his pocket. 'I think this is probably the gun you used. We may find your prints on it. But you're a professional, aren't you, Dennis? You don't make rookie mistakes like that. You've murdered enough people to know.'

Collins opens the evidence bag and takes out the gun. Megan stares at him in disbelief. *What's he playing at? More macho bullshit? Is this why he insisted on bagging the gun?*

Bridger glares at him. 'Seriously?'

Collins pulls back the slider and checks the chamber. 'Nice gun this, the Glock. I always liked them. Good safety system, means you can keep a round chambered in case you get taken by surprise.'

Megan's stomach lurches. She has to stop this.

'Jim—' she says.

'I'd be careful what you're up to with that, mate,' says Bridger. But Megan notices him edging backwards. He can sense the volatility in Collins too.

She's at least three metres away. She takes a step forward.

'Stand back, sergeant,' Collins says sharply. 'I know what I'm doing. You may think I'm a broken-down old fart, but I did ten years in the Met's tactical firearms unit back in the day.'

He raises the gun abruptly and points it straight at Bridger. Megan glances at Vish, who's staring open-mouthed. He's further away than her. They exchange panicked looks.

Oh shit. He wouldn't, would he?

'We were taught only to go for a head shot as a last resort. Is this a last resort, do you think?'

'Jim,' says Megan. 'Stop it! You can't do this. Lower the gun.'

Bridger's expression has changed to one of real apprehension. He's going red in the face, but he says, 'Nah, I know your game. You're not going to intimidate me—'

'That's not my intention,' says Collins calmly. 'My intention is to demonstrate to Mrs Lopez that saying "no comment" is not the sensible option here.'

'Jim, that's enough,' says Megan. 'Lower the gun. Now. Please.'

'I think a head shot is kinder,' says Collins.

Megan moves forward. She has no idea what she's going to do. *Grab his arm?* 'Jim, no!' she shouts.

But she's too far away.

Collins smiles and squeezes the trigger. The bullet hits Dennis Bridger squarely in the middle of his forehead and sends him flying backwards. He's dead before he hits the ground.

CHAPTER SIXTY-TWO

For several seconds no one moves. Megan stares in horror at Jim Collins. She never thought he'd do it. The look on his face is serene. A kind of release. She did suspect him of being corrupt, of helping Bridger years ago. Perhaps Ted did too. But that's completely wrong. He's a man driven by righteous anger. And despair.

'Give me the gun, Jim,' she says, holding out her hand.

But Collins steps away from her. 'I'm not finished yet,' he replies.

Megan glances at Vish. He's not close enough to grab Collins either and Collins could turn the gun on him. She can't risk it.

Bridger's corpse is sprawled on its back with blood puddling round the head. His hired hand is cowering in the corner. But Elena Lopez is standing and staring at Collins.

Collins steps backwards, repositioning himself so his back is to the wall. Then he points the gun at Elena Lopez.

'Not a bad shot after all these years,' he says. 'So, Mrs Lopez, I hope none of that got lost in translation.'

Elena juts out her chin and glares at him. 'You gonna shoot me?' she says. 'Why?'

'You did murder Greg Porter, didn't you?'

'What?' she says in astonishment. 'No, I did not! Why would I do that?'

'And procure the murder of his father?'

'What's "procure"?' she says with a sneer. 'I don't procure nothing.'

Megan takes a deep breath and steps between Elena and Collins.

'You can't shoot her, Jim,' she says. 'And any statement she makes under these circumstances will be obtained under duress, so it's inadmissible.'

Collins huffs.

'Money, lawyers. It's all a fix,' he says. 'CPS only prosecute what they think they'll win. You realise she'll probably walk away from this. And we'll still be pulling bodies out of the water from her little family business. Doesn't that bother you?'

'Of course it bothers me. But this isn't the answer,' says Megan.

'Bridger got five years, he's out in less than three and gets to commit more murders. Ted was a good copper. And he was right. We should've done this properly. Instead we rely on a load of high-tech bloody gizmos while Bridger runs rings round us? I'm sick of it.'

'We try harder,' says Megan. 'We make a better case. We're the police, that's our job. We're not judge and jury. And we're certainly not executioner.'

Collins shakes his head. He's pale and sweating.

'Why are you standing there and protecting her, Megan?' he says. 'Stand aside. Let me finish the job.'

'I'm not protecting her. I'm trying to protect you, Jim. Becoming like them is not the answer. In your heart you know that. It's not easy, it never will be. But you didn't become a police officer to murder people. Did you? Think about this, I'm begging you. This is wrong.'

He shakes his head again and sighs. The energy and the fight seem to have drained out of him. He turns the gun over and offers it to her by the pistol grip.

'You'd better arrest me, sergeant,' he says.

CHAPTER SIXTY-THREE

Wednesday, 2.32 p.m.

Megan lounges back in her desk chair. She stares up at the ceiling. It's been patched and re-plastered in various places. She lets her eye wander over it. Traces of some old water damage maybe, a bodged rewiring job? After the adrenaline rush of the morning, she felt shaky. Now she's flat and lethargic.

Could she have stopped Collins? No one has asked her outright. But she can't stop asking herself. Did she see it coming? Bridger's death has relieved her of one anxiety. The link with Zac Yilmaz. With Bridger dead, she's safer. In the split seconds she had to decide, did she realise that? Did it make her hesitate? She has no answer. Only a secret feeling of guilt.

Brittney walks across the room and places a mug of coffee on the desk in front of her.

'I brought you a refill,' she says.

Her colleagues are taking care of her. Although Megan's not sure she needs any more caffeine.

'Cheers,' she says. 'What's happening?'

'Elena is still denying any involvement in Greg Porter's murder. She says they weren't in a relationship. It was a business connection. She and her husband were investors in the flat development.'

'What about the boats and the people smuggling?'

'Complete denial. She just came over to see the show flat. That's her line.'

'What does Slater think?'

'She's hoping Lopez's prints will match the ones on the murder weapon. Then we'll have grounds to hold her,' says Brittney.

Megan sighs. 'I don't think they will,' she says.

'Why not?'

'Collins accused her,' says Megan. 'Her denial was spontaneous. No one's that good a liar.'

'You sure?' says Brittney.

Megan sips her coffee. 'No. But usually when people lie, there's a moment of hesitation, even if it's just a beat. It's there. Before they deliver the lie.'

Brittney grins. 'You know so much stuff. I'm really envious. How did you learn it all?'

'I'm not sure that's true,' says Megan. 'You just pick up bits as you go along.'

Brittney continues to beam at her from behind the owl glasses.

'You been out with that bloke yet?' says Megan. 'What was his name?'

'Matt. We've texted. But I haven't really had any time off.'

'You should find time,' says Megan. 'The job can swallow your life.'

She gets up. Her limbs feel heavy. 'I need to talk to Slater. Oh, and thanks for the coffee.'

Megan finds Laura Slater in her office; she taps on the open door.

'You got a minute, boss?'

Slater smiles. 'Certainly. Come in and sit down. How are you feeling?'

'I'm okay.'

'You really should go home,' says Slater. There's concern in her voice.

'No need,' says Megan. She doesn't mention that it's easier for her to wind down here in the office, where she doesn't need to explain herself.

'I've had a word with Rob Barker,' says Slater. 'It seems clear that Dennis Bridger killed both Barry Porter and Ted Jennings. Certainly we're not looking for anyone else.'

'Do you think we'll ever prove that he killed Barry for the Lopezes?' says Megan.

Slater sighs. 'I doubt it. Also Jim Collins has been taken to Exeter to be interviewed. Totally different team, no connections here. They'll probably want to talk to you at some point.'

Megan nods. 'I'm sorry,' she says. 'I should've seen it coming.'

'I don't see how,' says Slater.

'He was on a mission. People who need to prove they're right are dangerous. Also... if Bridger killed Ted. I should've told you that Ted was up to something. But Jim said he'd do it and I didn't want to undermine him.'

'Megan, it's a judgement call. Collins was much closer to the edge than any of us realised. You did the best you could. Go home and take a break.'

'I will. But first I want you to let me have another crack at Penny Reynolds.'

'Why?' says Slater. 'She's been quite co-operative about how the boat business was set up and the money channelled from the Lopezes through her bank. I'm not sure if it's quite enough at the moment to charge Elena and hold her. But Danny Ingram's working on it.'

Ever since she returned to the office a niggling thought has been growing in Megan's mind.

'There's something in the triangle between Penny and her sister Yvonne, and Greg,' she says. 'Marion Porter reckons her son only married Yvonne because Penny rejected him. Did Penny encourage her nephew to confess because she thought Yvonne had killed

Greg? Or was there another reason? I think we're not seeing the whole picture.'

Slater tilts her head and frowns.

'Okay,' she says. 'Go for it.'

CHAPTER SIXTY-FOUR

Wednesday, 3.05 p.m.

Megan waits outside the interview room for Ingram and Garcia to emerge.

The door opens. Garcia is first out. She rubs Megan's arm and says, 'Hey, how you doing?'

Ingram joins her. He smiles. 'I hear you had an interesting morning,' he says.

'Bit too interesting,' she replies.

'Are you all right?' he says.

She meets his gaze but he immediately looks away. She realises he's reverted to professional mode. She'd love a hug. That would certainly help. But he has his hands in his pockets and an antsy look on his face. It gives the impression he's got things to do and being polite to her is a distraction.

'Yeah. I'm fine,' she says.

'I talked to Vish,' says Garcia. 'He says at one point it looked like Collins would shoot you too.'

'That's an exaggeration,' says Megan. 'I don't think he would have.'

'When a cop loses it like that, you never know,' says Ingram with a sigh.

Megan wishes Garcia would go away and give her a chance to talk to him on his own. But what would she say? Don't blame me for this, don't blame us. You didn't take your eye off the ball. What's wrong with two people meeting and having a good time?

But Garcia hovers.

'Have you got a final body count yet?' asks Megan.

'Twelve adults and three children,' he says. 'Coastguard reckons some will have drifted on the ocean currents. They could turn up anywhere. Or sink, get eaten. French and Spanish authorities have put out an alert for the boats.'

'And they're still missing?' says Megan.

'Yeah. We're flying to Madrid tomorrow to talk to the Spanish police. See if we can start to join all this up from their end. They're looking for Javier Lopez.'

Megan nods. 'Have a good trip,' she says. He's still avoiding eye contact.

'Thanks,' he replies. Then, as an afterthought: 'Do you want one of us to sit in with you while you grill Reynolds?'

'Not necessary,' says Megan. 'Vish should be here in a minute.'

'Good luck, then,' says Danny Ingram. And with a curt nod he walks away.

It feels as final as it is abrupt and Megan's dismay must show on her face.

Garcia gives her a sheepish look. 'Don't take it personally,' she says. 'He's a bit preoccupied.'

'I'm fine,' says Megan. 'We've both got a job to do.'

He's retreating into what he knows: the job. Or maybe for him it was always a casual fling to pass the time.

She's aware of Garcia scanning her. She's not fine. Inside she's howling. *Not fair! Not again!*

But she paints on a smile and says, 'You take care of yourself, Sasha.'

*

Penny Reynolds sits with her steepled fingers resting on the table in front of her. The pose looks meditative but Megan wonders if it's more about control. She's back with Tim Wardell. His tie is askew and his notebook is a sea of messy scrawl. All of which must make Penny feel even more abandoned. Her posh lawyer is gone and the bank has cut her adrift. A bad apple, a corrupt employee, that will be their story. Any wrongdoing by the bank will be denied. New procedures will be put in place.

'When did you first meet Greg Porter?' says Megan.

Penny raises her eyebrows. 'Good Lord,' she says. 'Years ago. I can't remember exactly.'

'Before he married your sister?'

Penny looks at Megan and there it is, the moment of hesitation, the beat before the lie.

'I think maybe Yvonne brought him to meet the family,' she says.

'That's not what Marion Porter told us,' says Megan. 'She thinks her son wanted to marry you and when you turned him down he married your sister.'

Penny stares at the wall above Megan and Vish's heads. Her hands are clenched tightly. Megan glances sideways and catches Vish's eye. They wait.

'Is this true, Penny?' says Megan.

Penny unclenches her hands and folds her arms. It's as if she's holding on to herself, trying to cradle her own body. The life she had, the future she thought she had, is disappearing before her eyes. She's trying to save herself and realising she can't. Megan's seen it before. When the collapse comes, it's sudden.

'Did you have a relationship with Greg before he married your sister?' she says.

Penny is deathly pale. She tilts her head and sighs.

'Yes,' she says. 'He wanted to fuck me, he wanted to fuck us both, but he married Yvonne when she got pregnant. Barry told him he had to be a man and step up to his responsibilities.'

'Did he continue to have sex with you after he married your sister?' says Megan.

Penny nods.

'Could you answer out loud for the record,' says Megan.

Tears well in Penny's eyes, she swallows them down.

'Yes, he continued to fuck me,' she says angrily. 'In fact I think the secrecy turned him on. Greggy liked to be a bad boy, to break the rules. And he liked to have his cake and eat it. My sister didn't want four children. After Imogen, she was a mess. Physically and mentally. But Greg liked the idea of a big family because he was an only child. He got what he wanted. He expected it.'

'And you continued to have sex with him?' says Megan.

'I didn't want to. I tried to stop it several times. I walked away. But when I said no, he took it out on her. She never knew what was going on. We both lied to her. But he still made it her fault. Sounds mad, I know. But that's what he was like.'

'When you say he took it out on her, what did he do?'

'He beat her. Quite badly a couple of times. Then he'd cry and say how sorry he was.'

'He'd cry to her?'

'No, to me. He'd turn into a little boy and say how unfair it all was. How he wished he'd married me. Then he wouldn't have to be like that. Yvonne wound him up, he said. Because she was stupid. He always blamed someone else. Nothing was ever his fault.'

'Did he hit you?'

'Sometimes. Then I'd refuse to see him. Then he'd take it out on her and the whole pathetic cycle would start again. Round and round.'

'You don't think Yvonne ever knew?' says Megan.

'Not about me. She always thought he had other women because of the things he said to her.'

'What sort of things?'

'Just nasty, spiteful stuff. And when she drank, it gave him ammunition to undermine her even more. It was about power.'

'You understood all this,' says Megan. 'But you still let it continue. Why?'

'It wasn't that simple. I tried to encourage her to leave him. But she wouldn't. She thought it was her fault, that he behaved like that because she was a bad wife. So I tried other strategies.'

'Like what?'

'He wasn't much of a businessman, so I thought if I helped him it might take the pressure off things. And making serious money pleased him, so it did work for a while. He liked to think he was clever, a slick deal-maker.'

'And was he?'

'He could be charming. Quite good at selling his ideas. But he wanted it all to be easy. He thought that's what he deserved.'

'So you made it easier for him?'

'Yes.'

'Is that why you introduced him to the Lopezes?'

'There wasn't that much for him to do, he was just providing a front. I thought it would work. Easy money. Everyone wins.'

'But they didn't,' says Megan.

Penny shakes her head and sighs. Then she gives a sour laugh.

'Greg's vanity, that's what made it all go wrong,' she says.

'How do you mean?' asks Megan.

'He became fixated with Elena. He wanted her. Which was a joke. She was not remotely interested. She was married. And way out of his league. She'd flirt with him and Barry to keep them onside; that was strictly business. But he kept pushing me to set something up.'

'Did you tell Elena?'

'God no. If Javier found out, he would've…'

'Killed him?' says Megan.

Penny gives her a ghostly smile. 'Probably,' she says.

'Would it be fair to say that neither Greg nor Barry fully understood the kind of people the Lopezes were?' says Megan.

'Do you know how many of my bank's clients have some connection with organised crime?' says Penny.

'Quite a few I'd imagine,' says Megan.

'But we don't ask difficult questions, we provide respectability and we keep the money flowing.'

'Are you ever bothered by the morality of that?' says Megan.

'Morality!' says Penny, with a cynical laugh. 'Compared to what? Governments? The arms trade? I can see you're not a stupid woman, sergeant. You know there's no difference. Everyone's got their snout in the trough. Sometimes there's collateral damage. It's the price of doing business.'

'Not in my world,' says Megan.

Penny shrugs. Megan meets her gaze.

'What happened on that Tuesday night, Penny?' she says.

Tim Wardell shifts in his chair. 'You're not obliged to answer that,' he says.

Penny gives him a ghostly smile.

Suddenly the struggle in her eyes disappears and is replaced by a look of resignation.

'Greg had this totally daft plan to seduce Elena,' she says. 'He wanted to throw a party to celebrate the launch of the flats and he wanted me to make a pass at Javier. Then once Javier was out of the way, he could move in on Elena. I tried to explain to him how moronically stupid it was on so many levels. He accused me of being jealous of his interest in Elena. He kept pestering me, like a greedy child who must have his own way.'

'Where was he planning to do this? At his house?'

'God, no. He didn't want Yvonne and the kids in the way. He was talking about the golf club. He'd already booked it. The whole issue turned into an argument.'

'Where did this argument take place?'

Penny stares at the wall above Megan's head. Her eyes are glassy and blank.

'I'd come down to see the show flat. Why on earth he thought Elena would just fall into his arms…' She shakes her head in exasperation, then her tone becomes bitter. 'He thought all women would do what he wanted. The sheer arrogance of it! And he expected me to help him. He assumed I'd do what he wanted. Because I always had. And I realised how stupid I was for letting him do that to me. I realised how ridiculous he'd made my life. And what a fool I was to let a man like that control me.'

She dips her head. The tears are flowing. She wipes her face with the back of her hand.

Megan waits.

Then she says, 'What did you do, Penny?'

'I was so angry. I saw the hammer and I picked it up. And I hit him. And it felt like the best thing I'd ever done. For me. For Yvonne. So I just kept hitting him. And you know what, even now, there's not one part of me that regrets it. He was a worthless shit who deserved to die. No one can tell me it was wrong.'

Penny leans back in her chair, her arms are loose, her face streaked with tears. The tension of holding it all in is gone. Megan feels the relief too. Tim Wardell clears his throat. Vish folds his arms. No one speaks.

CHAPTER SIXTY-FIVE

Vish accompanies Megan to the Porters' house. They ring the doorbell but it goes unanswered. Vish leads the way; he knows where the side gate is. It takes them into the sizeable back garden.

They find Yvonne and her children beside the pool. The twins are playing under the supervision of their nanny. Imogen is sitting alone on the side, dangling her feet in the water. Aidan is on a lounger, eyes closed, headphones on. Yvonne is smothering her legs in suntan cream. She applies it slowly and methodically. Her hair is wound up in a scarf, her face concealed behind large black lenses with tortoiseshell frames.

Megan watches for a moment while she and Vish remain unnoticed.

'How the other half live, eh?' says Vish.

'You envious?' says Megan.

'Maybe a bit,' he replies. 'The pool and the house and the stuff. But it hasn't made them happy, has it?'

Megan chuckles, 'Plenty of rich people are quite happy. Why wouldn't they be?'

Megan and Vish follow a short path to the poolside. As soon as Yvonne Porter notices them she seems to freeze. She prods her son's arm, picks up a towel and wipes her hands. Aidan Porter opens his eyes and blinks at them.

'Hello, Yvonne,' says Megan. She glances at the children. 'Can we speak in private?'

'Why?' says Yvonne.

'We've come to tell you that a suspect has been charged in respect of your husband's death.'

'Oh,' says Yvonne.

'Who?' says Aidan. He sits up and pulls his headphones off.

Yvonne waves a hand at the nanny. 'Jamila, take the children in the kitchen and give them some ice cream.'

Jamila dips her head in acknowledgement of the instruction.

Megan waits. The nanny hustles Harry and Lucas out of the pool.

Imogen glares at her mother. 'I want to stay,' she says. 'I don't want ice cream.'

'Go with Jamila and don't argue,' says Yvonne without the least trace of warmth in her voice.

Imogen gets up slowly.

'Go, Imogen!' says Yvonne.

Megan watches the child. The look on her face is something between blankness and blind terror. *The children are always the hidden victims.*

Yvonne glances nervously at her son. It looks like he's been promoted to the role of the man in her life.

'I'm staying,' says Aidan.

Yvonne takes his hand and squeezes it.

Megan waits until Jamila and the children are out of earshot. Then she says, 'As I expect you know, we've been interviewing your sister, Penny Reynolds.'

Yvonne nods. 'About the smuggling and all those people that died.'

'Penny has made a full confession to your husband's murder. And forensic evidence related to the murder weapon confirms her account.'

'Oh,' says Yvonne. Her eyes are hidden behind the sunglasses.

Aidan stares at his mother and frowns. 'Why would she—' he says. 'I don't get it. She killed Dad? Why?'

'Well, you know, darling,' says Yvonne calmly. 'She's always been jealous of me.'

Megan watches the two of them. Mother and son. She's become still as a statue. He's a ball of furious energy.

He jumps up and rakes a hand through his hair. 'Fuck!' he exclaims. 'She told me I had to protect you!' He paces up and down.

Yvonne perches on the side of the sun lounger. Using the towel she wipes each of her fingers individually. She glances up at Megan. 'Don't you hate the stickiness of suntan cream?' she says. 'I'll have to go and wash my hands. Thank you for letting us know.'

'Wait a minute, Mum,' says Aidan. 'Don't you think there are some questions need answering?'

Megan and Vish exchange looks. *An understatement.*

'Did you know or suspect what your sister had done?' says Megan.

'I thought it was Elena,' says Yvonne with a shrug.

'Were you aware Penny and Greg were involved?' says Megan. *Does she know? She'll find out at the trial.*

Yvonne inhales, her upper body becomes rigid. She carefully folds the towel. 'Of course I was aware,' she replies. 'I'm not stupid. But he married me.'

'What involvement?' says Aidan. 'You mean like sex? Dad and Penny were screwing?'

'It was a casual thing, darling. It wasn't important. Your father's priority was us. He always put the family first.'

'He hit you, Mum! He beat you up.'

'Couples argue sometimes. That's not important either.'

Aidan turns to Megan. 'Can I see Penny? Talk to her?'

'Yes. If she agrees to see you—'

Yvonne stands up. 'No, Aidan! Absolutely not. I forbid it.'

'Why?' he says.

'That woman murdered my husband. She introduced him to criminals who murdered your grandfather. There is no way that I or you or any of my children will have anything to do with her ever again. She can rot in jail. It's what she deserves.' She turns to Megan. 'If that's everything, officer, I really must go and wash my hands. Do excuse me.'

Yvonne walks up the steps onto the terrace. Her chin is held high and her manner is regal. But it seems to Megan that she needs every ounce of her strength to keep her narrow frame upright. She disappears into the house.

Vish turns to Aidan. 'Are you going to be all right, mate?'

Aidan folds his arms and paces. 'Fucked if I know,' he says. He wipes the back of his hand across his face. He's crying.

'You sure it was Penny?' he says. 'I always thought she really loved us.'

'Perhaps she does,' says Megan.

He shakes his head and runs up the steps towards the house.

Vish sighs. 'That was a bit intense,' he says. 'Do you think she knew her sister and her husband had been at it for years?'

'Your guess is as good as mine,' says Megan.

EPILOGUE

Debbie pours red wine into Megan's glass. They're sitting at the kitchen table. Evening sun streams across it from the window.

'Killed by the sister-in-law he was screwing? It's sort of bizarre, don't you think?' says Debbie.

'Complicated family,' says Megan.

'What will happen to her?'

Megan picks up her glass. 'She's got money, she can get herself a smart lawyer.'

'You don't seem very sympathetic. Sounds like Greg had a pretty abusive relationship with her and with his wife.'

Megan sips her wine. 'Yes. But it's not straightforward coercive control. If Yvonne had killed him, you could've probably argued that as a defence. But Penny? She wasn't isolated and trapped by him.'

'You said she kept coming back because, if she didn't, he'd take it out on Yvonne. I can believe that. He was a total arsehole who just bullied everyone.'

Megan scans her sister. The pain is still there in her face. It seems unlikely she'll forget what Greg Porter did to her any time soon.

'I dunno, Deb. I'm not a lawyer.'

'The people smuggling thing, that's awful,' says Debbie. 'She should go down for that. 'Cause she actually made that happen. She was the go-between.'

'Ironically,' says Megan, 'her culpability for that'll be much harder to prove.'

'The system sucks,' says Debbie.

Megan smiles to herself. *Jim Collins would agree with that.*

They both sip their wine. Megan watches the motes of dust dancing on the table in the sunlight. She looks across at the dog in his basket. Scout raises his head.

Debbie glances at her watch. 'Hey,' she says. 'C'mon, it's time!'

She jumps up and heads into the sitting room.

Megan gets up slowly and follows.

The three children are seated in a tight line on the sofa. Amber is in the centre. She's in charge of the laptop. It's open on the coffee table in front of them.

Mark is on screen. He's smiling and waving. 'Hey, everyone.'

'Daddy!' shouts Ruby.

'Hi, Dad!' Kyle and Amber chorus.

'Where's your mother?' says Mark.

'I'm here! I'm here!' says Debbie as she plonks down next to Ruby and leans in.

'How are you all?' says Mark. 'What've you been doing?'

The kids all answer at once in a cacophony of voices.

'One at a time!' says Mark. 'I can't hear you. Ruby, what did you have for tea?'

'We had sausages and beans,' says Ruby.

'And chips,' says Kyle.

'Kyle ate all the chips,' says Amber.

'Well, he's a growing lad,' says Mark.

Megan watches from the doorway. The backs of the children's heads bobbing up and down in excitement on the sofa. Debbie next to them with her arm round her brood. Mark, on screen, but many miles away, beaming with pleasure at the sight of his family.

Megan sips her wine.

Debbie turns her head and glances over the back of the sofa towards her sister. 'Meg, c'mon!' she says.

Megan shakes her head. 'I'm fine,' she says. 'There's not enough room.'

'Don't be silly, Meg,' says Debbie. 'Of course there's room. Get over here! Now! You're family.'

A LETTER FROM SUSAN

I want to say a huge thank you for choosing to read *Close to the Bone*. If you did enjoy it, and want to keep up to date with all my latest releases, just sign up at the following link. Your email address will never be shared and you can unsubscribe at any time.

www.bookouture.com/susan-wilkins

I have loved writing Megan Thomas and I've tried to create a character to fit the mood of the times. She's far from perfect but she's doing the best she can; like me, like you, like most of us. And these are very strange times. But the police, in particular, have been faced with unprecedented challenges. I've been wondering how Megan would cope and perhaps you have too. So if you'd like to catch up with Megan and all her colleagues in the time of Covid, I'm offering readers a short story. It's free. You can get a copy by going to my author website:

www.susanwilkins.co.uk

Do let me know what you thought of *Close to the Bone*. Writing can be a lonely job and I love to connect with readers. You can find me in the usual places: Facebook, Twitter, my website and Instagram.

Also if you feel like writing a review I'd be most grateful. There's a sea of books out there and reviews definitely help new readers discover one of my books for the first time.

Happy reading!

Thanks,
Susan Wilkins

f @susanwilkinsauthor

🐦 @susanwilkins32

🖥 www.susanwilkins.co.uk

📷 susan_wilkins32

ACKNOWLEDGEMENTS

Huge thanks to the experts who've guided me, making sure I know how the police would proceed, and for understanding when I've twisted their advice for the purposes of drama. Colin James is brilliant, inventive and patient. Again he should take credit for some of my better ideas. Kate Bendelow is the go-to expert on forensics and endlessly generous with her time. Graham Bartlett is always my fallback, because if he doesn't know, he knows a person who does. Alex Doughty has added her expertise and, in particular, her knowledge of policing in Devon.

Thanks to the wonderful team at Bookouture for launching me on the next stage of my crime-writing journey. Thanks to Alexandra Holmes and Jennie Ayres for the careful copyediting. And extra special thanks to my editor, Ruth Tross. Once again I've relied on her smart and incisive editing and her encyclopaedic knowledge of crime fiction.

As ever I am lucky enough to have a back-up crew of fellow crime writers who are always generous with advice, support and encouragement. So thanks to the usual suspects, you know who you are. And loads of love and hugs to my friends and family for putting up with the ups and downs of the writing life. Last but never least, my two first readers: Jenny Kenyon and Sue Kenyon.

Made in the USA
Las Vegas, NV
10 April 2021